"Did you ever think about how Colombian cartels, paramilitaries, and shady U.S. operations could be involved with artwork? . . . Linda Moore has written a wonderfully taut thriller that shows just how dangerous that world can be. Moore is a helluva writer. She makes the plot zip by while she immerses you in the setting and her deep knowledge of the art world. Take a breath, you'll need it."
—Carl Vonderau, award winning author of
Murderabilia and *Saving Myles*

". . . a masterclass in immersive storytelling. With vivid prose that transports you to the heart of Colombia's bustling art world, Moore crafts a thrilling tale of intrigue and betrayal . . . a cinematic experience waiting to unfold, and I can't recommend it enough."
—Jesse Leon, author of *I'm Not Broken*
and *No Estoy Roto*

T0051212

FIVE DAYS IN BOGOTÁ

Also by Linda Moore

Attribution

FIVE DAYS IN BOGOTÁ

A NOVEL

LINDA MOORE

SHE WRITES PRESS

Published 2024
Printed in the United States of America
Print ISBN: 978-1-64742-612-5
E-ISBN: 978-1-64742-613-2
Library of Congress Control Number: 2023915530

For information, address:
She Writes Press
1569 Solano Ave #546
Berkeley, CA 94707

Interior Design by Tabitha Lahr

She Writes Press is a division of SparkPoint Studio, LLC.

For Terry, Adrienne, and Craig

What matters is not what happened,
but how you remember what happened.

—GABRIEL GARCÍA MÁRQUEZ

DAY 1

CHAPTER 1

ALLY BLAKE JOINED THE LINE, if you could call it that, and jostled her way toward the front to claim her two art crates. Bogotá customs held her artworks hostage somewhere in this building along with the freight of the other weary travelers crowding the counter. Together they endured the smell of diesel fumes that belched from a bus outside. Those odors merged into a noxious mix of cigarette smoke and mildew making it difficult to breathe.

A clerk at the counter demanded everyone move back and take a seat. Ally helped a woman struggling with crutches find a chair next to a scratched and stained table. Reading material or perhaps discarded trash, including a newspaper a few weeks old, dated November 21, 1990, littered the floor. A headline in two-inch type screamed 'KIDNAPPED' followed by a photo of a body next to a colonial fountain, bubbling unawares as it had done for centuries. The body, which seemed more corpse than kidnap victim, added to her apprehension about the realities of Colombia and how much she'd chosen to ignore.

Financial necessity had landed her in this strange place for the Bogotá Art Fair. She had navigated many South American countries, each with its unique brand of turmoil, and recognized that Colombia was a special case. Going forward, she'd move with more caution, heed warnings, and do everything to return to her children in California in one piece.

She flipped the newspaper to the sports page with a soccer score broadcasting a big win for Atlético Nacional over a rival, in the same large type as the kidnap story. Colombia boasted its wins and its losses as though they were equivalent, at least in headline size. She tossed the paper onto the table out of view.

Her singular goal to exhibit her gallery's art in an elegant art fair with collectors ready to love her artists and buy their works, sprung from a crisis too. When the life insurance company failed to pay her husband's death claim, her family's finances went into a tailspin. Without Nick's high income, gallery sales became her only source of money to pay the household bills, especially the mortgage. Those art fair sales could only happen if her art crates were released.

She rose from the egg-shaped chair rattling three others ganged together in plastic unity and approached the clerk at the shabby counter. "Excuse me, did you find the paperwork for our shipment?"

The clerk rose from his desk and appeared ready to reprimand her for leaving her seat. Instead, he paused, glared at her, and then rifled through a stack of papers. He pulled out three pages in the yellow color the U.S. Government called goldenrod, the same color of the forms she'd handled when she worked at the State Department.

"Here is your document." He flicked the pages at her and added, "Missss All-eee-son." His voice carried over the heads of chatting supplicants who had again crowded the desk without a queue.

The word *Miss* rankled her. She twisted Nick's wedding ring that she'd kept on her left hand.

The clerk made illegible scribbles on her paperwork and handed the forms to her.

"Gracias." She smiled to hide her frustration about unanswered questions. "Will you release my crates and deliver them to the convention center?" She aimed for a sincere and grateful tone.

The clerk turned up the music on an old radio on top of a file cabinet, sat down at his desk, and lowered his head. Her question dangled in the air like an empty hammock.

She sighed and shook her head. He's trying to do a job. Earn a living. Feed his family. Just like she was.

"Excuse me, perdón. Please can you help me understand?"

He shuffled papers on his desk, lit a cigarette, and dialed the phone. Colombians waiting in line smirked at the interchange.

Funcionario. Bureaucrat. Such a good word. Just to say it is to expel spit and anger.

Fuuuuun siiiiiinnnn ario. Her Spanish was passable, she'd thought, but every country had its words, phrases, and nuances. Subtlety of meaning could result in disastrous misunderstandings, and in this situation, she needed to understand and be understood.

The clerk issued another command to disperse the line. Some returned to sit on the plastic chairs. Others left the stuffy room to stand outside and smoke. The waiting room filled with lively conversations between Colombians who either accepted the reality of interminable waits or had no urgency to retrieve their goods . . . or both.

She remained at the counter and tried again. "The forms say the art crates were transferred to *Sub-estación* 1109. Is that here or somewhere else?" She had no clue what to do next. "Is there an address? Are they open now?"

She pointed to page three and stood, silent, waiting, hoping he'd respond.

He shook his head.

She took that to mean . . . well, nothing.

Who smuggles anything *into* Colombia? She couldn't imagine why crates of original artworks, most not valued over $10,000 would create an import problem or be attractive to steal. If thieves knew where to sell the paintings, she'd like to hire them to work in her gallery.

She stuffed the forms in her purse, gathered up her briefcase, and left to find the friendly driver who was parked outside. A chaos of horse carts, a cow sleeping on the median of the road, and vendors pushing useless things at her cluttered the pathway to the car. These sellers called out desperate to make a deal, foreshadowing herself at the art fair. A sardonic smile lifted her tired face.

Despite these noisy, smelly surroundings, the driver slept. She nudged him awake like he was one of her sleepy children.

He lifted his head, without apology or regret, and got out to open the door. He demonstrated a kind attitude as though he practiced this sleep-to-fully-functioning transition often.

She sat in the back seat, envious that after the long flight and the struggle in customs, she had not spent the last two hours the same way he had.

The driver fumbled for the keys to start the engine and asked where they were going.

"Tequendama Hotel. To check in."

He drove through a slalom of obstacles and open spaces in the parking area and finally entered a ramp of the main freeway to central Bogotá.

She stared out the window, studying the surroundings of this unfamiliar city. Worry about whether this gamble would pay off, whether the high cost of leaving her sad children would reward them all with financial security, filled her thoughts. Her tired head slipped to the back of the seat and sleep took over.

SCREECHING BRAKES JERKED HER awake as the driver left the lullaby of the highway to enter the city streets. Pedestrians, not vehicles, controlled the road. Men dressed in elegant suits, alone or with fashionista women on their arms, exited their limos leaving their drivers blocking traffic. In the shadows, ragged beggars, especially women with babies at their breasts, had their hands outstretched for coins. She ignored the faces begging at the car window and focused her eyes on the streets ahead.

In a couple of blocks, the car entered a driveway and stopped in front of a doorman in a gold-buttoned jacket. He opened the car door and she paid the driver before she stepped out. The doorman directed the bellman to take the luggage, but she stayed near her belongings, following them into the hotel.

Vehicle exhaust and blaring street noises undermined the elegant arrival. Guards, police, military, everywhere, serious guys with rifles or machine guns, she couldn't tell which was which. Their camouflage uniforms differed from the spotless and neatly pressed one the doorman wore. Their dirty, torn, and mismatched gear had seen action. Recently.

She hustled to the door, out of range of the chaos of taxis, soldiers, and hawkers of everything from woven shawls to suitcases.

Inside, she paused by the reception desk, which provided a familiar moorage to anchor herself and take a breath. Classical music piped through speakers and drifted over the bustle of people. The pristine lobby, free of debris, displayed well-groomed plants and dated but elegant decor including a beautiful mural on the far wall. The place smelled of a blend of soap and bleach, a good thing.

A young woman in a grey uniform stood upright behind the counter. Her nametag read Maria. Beneath that, it said 'Trainee' in Spanish.

Ally managed a smile and presented her passport. "Checking in. Reservation for Allison Blake."

"Check-in 4:00 p.m. Would you like to wait in the bar?"

Ally checked her watch: fifteen minutes to four. She considered pointing an angry finger at the time but was too exhausted to fight about fifteen minutes and did not want to start with a bad impression. She summoned patience and kindness with the prospect a drink could take the edge off.

"We can store your luggage until your room is ready."

"No, I'll keep my things." She couldn't face more disappeared belongings and lifted her suitcase, duffle, briefcase, and a tube of rolled art works struggling like an overloaded camel. The three-foot tube was awkward to handle, but if the crates were never delivered, the tube contained the only art she had to sell in Bogotá.

She rested near a bench by the elevator to collect herself, place her duffle on top of the rolling suitcase, and organize her load. A potted plant and a large globe of the world crowded the sides of the bench. The globe displayed a red arrow pointing at Bogotá, in case a guest might not know where to find one of the largest cities in South America.

That morning her children, at five and eight, still small and fragile, had sat teary-eyed on the couch of Nick's office. The three of them gathered in this room where they felt close to him, a place that smelled of him, with piles of papers he had touched and stacked with a purpose. Claire ran across the room to the large globe next to Nick's mahogany desk. "Show us again. The place you are going."

Ally helped Claire twirl the world to find Bogotá, spinning and stopping it with her finger, trying to hit the spot. She guided Claire's thumb to rest on San Diego. Claire stretched her index finger, but her small hand could not reach Bogotá.

"So far away." Claire's voice quavered, and she turned her face toward her only surviving parent.

Ally pulled Claire, her little worrier, closer, drawing her into a hug. Mikey snuggled himself into the middle and Ally encircled them both still dressed in their matching dinosaur pajamas.

The decision between securing income for her family or staying beside grief-stricken Claire and Mikey ripped her heart out. But she'd had no choice. Too young to understand the difference between leaving and dying, the two of them stood on the curb and waved at the taxi. She had blown kisses at them through the rear window until she could see them no more.

The elevator door pinged and rattled open. She stood aside to let an elegant couple get off and then gave the globe a twirl. She picked up her things and moved forward with new resolve. Five days was not long. She could do this one thing to gain financial security, protect their family, and make Nick proud. At least, she hoped he would be proud. He often nagged her to close the gallery because it never made much money. She pushed back, and thank God she had. Now the gallery, the art and the artists were her only lifeline.

A man stood near the entrance of the bar with his back to her. She didn't need to see Mateo's face because she recognized his artist's uniform: shredded jeans, black t-shirt, and Converse tennis shoes, covered in paint spots like some Jackson Pollock designed footwear. Other males in the lobby had that GQ elegance expected of Latin American men of wealth. Amazing what an Italian suit, cufflinks, and a silk tie could do for an ordinary man. She tried to picture him like them but couldn't. His rebel style, his don't-give-a-shit attitude, his candid remarks made her respect him as a person even more than she admired his art.

"Mateo." She put her arms out. "Great to see you." She meant it and squeezed him in a bear hug.

He bent down to give her one kiss, Uruguayan style. "Bogotá. Wouldn't miss a chance to visit the planet's most violent city." He chuckled.

She smiled and responded with another hug. "Thanks for coming, for helping me." Her voice cracked when she said the words.

His cheerful face disappeared. "Tragic about Nick. How are you doing? And the kids?" He held her shoulders with both hands, and she looked up at his face, a foot above hers.

"Struggling, Mikey can't stop crying and Claire barely speaks, which is worse. And me, no time for emotions. So many challenges, especially money."

Her kids loved Mateo. He spent a month with them last year, painting for his exhibit in her gallery. Despite his limited but improving English, he had them laughing at the littlest things. Nick too. Nick didn't take to all her artists, but Mateo had won him over.

Mateo took a couple of steps pulling her away from the door to let several customers enter. "We got this, *jefa*. We're going home with suitcases of cash."

She smirked. "We're starting out, no bueno. Customs won't release our crates."

"*¿En serio?* Customs hassled me too. Pulled me out of line because of the white stuff on the back of my canvases."

"White stuff? Mateo, you didn't!"

"No, no. I pin the large canvases to the plaster walls in my apartment. The wet gesso base bleeds through, makes the walls damp, and the plaster attaches to the back of the canvas. White stuff, get it?"

"Got it." She shook her head. "What did they do?"

"Bureaucrats. Big delay to justify their jobs. Then, nothing."

"Thank God. I could not have faced getting you and the crates out of jail." This place was a minefield, a misstep could result in catastrophe.

Mateo shifted from one foot to the other. Whether he was uncomfortable with the memory, fears he would joke about and never own, or just wanted a cigarette, she couldn't tell.

"The real dealers—over there." He nodded his head toward the men at the bar. "Narcos in their fancy-pants suits, reap the big money."

"Let's grab a booth." They entered the bar. Leaning closer as they walked toward the tables, she whispered, "No rants. Don't earn us enemies. Those guys at the bar could be art collectors."

Mateo Lugano, the *infante terrible,* created challenges, but also earned her respect as a talented artist with outrageous paintings that grabbed collectors' attention. In a six-by-eight-foot canvas, a giant penis wrapped in floral garlands, stood up between a reclining, frozen, almost dead-looking couple. Mateo entitled it *The Marriage Bed,* a cynical commentary from a bachelor who thought he understood marriage. A female doctor bought the provocative work. After she got married, the doctor phoned hysterical, complaining the painting made her new husband nervous. Ally, amused at that reaction, arranged a swift donation of the work to a Florida museum. She hadn't told Mateo. She expected he'd find the story funny, but she could never predict his response.

Mateo led the way to a small booth near the wall and motioned for her to move into the banquette first. A waiter appeared, pen and pad at the ready.

"Beer for me. Campari for you?" asked Mateo.

"With soda and a lemon twist." The acrid, medicinal taste of the Campari was perfect for her mood. When the waiter left, she slipped Mateo five twenties under the table. "For expenses." In Colombia, women, or women from good families, didn't go to bars alone, did not order, nor pay the bill.

Mateo took the cash without a word. He had nothing on him, she was certain. The last time she'd visited his apartment, the fridge contained a bottle of water and one egg. An airline ticket from Uruguay to Bogotá for Mateo to bring a tube of un-stretched canvases with him would be less than shipping costs. He had embraced the idea of visiting a city that might provide new material for his cynical paintings and relished the opportunity to observe the truth about Colombian violence that made the daily news in Montevideo. And a chance to show his paintings and perhaps sell one or two. Yes, that was most important.

He gulped his beer, and she sipped her Campari, and then took a big swallow.

"What happened to you in customs?"

"I was told to go to this building to claim the crates. Spent two hours and got some paperwork stamped. But no art." She pulled the goldenrod pages from her purse. "Maybe you can understand what it says."

He flipped through the forms and shook his head. "These don't say anything." He tossed them back on the table. "But we do have art. . . . my art, more than enough to fill the booth. It'll be a one-man show, a Mateo exhibit." He laughed, lightened her mood, and reminded her how their carefree banter lifted her spirits. "I also brought a few new paintings from Morini's studio, the brown-Torres-Garcia-palette ones you like. They'll sell."

She'd forgotten he was bringing the Morini's, but those paintings were not enough to make the numbers work without the art in the crates. She pictured a strange exhibition: Morini's muddy Rio de la Plata palette alongside Mateo's color explosions. The difference between the two artists reminded her and the world that Latin American artists had diverse and complex styles. The catchall phrase 'Latin American' didn't describe a consistent style or any connection except geography.

She added the dollars in her head. The Morinis would sell, but the three or four works Mateo brought weren't enough to pay the cost of the fair and the travel to get here. They needed the larger artworks in those crates to make the big sales to keep the gallery open and pay the bills for the Blake household.

She ran her hands through her hair and left her palms on her temples to ease the throbbing.

Mateo craned his neck forward to study the paneling behind her. "Look at these walls. Zebra stripes."

She turned her head to look at the wall behind their booth. Panels of exotic hardwood reached to the ceiling, probably from endangered trees, but no one called them that. Colombia had many problems, including rebels, civil war, drug lords and drug kings, corruption, all threatening mayhem every day. Environmental concerns didn't even make the top ten of government priorities.

Mateo ran his hand along the wood next to the booth, admiring nature's art.

She welcomed his adept distraction from her worries, perhaps well-practiced as he dealt with his own substantial financial challenges.

They rested in tranquil silence until a disturbing but familiar squeal came from across the room.

CHAPTER 2

SANTIAGO NAVARRO SANG OUT, "*Guapa, guapa,* pretty lady." He sashayed toward them with a bounce in his step, a unique gait she applauded but couldn't imagine replicating. Men at the bar turned, gawked, and rolled their eyes as though disapproving of him would affirm their own manhood.

Santi, as everyone in New York called him, found his way to their booth. She laughed just to see him and stood to hug this dependable friend. He planted so many kisses on her cheeks she lost count and blushed. When their reunion excitement subsided, she stretched her arm toward Mateo who by now, was standing, waiting to be introduced. "You remember Mateo, the artist—"

Santi finished her sentence, "Best new talent at the Cuenca Biennial."

Mateo put out his hand, but Santi was having none of that. The New Yorker surprised him with a bear hug, and Mateo reacted with his arms pinned to his sides and a crimson face. This was going to be a long fair if the two of them didn't get on.

Santi's choice of a purple Versace blazer with a paisley ascot set him apart from the other bar patrons. "Look at you. No boring black for this New York art guy." She stroked the velvet sleeve of his jacket.

Santi smiled, apparently pleased that his choices impressed her. He'd be a stand-out at the fair too, as it was a rare day when an art dealer wore something beyond black grayscale. Limited color wardrobe choice had not been her preference. But over time it made sense to her, spending all day considering color and form in artists' work. Black eliminated choices. By removing what-to-wear deliberations, her mind opened to a myriad of decisions that mattered, hard choices like coming to Colombia.

The idea of exhibiting at the Bogotá Art Fair had come from Santi. Colombian artists filled his gallery roster and he'd been invited to become a member of the first art fair organizing committee, a role he regretted. He'd explained to her a year ago his primary function was to convince American gallerists to exhibit at the fair. Colombia was considered too dangerous even by money hungry gallery owners, and everyone had declined.

The bar was filling up, and they waited for the waiter. Was that why they were called 'waiters?'

She toyed with the plastic stick in the Campari and waited to drink, considering it rude to drink when Santi hadn't been served. She pointed to the wall behind them. "We were admiring the unique wood paneling. Do you know what it is?"

Santi turned his head and nodded. "Beautiful, isn't it? Panels from the tigerwood tree. Gorgeous yellow flower and striped wood."

"Does it grow here?" She lifted her glass, set it down without drinking, and searched the bar for the waiter.

"Yes. There's a small grove up in the mountains about five miles from Bogotá and maybe a few elsewhere. A sculptor uses it for his pieces, gorgeous work. The wood has been labeled endangered."

Hard to imagine sophisticated Santi in a forest of trees. He ran with that crazy Warhol crowd, even after Andy died. Santi probably had some good Warhol paintings stored away that he could sell for major money. But he was more than a dealer who flipped works for cash. Santi's eye for spotting new talent, a special skill few art dealers had, earned her respect and that of many others.

A waiter arrived, finally recognizing a new guest had joined their table.

"What are you drinking?" Mateo asked, performing the host's role.

"Can't get absinthe here." Santi pouted. "I'll have Pernod. With a pitcher of iced, very cold, cold water." The waiter nodded and left for the bar.

"Why not *aguardiente-guaro*?" Mateo suggested. "Licorice taste, right?"

Santi laughed. "Good idea. Start with Pernod and move on to guaro."

She stirred the straw in her Campari, and her mind returned to the crates. A mirrored border on the wall behind their table reflected her face with the two vertical lines between her eyebrows, her worry grooves, she called them. She rubbed the lines with her thumbs.

Santi noticed too. "Why you look so down, little lady? No, no, no, must not wrinkle your face." He reached his two thumbs to her forehead and stretched the groove between her eyes until the skin laid flat. No one was allowed to be troubled in Santi's world, a quality that endeared him to her, but could be exhausting for an ordinary human.

"Customs. Our crates. They're here, but not here, here. I'm afraid we won't get them in time." Her worry lines returned, and she stopped trying to hide them.

Santi, with his wrinkle-free forehead, appeared unconcerned. "So, *chica*, was your bribe not enough?"

"What bribe?"

"Please. You Californians have no street smarts, like us New Yorkers. A customs guy makes a dollar an hour. How do you expect him to live? Bribes feed the Colombian GNP and its people too."

The grimace on Mateo's face revealed he'd guessed what she was thinking, not like doing business in the U.S. or Uruguay. Bribes were not in Mateo's repertoire either, but maybe worry wrinkles were.

Ally shook her head. "What if some Colombian official complains to the U.S. Government? I'd get thrown into prison here. I'd need an even bigger bribe, which by the way, I do not have. The point is to make money, not spend it."

Santi stopped. He reached his arms around her, drew her to him, and squeezed. "Dear Ally, so sad about Nicholas, so young." Santi lifted his hand pulled her head closer and stroked her hair. "Sorry, sorry, *querida*."

She felt loved by him, like a brother that stayed close and loyal. She tried to calm the wave that swept over her and brought the glass to her lips to quiet their quivering. "Tell me what to do."

He sat up straight. "We got this. You don't offer the bribe. The broker clearing the crates pays whatever is necessary and adds a miscellaneous charge to your bill." He said with a wink, wink that made his message clear, if it wasn't already.

"We've got no money for brokers or funds to burn like New York galleries looking for losses to get a tax break. You've got deep pockets for your $20,000 a month rent and handle expensive works to pay it. We hope, no, we need to make money, an actual profit to pay the bills. We'd happily pay taxes because taxes would mean we had made a profit."

She regretted her snarky words as soon as she'd said them. She'd been unfair. Santi didn't deserve projected anger that belonged to the Colombian customs bureaucracy.

Santi recovered and spoke first. "Sheeet, Doña Ally. Who pays so little for rent? You Californians have no clue."

San Diego was not New York, she knew that, and didn't need it thrown in her face. Sometimes Santi was annoying, but this sarcasm toward her had been earned. "Sorry, I'm frustrated . . . and tired."

"Well, let me fix that." Santi turned to the waiter who'd arrived with his drink and ordered another round for the three of them.

She raised her glass toward Santi and Mateo. "Here's to getting our crates and selling lots of art."

"*Salud* and sales," Mateo said laughing and lifting his glass.

They chuckled with him, and moods shifted again. "I haven't seen you since the party in New York." She sipped her Campari.

Santi drizzled the ice water into the Pernod, tasted, and added more. "Sí, Mami. A special night that sings in my memory."

After seeing Mateo's raised eyebrows, she added, "A surreal gathering of Colombian luminaries."

He raised his hands, palms up, moving his fingers in the universal sign asking for more information.

Last January, she'd gone to New York to make the rounds of new gallery exhibitions. Santi had hosted a dinner for the Colombian United Nations delegation. His tiny apartment in the old police building in SoHo had no dining room, and they sat on silk cushions on the floor, eating take-out Chinese. A classic Santi event with his special touch of breaking social conventions between strangers to open the human connections. Across the room, Santi's partner Tom and some Colombian artists danced to cumbia music. Selena Quintanilla had brought these irresistible rhythms to the American audience, and Ally found such joy in them. She joined the dancing, learning the steps, throwing her whole body into it until her head swirled from too many glasses of *guaro*. She stumbled and landed to rest on the cushions.

Santi confided his challenges about the Bogotá Fair, shouting over the throbbing beat. "U.S. galleries don't want to come to FIART to exhibit in Bogotá. Too dangerous, they think. Murders, torture, kidnappings."

"The way you describe it, I wouldn't go either." She'd lowered her voice so that the Colombians wouldn't hear.

"I understand. Bad guys blew up the Supreme Court building and assassinated a presidential candidate. Life is dangerous, no?" He tried a smile and then turned somber. "I need you. A woman gallerist could lead the way to influence others to sign on. We'll have exceptional security to protect you."

She'd looked across Santi's apartment at the Colombians enjoying themselves and questioned how they managed. Their world existed in the now. The epidemic of violence happening in their country did not enter the joy of this moment.

"These guerillas, narcos, whatever, their fight is not with us. Art happens in the intersection of places of tension: Berlin, Cuba, and yes, Bogotá. Be part of it. It will become part of you."

Not her world. She'd traveled a lot, done art fairs on four continents. In the past, Nick, with Margarita's help, had cared for Claire and Mikey while she'd been away, a gift to allow her to focus on the crazy art world without worrying about home, about them.

She'd been to many Latin America countries, but not Colombia. The violence had put her off, too, but she recognized the troubles were a mix of good intentions to fight poverty, the repression of autocratic regimes, and the greed of criminal elements including corrupt officials. Drug cartels, the military, the FARC communist rebels combined into a toxic soup, a terrible civil war with confused battle lines that enveloped the whole country.

"The gallery schedule has exhibitions through January," she'd told him, shaking her head.

Santi repeated that there would be *fah-boo-lowss* parties. She smiled at how different his priorities were. He had also promised wealthy collectors and cheap prices on the five-star hotel where they could stay.

"I'll look at the schedule, develop a budget, and see if it works. If I do it, you must stop calling me Mami."

"You have kids, you are a mommy. Right?"

She'd given him that look that told him to back off. "Call me Ally."

"Ok, Allison." Santi pinched her cheek. "Please agree we'll meet in *fantástica* Bogotá."

Then Nick died. And here she was in the Colombian capital, not out of choice as she might have been, but of necessity. She'd postponed one exhibition and left the gallery with a part-time sitter to keep the doors open but didn't expect the sitter would sell anything. Margarita would be Ally's co-madre and care for the kids with their aunt Dawn backing Margi up from a distance in Los Angeles. Everything was on the line to make some real money at this art fair.

Santi finished his drink and turned to her. "Look, talk to Enrique Rodriquez. He's the head of the fair organizing committee. You know him and his gallery, right? He might have a connection to get your crates."

Enrique had a serious art gallery in Bogotá, was married to an actress who ran with a wild crowd of entertainment types. His father-in-law, Ponce Goméz, created paintings that commanded serious money in the international market, but Ponce didn't show his works in Enrique's gallery.

"Can Enrique help with this?"

Santi set down his neon green Pernod. "The fair cannot allow the exhibitors to suffer from local, shall we say, practices. By the way, your booth at the fair is on a corner where two aisles meet, great location for collector visibility and traffic. What artists did you bring, or . . . ah when you get the crates, what art is in them?"

"McGraw, a Californian, did some encaustics with themes related to García Márquez's novels. Maybe Colombian collectors will relate to the content. What do you think?"

"Good plan. What else?"

"Some safe sales like Morini paintings, some more risky." She looked at Mateo.

"Morinis will sell, but for me, they're boring. I'd rather see the craziesies. Show what you love."

Mateo lifted his hand to high five Santi. "Yes. My new friend."

Great. Common ground between the two of them. She made a mental note to allocate high visibility space to Mateo's paintings no matter who might be offended. He was helping her with the other artists, and she needed to give him a shot. "Maybe you can send me some buyers for the crazy art?"

"Sure, of course. Let's see who shows up."

Santi got it. What was the point of a gallery if unknown artists couldn't add their unconventional ideas? He'd organized a New York exhibition of three very different, but terrific Colombian artists, some who were at that party a year ago. The artists were riding high from their first show. Santi would take the momentum from these artists' exhibitions into Bogotá, hopefully without the cocaine they consumed. Some careers could soar to the stratosphere in just a few days. An art fair could do that for an artist.

The Latin American auctions in New York had just finished the first week of November and dealers analyzed the sales results to predict the mood of collectors. She'd barely had time to open her mail much less keep track of the results. "How did the Ponce paintings do at auction?"

"Ponce prices—*desorbitados.*"

Santi made her laugh. Values out of orbit, or on the moon, told her everything she needed without studying price sheets.

Mateo perked up his ears, no doubt dreaming someday he could make that kind of money and asked, "Ponce's auction prices increased again? New records?"

Santi nodded. Rumors circulated about the source of collectors' funds who'd bought Ponce's cartoonish paintings of anorexic figures with huge feet. His last sale at Ellsworth's Auction in New York hit eight digits.

"Ellsworth is happy. Ponce is happy. Who cares if . . ." He leaned to whisper the rest of his sentence, an unusual moment when he did not want to be heard. ". . . who cares if the narco guys buy his paintings to launder their money?"

A man in a suit with the telltale earpiece sat down on a bench near their booth.

Santi stopped talking. He communicated by nodding his head over his shoulder toward the man. His mood turned serious, and he added in a normal voice, "Let's focus on getting the crates pried out of customs' claws."

She was grateful to put their attention to solving the crate problem. "When does customs close?"

Santi shook his head and finished the last gulp of his Pernod. "For a price, never."

Maria from the front desk stood three feet from their table, waiting for a break in the conversation. They looked up and seeing Maria, without speaking, they stood up to leave. Eager patrons from the standing room only bar, swarmed to grab their seats.

Maria approached and said, "Señora, your room is ready. The reception manager awaits you."

Ally turned to the guys. "I'll change out of these travel clothes and meet you in the lobby in 30 minutes. Let's go to the Convention Center, talk to Enrique to track down our crates."

CHAPTER 3

A SWARTHY MAN BEHIND THE CHECK-IN counter looked at her in an up and down sort of way and held out an official-looking envelope.

He pushed the envelope toward her. "A package from the U.S. Embassy for Allison Blake." The young man in his well-pressed shirt and tie had an odd look, but his Puig cologne distracted her from his attitude. He smelled like Barcelona, not a bad thing.

"I'm not with the embassy or the U.S. Government." She handed the envelope back to him. "It's a mistake."

"It's addressed to you. I can't give you a key until you sign for it." He handed her a pen.

People stopped talking and the lobby grew quiet. South Americans suspected every American working in the region of being CIA, but surely there were some who did not suspect all Americans. Those who knew her, like Mateo and the other art dealers trusted that she had nothing to do with the U.S. Government. Collectors didn't care.

Too tired to argue and impatient to get to her room, she scribbled her name on the receipt. She juggled her passport, credit card, and wallet trying to put them into her bag with the large envelope and pick up the art tube and her suitcase.

The clerk stepped away from the counter and turned his back to work on something else.

She spoke to the clerk's back. "Ah, could you please call the bellman?"

Without turning around, he rang a small buzzer and even that was with a bit of drama that made no sense to her. Maybe he disliked Americans, because of ancient history. The U.S. helped Panama become independent from Colombia, a wound still raw from the early 1900s. No doubt, a long history of arrogant actions by the U.S. provoked everyone in the region and in the entire continent.

"Take madam to room 934."

The cologne followed her and the bellman as they left the desk and walked through the now noisy lobby. The bellman rode the elevator with her in silence.

The drab room didn't surprise her. When international chains took over these old hotels, they decorated the rooms in bland, outdated colors, that set standard expectations for all hotels on the continent, chains or not.

She had bigger problems to handle than an unpleasant room. But the visual aesthetic mattered, it was in her DNA to want a nice room to relax, kill stress, and—yes—even sleep. She'd learned to add taking care of herself to the top ten list for surviving an art fair anywhere. "Is this room the same as all the other rooms?" Maybe she could change rooms.

"Sí, except the penthouse suite. She is not happy with the room?"

She abandoned the idea. "No, it will be fine." She handed the young guy a twenty-dollar bill, probably a day's pay for him.

There were practical reasons to be generous when she couldn't afford it. Before the elevator hit the lobby, the hotel staff would know there was a lady who tipped well on the ninth floor. This gesture might buy prompt responses and establish a helpful home base to balance the mad pace she'd face for the next five days. The money would be worth it. She made a silent promise to herself, don't think about money.

The bellman returned with a bucket of ice.

She checked her watch, poured a glass of water, sat down, and kicked off her shoes. "What's interesting in Bogotá?" She studied his nametag and added, "Frederico."

"Casa Bolivar. Lots of history and emerald stores there. You like emeralds?"

"Emeralds are expensive." She rubbed her fingers together in the universal symbol of money. Perhaps the tip had left the wrong impression.

She continued. "I have clients who are interested in pre-Colombian artifacts."

A good collector of her gallery's Latin American art had a passion for pre-Colombian history and had approached her when he'd heard she was traveling to Bogotá. He'd been on a dig in central America, a volunteer archeologist, and participated in writing a monograph. He ticked off a list of unfamiliar pre-Colombian cultures. When she'd asked him about the laws related to removing historical objects from the country, he brushed her off by remarking small things can be found in marketplaces. He added he'd be glad to buy them, authentic or not. She warned him she knew little about pre-Colombian cultures but would be on the look-out for objects like he described.

"Artifacts?" The bellman shook his head. "Government prohibits certain things to leave the country. *Guaqueros,* gravediggers poke the ground with sticks and find graves. If you are interested, I will ask."

She couldn't reconcile his last comment with the remark about government prohibitions but had more important things, like her crate, to deal with. Frederico left the room, offering to help her with whatever she needed, and closed the door behind him.

She washed her face and let the cool washcloth linger on her temples and forehead, drawing out the tension. After she'd dried her face and brushed her teeth, she rifled through her suitcase and pulled out the one thing she could not travel without: the photo of Claire and Mikey. She placed her palm on the glass of the little frame as though she could touch their cheeks. Soon, she told them, soon, she'd be home.

A hard desk chair, the only chair available, provided a perch to rub her swollen feet. She poured more water from the bottle that sat on the desk next to where she'd tossed the mysterious embassy packet.

The envelope contained a letter on embassy stationary, with a salutation addressed to her. Last month, she'd reached out to the U.S. Cultural Attaché requesting that the embassy invite García Márquez to the art fair to view McGraw's paintings, a tribute to his book, *One Hundred Years of Solitude*. The embassy responded that Gabo, as his friends called him, was unavailable. He'd been scheduled to accompany the Colombian president who was hosting five Latin American presidents at a Medellín summit. Seriously five presidents? It had been a wild ass idea to invite him in the first place. Regardless, McGraw was thrilled to learn that his name and the painting series had gotten in front of the Nobel prize-winning author. So was she.

The embassy packet letter read:

Dear Ms. Blake,
Congratulations on being selected to bring artwork from the United States to the *Feria Internacional de Arte* (FIART). As part of our efforts to promote cultural exchange between the United States and Colombia, we want your visit to succeed.

Hard to stomach that one. The U.S. didn't help art dealers promote their artists abroad. Every foreign gallery had artists' catalogues, booth space, shipping costs, and sometimes airfare and hotels, all paid by their governments if they exhibited their country's artists. U.S. galleries got zero, nada.

Colombia is extremely dangerous for American citizens. The Department of State has placed Colombia on the Travel Advisory list with a Do Not Travel designation. Violence by narco-terrorist groups and other criminal elements continues to affect urban, rural, and coastal regions of the country. United States citizens have been victims of muggings, kidnappings, and other acts of violence. Since 1990, thirty-two Americans have been reported kidnapped.

The U.S. Government places the highest priority on the safe recovery of kidnapped Americans. However, U.S. policy prohibits negotiation with terrorists and the U.S. Government has limited ability to assist American citizens.

Covering their tails. If she was kidnapped or the victim of an assault, they could say to her family or to some senator who might inquire, we warned her, waving the signed receipt still reeking of the Puig cologne.

Read the Alerts below. Always carry the 24-hour emergency number with you. Have a successful and enjoyable stay in Colombia.

She turned the letter over, but it was blank. Inside the envelope was a small business card with a phone number and a page of letterhead from the Regional Security Office, United States Embassy with the subject title *Alerts*.

She took a sip of water and continued to read.

ITEM 1: If someone in a uniform stops you and asks
for identification, walk away, get to safety. Do not
stop for any reason.

Meaning what? Get shot? The alert went on to say Americans had been kidnapped when a police imposter studied
their identification. The imposter would tell the American
that there was a problem with their papers, and they needed
to go to the station house to clear it up. If the victim resisted,
kidnappers in a nearby car would grab them. *Desaparecido*
. . . disappeared, a common Latin American tale.

ITEM 2: When in a bar or public eating place, never lose
sight of your drink. Several American women have
reported a drug, identified as *plucho*, in their drinks.
They have been raped and robbed. The Embassy urges
you to consume drinks only from unopened bottles.

The phone rang.

Mateo's tone sounded urgent. "Are you coming downstairs?
This place is like a war zone. Loud pops. The front desk clerk
said 'Gunshots' without even looking up. Like it happens all
the time."

"What? Real shooting, outside the hotel?" Her voice
trembled. "Are you and Santi okay? Was anyone hurt?"

Mateo often exaggerated. This time she hoped he had.
Before he could answer, she hung up and tossed the packet
with unread warnings onto the desk, grabbed her purse, and
headed for the lobby.

CHAPTER 4

THE LOBBY BUZZED WITH PEOPLE, including Mateo and Santi who laughed from some amusement she could not imagine. She wanted to join their festive mood, but a dark cloud floated over her. "What's funny?"

"Art fairs are funny. Colombia is funny. Strange and funny," Mateo replied.

"Gun shots, lost crates, financial challenges—funny? Really?" She regretted throwing cold water on their joke, but seriously?

Fresh air beyond the cigarettes and confines of the hotel appealed to her. "The Convention Center is down the block and across the street. Let's walk."

Santi gave her a disapproving look. "No, no. We'll go with my driver, waiting out there." Santi did that thing with his hands, something between pointing and flapping, that said 'don't bother to argue.'

In her fatigue, she agreed with a quick nod.

Three men rushed to open the hotel door for her, and she forced a smile at their attentiveness. She and most modern women recognized this effort as a hollow gesture in a country where women struggled to be equal. She supposed American women would not sacrifice hard-won freedoms for small tokens. But maybe some would.

Outside, a cacophony of car horns sounded, vendors hawked their goods, and military men shouted, all a contrast to the relative calm inside the lobby. With Mateo next to her, she followed Santi to the white stretch limo where a guy in a silly uniform waited for them.

She shook her head, worried the limo would make them a target for thieves, a hijacking, or worse. "Of course, an important New York dealer must arrive in style. *Correcto*, Santi?"

Santi waved his arm with a flair and replied, "For Mateo Lugano, Best New Artist at the Cuenca Biennial." Santi had found the sweet spot to pump up Mateo's confidence.

A descendant of northern Italians, Mateo's light-skinned cheeks glowed in embarrassment.

Bogotá could be a great time. In her head, she said it again as though repetition boosted the possibility that she could enjoy herself without fretting.

They drove through the hotel turnaround, and before they exited to the street, Santi was flirting with the driver— a skinny fellow with the unlikely name Brutus. Through the back window, soldiers ran after the car with rifles at the ready.

She shrieked to get Santi's attention. "What the hell? Stop. They're going to shoot. Stop."

Santi turned to see the soldiers running and scoffed, "They get their panties in a bunch when we don't stop. We never stop. Somebody probably bribes them to hassle us. Think of the military here as toy soldiers—don't take them seriously. If we stop, we also got to pay the Man."

She wrinkled her brow again. "The *Man*?"

"Everyone here wants or needs a bribe to leave you alone, to get things done, whatever. I told you it's the minimum wage. Embrace it. Things will be easier for you."

Santi knew the system and used his knowledge to navigate these different cultural rules. The information helped her understand the place, but complicity in corruption regardless of Colombia's conventional practices, felt like moral compromise. Quick fixes could lead to potential perils that would never end.

During the short ride, daylight disappeared over the mountains surrounding the city and their silhouettes appeared closer. The yellowed landscape, now turned to black with the evening sky, raised the tension about what was hidden in those hills.

The limo pulled into a circular drive and stopped at the glass doors of a grimy building. The architecture of the *Centro de Convenciones Gonzalo Jiménez de Quesada* represented a failed attempt at modernism.

"Gonzalo who?"

Santi rolled his eyes as though he expected more from her. Even with graduate work in Latin American politics, her knowledge had limits. So many countries, different cultures, many histories and heroes.

"A dead man who founded Bogotá. A Don Quixote guy, looking for El Dorado. Just like us, Ally, we're here for the El Dorado of art." He put his arm around her, squeezed her shoulders. "Your gallery is going to be a huge success at the fair."

A buzz of preshow activity, a familiar chaos that reduced her anxiety, filled the convention center. Workers in jeans and t-shirts ran back and forth with crates, parcels, toolboxes, and ladders. Forklifts cut a path wherever they could fit, sometimes threading a needle avoiding a near collision. Exhibitors had less than twenty-four hours to retrieve, unpack, organize, hang, and label their gallery's art. For her, that crazy work would be followed by a Cinderella transformation into a glamorous dealer who could greet the moneyed class of the Americas.

"Señora Allison Blake?"

An elegant Colombia woman, a girl really, greeted her. The girl's clothes and jewelry were, well . . . wow. *Hija de papa*, her father's daughter, this young woman had been permitted to do socially acceptable work until she married. For her parents, the best result would be work that would introduce her to a rich husband.

Confronted by haute couture on a kid, Ally glanced down at her own black turtleneck, black blazer, and black pants. She judged herself acceptable, but not showy. An art dealer dressed in black could go anywhere but needed to avoid messages of excessive wealth (the artworks are overpriced) or desperate finances (no one's buying her artists).

"Welcome to Colombia. I'm Maripaz, your concierge. I have your credentials."

Maripaz presented exhibitor credentials to her and Mateo and handed her the usual everything-you-need-to-know-about-this-art-fair notebook in two languages. Before Ally could thank her, Santi steered her by elbow toward the corner booth already labeled ALLISON BLAKE GALLERY, CALIFORNIA, USA.

"This *is* a terrific space." She stood back and took it in. "I can visualize where the canvases will go. If we ever get the crates—" A large crate at the back of the booth drew her attention.

"Mateo, Santi, a crate arrived! Is the other one here somewhere?" She surveyed the small space, including the storage closet positioned inside the booth. Nothing.

She returned to the one crate. "What's the number on this crate?"

Mateo pulled it away from the wall and checked the back side. "It's marked '#2'."

"It's not the one with the big art." Her excitement disappeared. "At least we have the tools and supplies and some of the small McGraws. The big money art is in the other crate."

Santi looked around the outside of the booth to see if it was in the aisle. "Customs has a substation here at the Centro for exhibitor's shipments. It might still be there waiting for a forklift to bring it up."

Substation 1109. Things were looking up.

"Mateo, try to find some tools to open that crate. I'm going to find Enrique to see if he can help me get the other one. Santi, will we see you later?"

"I'll see you at Enrique's dinner." Santi bowed with a grand sweep of his arm.

"Wait. What dinner?"

"Everyone's invited. Your invitation—there on the table."

She turned to a little reception table placed in her booth to see not one, but a stack of invitations. Santi flicked through them and handed her the one to Enrique's *cena*.

Supper at eleven p.m. A response to the invitation was required. She'd tell Enrique when she saw him.

Eleven p.m., how did they do it? Eating so late, it took all she had to keep her face from falling into the plate. And they'd all be up and ready to work in the morning. Latinos had that party gene, something missing from WASPs like her who could only aspire to the Latino capacity for late night living.

Promising to see them later, Santi blew kisses and urged them to find him if they needed anything.

When he was gone, she strolled the aisles, checking the art in competitors' booths and hoping she'd run into Enrique. It didn't take long. "California Allison," called a familiar voice. She turned and there was Enrique loping toward her, his arms extended. "You made it."

She'd always been fond of Enrique, but she was surprised by how happy she was to see him. He was friendly, hard-working, and dedicated to his artists, but he had an inner sadness, an old soul she was drawn to. She also liked the sophisticated way he dressed. Even here, installing art, he was as elegant—crisp shirt, silk tie—as the art in his booth.

She kissed his cheeks. "Enrique, hello. And yes, I'd love to come to your party tonight." She pulled the invitation from her purse and held it up. "I hope it's not too late to respond."

"Of course, not," he assured her. "Your name goes right to the top of the list."

"Can I bring Mateo Lugano? You remember him, right? From the Cuenca Biennale."

"Of course, he's welcome." He added, "Bring your IDs. Security will be tight. For your protection, you understand. Come see my booth."

She continued to talk while they walked. "Can I ask for your help? I'm having trouble getting customs to release my crates," she told him. "Well, one crate arrived, but the other has been taken prisoner."

He sighed but didn't seem surprised. "Did you go to the customs station here, adjacent to the parking garage?"

"Not yet. Do you know anyone who could help?"

"Ask for Jose," he said, packing up his briefcase. "Tell him I myself authorize him to release the art, and I'll sign the paperwork in the morning. I'd go with you, but I must hurry home to supervise the caterers."

"Where's Helena?"

"She's doing an interview on television. She won't be coming to the fair."

"I apologize to add my crate problem to your very full plate."

He shook his head. "Speak no more about it. I'm your host in Bogotá, it's my pleasure to make your experience a success." He rolled down his sleeves, fiddled to insert his cufflinks, and put on his jacket. Picking up his briefcase, he tossed a white scarf around his neck with a dramatic flair. She watched him until he disappeared out the exit.

The directional signs had an arrow pointing to the parking garage. She was determined to find the substation and resolve the crate issue. Equipped with José's name and Enrique's support, she forged ahead to retrieve the crate. Inside the door, a staircase led to another door that opened into a dark tunnel, leading to an empty garage. She wished that there were more people around or that Mateo had come with her.

The echo of her heels on the concrete sounded throughout the silent space. She stopped, listened, and kept walking, faster.

Against the back wall of the parking structure, there was an enclosure made from chain link fencing. She read the sign that said customs and, hallelujah! Substation 1109. At last.

"Hola. José? Hello."

Hearing no answer, she pushed the enclosure gate open. The noise of the rusted gate creaked throughout the basement. She wandered in and surveyed what was locked in a separate cage at the back. She caught a glimpse of several crates that were like the ones they'd shipped. She craned her neck to look for markings that would identify one of the large wooden boxes as belonging to her gallery.

"*¿Qué quiere?*" A gruff voice, a kind of a growl came from behind the stacked crates. She jumped, surprised, and reacted with a nervous giggle at his odd snarl.

When his face came into the light, the dour man was not amused. Not at all.

"Are you José?"

He growled, "José, gone home."

"Allison Blake, exhibitor." She waved her badge in his direction and reached out to shake his hand.

He ignored her hand and asked her again what she wanted.

Okay, down to business. "Do you have this crate?" She handed him the goldenrod pages from the customs office. "Airport customs said it was here in your substation."

"Who is your broker?" He looked at her, waiting in silence. Perhaps he wanted a bribe.

"We don't have a broker." Without any money to offer him, she'd use what she had. "Enrique Rodriquez from FIART said to tell José that he authorizes this crate and will complete the paperwork in the morning." She stumbled on the unfamiliar dialogue, searching for the words to communicate bribe money would be paid.

"I know nothing about this." The man looked away.

Ok. Did this guy need a bribe different from the one José would get? Maybe she should have been more specific—like 'take care of José and you' or something else, that would include this man in the offer. "I know Mr. Rodriquez will take care of you." She shrugged wondering if pleading might help.

He growled back. "Where you are standing is not Colombia. While they wait to be inspected, your crates are not in the country. The *jefe* must sign before they can pass customs."

She'd hoped José was the *jefe*, but maybe not. "Please can I talk to the *jefe*?"

Silence. He turned his back to do some other work, ignoring her, just like the guy at the airport. *Strong women, not welcome here.* Or maybe it was that she was a Yankee. She needed a new approach, reconsidered, and rejected all the choices, including crying.

He closed the big chain link gate, sweeping her out of the space, and added, "We are finished, señora."

She placed her hands on the gate and planted her feet to stop him from closing her out.

He pushed harder and closed it, locking it with the big padlock.

She tried again, shaking the gate to get his attention. From outside the enclosure, she tried one more time. "Señor Rodriquez will not be happy about this."

Unmoved, he ignored her and disappeared behind the shelves of boxes and crates.

She walked back up the ramp, her frustrations and exhaustion turning to tears. Time was running out. The small McGraws might work if hung as a group, but the great white walls needed large pieces to make an impact. At most fairs it took a whole day to hang an exhibit, sometimes rehanging to make it look balanced and to draw in the collectors. She tried to organize the artworks they had in a mental display, and landed in the same place: there were not enough large pieces to create a substantial display.

The dark passage that had frightened her on the way down became a refuge, providing privacy to get a grip on her fragile emotions. The ramp was so dark she bumped into a planter or a high curb, she wasn't sure. She sat down, taking a moment to recover before entering the art fair space. Becoming the center of fair gossip and being labeled a weepy art dealer was not the introduction she wanted.

If the game wasn't bribes for the customs people, she couldn't understand what the motive was. She had fair bills to be paid, artists who depended on her for their survival, no money to pay the mortgage, the damn life insurance people sitting on her appeal. The worst, she had no partner, no Nick for support, to carry half, well, more than half the burden. Two *was* better than one. Heavy sobs, punctuated by gasps for air, echoed in the tunnel.

It's only an art crate, only an art crate. If Nick was still with her, she'd call him after the kids were asleep to review the challenges of his day and of her day. He'd listen and share calm words that took the edge off. She had no one to call, now.

She stopped crying long enough to draw in some yoga breaths, visualizing all the toxins and stress leaving her body. Find a perfect happy place—your escape place, she said mimicking her yoga instructor. Those happy places became more difficult to imagine.

Images of her children's faces, so perfect, so innocent in the arms of their dad appeared behind her closed eyes, the sounds of their laughter and the smell of their sweaty foreheads from horseplay and finally, a happy collapse exhausted from joy.

She opened her eyes. She needed the art sales so badly she'd left her precious children alone with Margarita, a loving house-keeper. But Margi had limitations. When Nick was alive, she would never consider leaving them for days with Margarita.

That crate contained potential art sales of tens of thousands. To save money, she'd bought the minimum coverage insurance policy for the crate's contents. If the crate never showed up, she'd not only lose the sales, but would have to pay her artists for their missing works without much help from the insurance company. A double disaster.

She searched her purse for a tissue. Never had one when she needed it. She covered her red eyes with her sunglasses which only made the creepy tunnel darker. She paused for a moment and then reopened her purse to take out her keys. She clutched them in her hand like a weapon, the way she'd been taught in self-defense class.

Armed with keys, she crossed the parking garage. Loud footsteps came from behind synced to the rhythm of her steps. She cringed but didn't want to turn and look. Instead, she quickened her step.

The steps behind her increased, came faster, closing the gap between them.

Now almost running, she rounded the ramp. With no clue how far she had to go, she saw a light from the bottom of a metal door on the back wall of the basement. The door to the convention hall wasn't far. She might make it.

A glance, a quick look over her shoulder.

The surly guy from the substation was walking ten paces behind her, but the door remained too far to reach it before he would catch her.

Running was useless. She stopped, turned to confront him. "Did you want to speak to me?" she yelled at him in Spanish. Fear smells like vulnerability; confidence intimidates, as she learned from New Yorkers like Santi.

The guy smirked. He walked past her without responding, like he was on his way to somewhere that had nothing to do with her. What the heck?

He threw open the door and light filled the parking garage with safety and relief. She followed, walking behind him into the convention arena.

Her heart pumping still, she made her way through the fair, rushing, just short of running through the aisles to her booth, home base. She collapsed in a chair to catch her breath.

Mateo lifted his head from a toolbox and looked at her. "Why are you wearing sunglasses?" When she didn't answer, he returned to searching for a hammer.

She gasped for air, turned around to survey the booth, and hid her swollen face from him. He didn't know this fragile art dealer she'd become in the last year, and she preferred he would never meet her. "Look how much you have hung!" she said between heavy breaths.

Mateo had installed some of the works that had arrived and was transforming the bare walls of the booth into an art exhibit. Maybe they could be ready for an art fair to happen in twenty hours. They were still missing the big money pieces, but at least they had some art to sell.

He bent back over the crate, which was almost emptied. When he stood up, he stared at her puffy face. He didn't ask, but maybe drew his own conclusions. "You didn't find the other crate?"

She couldn't lie, not to him. She pretended to search the supply box and found flannel cloths to wipe her face. She took the bottle of hospitality water left by Maripaz and poured some on to the cloth and dabbed her cheeks.

Mateo stood up behind her. "You don't have to do it alone." The comment showed some rare empathy on his part; he wasn't all cynicism and sarcasm.

"I know. I know." She held back and didn't say more. Her new reality, her truth was that she was alone, profoundly alone.

He looked away. "We need to get to Enrique's supper. Aren't you hungry?" He'd moved on, exhausted his quota of sensitivity. He was right. Best to move on, nothing more to do, until tomorrow. A distraction was just what she needed.

She couldn't ask for sympathy and add her problems to his own list. Mateo had watched fellow artists survive political suppression and even torture by the Uruguayan dictatorship because of their ideas. He lived in near starvation to make art that mattered. Her problems, her crate, her finances were petty challenges by comparison. She shook it off, embarrassed that she'd melted down over so little.

"Did you learn anything about the other crate?"

She exhaled and looked away.

Mateo put on his hoodie, signaling he wanted to leave. "I'm hungry. Let's go."

She picked up her purse. "Tomorrow, we'll hire a broker."

CHAPTER 5

ALLY WASTED NO TIME DRESSING FOR Enrique's party, throwing clothes on the beds, on the floor. She grabbed a black dress and put it on with the adrenaline rush of a costume change between acts of a stage play. No time to pause, or yield to exhaustion, or feel anything before she stumbled onto the stage.

She made her way to the lobby and hoped the hotel would have a safe car for them, especially after the warnings from the embassy. But Mateo was way ahead of her, at the front desk asking for a car and driver. The doorman appeared within seconds and ushered them to the car, bypassing taxis and other private drivers not approved as safe by the hotel.

They settled into the comfortable sedan that smelled of new leather. If everything from now on went so well, she'd be over the moon. She rested her head on the back of the seat, closed her eyes. In what seemed a micro minute, the driver slammed on the brakes and pulled off the road. She sat up straight, alert and watching.

The driver guided the car onto the gravel shoulder. He avoided hitting a uniformed guard and announced to the back seat, "A checkpoint."

"No one stops at checkpoints," she quoted Santi and remembered the unusual cautions in the State Department Alerts.

The driver replied with a non-negotiable, "I must."

Mateo leaned over the front seat and whispered to the driver. "Why? What are they looking for?"

The driver answered over his shoulder, out of the corner of his mouth. "Rebels. Military posted to keep the FARC rebels out of the city."

She interrupted him. "Maybe the guards are thieves, kidnappers, or paramilitary about to kill us. Maybe they're FARC."

Mateo flashed a look asking her to be silent. Even though Mateo had not seen the embassy letter, he had more experience in places like Colombia than she did, and he probably had more understanding than embassy staff.

The driver didn't answer and turned his attention to a rough-looking guard standing at his window.

Dressed in half a uniform with a battered camouflage jacket that hung unbuttoned over a t-shirt, the guard spoke with the driver in a low voice and then issued a command. "Get out." Barely old enough to shave, he wore dirty cargo pants, worse than the military guys outside the hotel. That the Colombian military were so ill-equipped resulted in an assumption that they were either random recruits or not military at all.

Mateo gave her that skeptical look he displayed when he had a lot to say but didn't. He got out and held the door for her.

She stepped onto the dark shoulder of the road, crunching the gravel under her feet, and made herself as tall as she could. The cold night wind stung her face. She clenched her hands in front of her to quiet their trembling and could not look at Mateo.

Another military, or not military man who smelled like sweat and dirt, put a flashlight close on their faces. "*Identificación!*"

She fumbled inside her clothes for the little pouch that contained her passport, some cash and a credit card, a separate stash that had become her routine wherever she traveled. The just-in-case-Plan-B-emergency-kit had been honed from her days working for the State Department, a work history she had put behind her and would never share in this situation.

Mateo, who towered over the soldier, pulled his ID from the pocket of his jacket. The guard shined a flashlight on his face and then on his passport, comparing the photo to the reality.

The guard took her U.S. passport and repeated the same comparison.

She studied him and declared the obvious, "I'm an American citizen."

Mateo squeezed her arm, a wordless message to be silent.

She searched her memory for something from the embassy packet about checkpoints and wished she'd brought that card with the emergency number, not that there was a telephone she could use.

The hotel driver sat in the car and looked in the opposite direction, fiddling with a cigarette lighter, maybe complicit in this . . . she didn't know what to call it . . . shakedown.

The soldier, rebel, criminal, whatever, turned to confer with his comrade; then he abruptly handed the passports back to the driver.

The driver got out for the first time and barked an order. "Get back in the car." He opened the door and almost shoved them into the back seat.

The car tires sprayed gravel as the driver headed onto the road and held their passports over his right shoulder. They took the identification papers, stowed them, and rode in silence. In another time and place, Mateo would have been loud and outraged. The whole thing made no sense. The mood in the car converted from fear to relief as kilometers fell away between them and the checkpoint if that's what it was.

The driver turned on the radio and sang along, perhaps to avoid questions from the back seat. His pleasant voice offered a nice distraction for them and maybe for him, too. The upbeat song ended, and the hopeful energy died. Even the lyrical canto could not cover the stench of danger hanging in the air along with the stale smell of cigarettes the driver smoked. Relief dissipated into the darkness, and her anxiety returned.

She never trusted drivers without having some sense of where they were headed. There'd been no time between acts to do her usual careful hiring of cars, with drivers employed by the hotel and directions to the destination given by hotel personnel. A doorman should record the license numbers like they did at the Alvear Palace Hotel in Buenos Aires. She studied the neighborhood they were driving through and concluded nothing about the dark streets. It seemed a quiet neighborhood of mostly houses where the unlit windows indicated the occupants had gone to bed. Still, she'd find alternative transportation for the return trip if she could.

Other worries outweighed the suspicious ride. To come to such a dangerous place was the gamble of her life, but Santi and others said the press overstated everything. The fair would be safe. She'd borrowed on the credit cards to make the gallery payroll and to fund the expenses for the booth rental, shipping crates, airfare for both her and Mateo, and of course, the hotel, food, and private car rentals.

The precarious nature of her own finances and the opulent wealth of the art scene required her best acting role yet. With the aplomb and confidence of a hugely successful gallerist from California, she'd proceed to make what was a fiction into reality. She had to.

She pushed aside her misplaced anger at Nick, something that came and went in brief moments that ended in her chastising herself. It wasn't Nick's fault. Regardless, he'd left a mess of bills he planned to pay when he got his bonus, something that didn't happen before he died.

Finances were not even the biggest challenge. No, the darkest obstacle came with worries about the future for vulnerable

Mikey and Claire. Their world, their future without a father looked very different than it had before Nick died. And now, at least for the next five days, they had no mother either.

She needed to regain her composure. Opportunities to meet collectors waited at Enrique's party, a networking scene that required complete focus and a magnetic presence she'd need to muster to succeed.

The driver slowed to enter yet another too dark street. He didn't need directions, he'd said, because he knew the building. Helena and Enrique were minor celebrities or maybe major celebs in Bogotá. Ponce designed the seven-story structure for his family. He might have been a competent painter, but he was no Frank Gehry. In the distance, a rectangular tower stood above the two-story neighborhood. The ugly box had balconies stuck on it like birthday cake decorations. Each of Ponce's adult children occupied a single floor. The artist and his wife resided in the penthouse like some architectural family tree. Helena and Enrique lived on the fourth floor, reflecting the birth order of the many siblings.

"Shit." Mateo shook her and pointed her head toward the window on the opposite side of the car.

She gasped at the scene ahead. A fortress a bit like the Brandenburg Gate before the Berlin Wall came down loomed above the street of single-story houses. Two guard towers rose on either side of a fortified entrance, staffed with four men, each armed with an automatic weapon of some sort, she couldn't tell one gun from another. Twisted razor wire and chipped glass covered the top of the wall. German shepherds pulled at leashes tethered to a metal ring at the gate.

"They live here? Like prisoners, prisoners of their own success."

"Shh, Mateo. Don't say anything." She'd become the shusher now.

"Let's go back. I'm not *that* hungry." Mateo's concerns set off alarms for her.

She ignored them. "You intimidated? Impossible. Can't believe you don't want to see where the Ponces hang out."

The driver turned to them, asking for their documents, again. His tone made it clear there'd be no discussion.

A guard took out a clipboard and shined a flashlight on their passports.

Oh yes, the list, the one Enrique claimed protected them.

The driver produced his credentials as well. Mateo thrummed his fingertips on the seat and his knee shook. No doubt memories of what had happened to his friends during the Uruguayan dictatorship plagued him. One of the armed guards got into the front seat next to the driver and rode with them to the next gate where they all got out. Their driver said he would wait for them in a guarded parking area. She said nothing, but reminded herself that she'd find a different, safer way home.

"Ready for a party?" she whispered to Mateo, trying to sound upbeat.

He sighed.

The guard hustled them to the portal. Inside the building, another guard checked another list and directed them to an elevator. The elevator car was paneled in brocade silk and had an inlaid marble floor. The operator pushed a button to take them up, and Ally couldn't wait to sit down and relax with a drink.

An elegant woman with delicate skin stood inside the elevator, staring at the ceiling and then the floor, presumably to avoid talking with them. Ally could only see her sagging neck, but even there, the woman tried, tried too hard, to hide what the years had taken. Her jewelry said major money. Definitely New York. Harry Winston necklace, Judith Leiber bag. Manolos on her feet.

Many art dealers considered assessing a potential client's wealth essential to 'qualify them.' Real money didn't need expensive trappings and the wealthiest clients she knew were understated to a fault. They drove Fords, carried department store purses, and never had a logo anywhere. One client commented, "Why should I provide them with free advertising?"

This woman in the elevator needed to be acknowledged, because she had an agenda or a personality flaw or both. Her ornaments proved nothing about personal wealth, only about choices and priorities the owner clung to for a multitude of reasons.

Ally played that game, even though she considered it shallow. She ran her fingers over the alligator skin of her Hermes bag—or accurately, her faux Hermes with real alligator skin. A Frenchman in Buenos Aires had worked for the leather firm in Paris and made perfect copies with the exact Hermes hardware for the clasp and the little lock. A real purse cost about $10K, hers cost $200, still a stretch for her, a gift to herself. It had passed the test of discriminating eyes and that pleased her.

The emaciated woman looked down, still avoiding eye contact in this slow elevator. Finally, Ally got a good look at her full face and recognized her immediately.

"Laura, I'm so sorry I didn't recognize you when we got in the elevator."

"Pardon?" The woman answered.

"Allison Blake from Blake Gallery, San Diego." She put out her hand trying to reduce the awkwardness.

She'd been introduced to Laura Ellsworth at least ten times, but Laura never remembered a poor gallery owner from San Diego. These games would be amusing if they didn't cut her out of certain collector circles. When she refused to give Laura a work by her artist Morini for Ellsworth Auction's Latin American sale, somehow Laura forgot who she was.

"Oh yes. Of course. How are you, dear?" Laura gave her a limp hand.

Ugh. She hated to be called dear. "Surprised you are in Bogotá."

"We've important collectors here."

Yes, she believed Laura on that, especially since they were selling Ponce's work at such high prices.

Mateo's face mouthed the words BEE-ATCH.

Ally suppressed her laugh with a fake cough and quickly added, "Laura I'd like to introduce Mateo Lugano, Uruguayan painter."

Laura offered Mateo the same limp hand, mumbling something about Cuenca. The elevator door opened, and they stood aside to let Laura exit first. Laura looked straight ahead and, without turning, said, "Beautiful bag, Allison."

Ally winked at Mateo.

Maripaz greeted the three of them. "Ms. Blake. Buenas noches, Señor Lugano." She held a clipboard with another list and turned to Laura. "Good evening, madam, may I know your name?"

Maripaz had committed the ultimate blunder: failing to recognize the arrogant Laura.

Mateo stuffed a cigarette in his lips and stepped away, pretending to light it, but Ally could see his back shaking with laughter. She turned away or she'd lose it too.

Laura strutted past, ignoring Maripaz, making it clear she would not bother with someone so small in Ellsworth's world hierarchy.

They waited in silence, pretending not to notice Laura's futile attempt to cover her embarrassment. Mateo greeted Maripaz like an old friend and whispered Laura Ellsworth's name so that the young gal could check her off the list.

Maripaz smiled and reciprocated by waiving off their identification check. "Enjoy the evening." She winked.

CHAPTER 6

PARTY CONVERSATION BUBBLED LIKE the champagne sparkling on large trays carried by waiters. The motionless waiter in the entrance offered them his tray to grab a drink. She helped herself. Mateo took a glass too and made a direct line through the crowd toward an attractive curator from the Wilson Institute. Ally couldn't tell if Mateo was in pursuit of an exhibit for himself or something else.

She stayed behind in the small foyer to survey the Rodriquez's apartment. It had an elegant old money vibe even though the money wasn't old, and the furnishings probably weren't either. A huge Ponce painting, a stylized portrait of his daughter, Helena Rodriquez, depicted as a very skinny girl with sad eyes and huge feet, loomed over the tiny entrance. She could understand why it was hung here, where Helena would only see it once or twice a day and most visitors would miss it completely when the elevator door was open.

The real Helena stood in the center of the next room, holding court near a small trio that played quiet ballads. The funky painting didn't do her justice. She wore a simple Chanel dress, accessorized with diamond earrings and her own laughter. Acting the queen's role, Helena projected a glow on those around her. And her subjects adored her. Ally pondered whether she could have been Helena, in a different world, a different time, but abandoned the idea as improbable and, for her, unappealing.

Just off the entry sitting area, a forlorn-looking Enrique stood in the library holding a crystal Old-fashioned glass filled with Scotch, no ice.

Ally made it through the crowd to his side. "Sorry we're late."

Enrique kissed both her cheeks in a European, Hollywood-type greeting. "There's no late in Colombia. Did you get your crate?"

She shook her head. "José wasn't there. A different guy. Surly. Hmmm, not helpful." She didn't want to spoil the evening by revisiting the dark garage or revealing how worried she was about getting the art.

"I'll investigate it myself in the morning. Hopefully, it will be delivered to your booth tonight, and you'll have your art before the opening."

"Your words to God's ears." She mustered a smile. "What an interesting room. Feels like we've been dropped into a European palace."

The library shelves held an amazing collection of leather-bound books, with gold-embossed lettering on the spines, rising to the top of the twelve-foot ceiling. A 17th century globe stood next to a French writing desk that could have belonged to Louis XV or maybe it was Louis XVI. One of them anyway. Claire's little hand could never have reached Bogotá on this globe if Colombia was even recorded on the map. But Nick would have loved the details and coloring on the geographically misplaced and mislabeled countries that history had revised over the centuries.

"Are you a book collector?"

"No. Ponce got tired of these. Gave us the entire room, including the wood paneling. Well, in truth, he gave it to Helena."

"Whoever put it together, it's impressive." She paused and took a sip of her champagne. "Is it strange to be his son-in-law?"

He turned toward the books, pulled a volume from a shelf, and mumbled as he thumbed through the pages. He looked up. "You cannot imagine."

She waited in silence. People cannot tolerate silence; every salesperson knows that. She wanted to console him and found it difficult to stay quiet. Eventually, Enrique would fill the void with his full meaning or as much of it as he wanted to share.

An awkward moment passed, and then Enrique continued. "Now it is difficult. Laura Ellsworth is demanding that I give her a Ponce for her Spring sale in New York. I don't have one. She's threatened to pull the Bravos I have in the sale unless she gets one. Can you imagine? If she pulls those drawings, everyone will start the gossip machine, about Bravo's values, and me as his dealer."

Mateo was right. Laura was a bitch with powerful leverage. Sometimes dealers and artists could never come back after something like Enrique described. She didn't work with Laura or other auction houses, exactly because she didn't want to play these games.

"Can't you get Ponce to give you a painting or get one on the secondary?"

"No. Many reasons, but now . . ." His voice cracked. "Helena and I aren't good right now. I can't ask her father, and I can't ask her to approach him."

She put her hand on his.

He pinched his lips together and nodded at her empty champagne glass. "You need another drink."

He guided her into a large room with crystal chandeliers and a marble fireplace. The mantle and the inlaid wooden floors had been purchased from a chateau in France. A fashionably hip dressed man standing near the mantle approached Enrique.

"Allison, meet Esteban Lobo. Lobo studied painting in the Bay Area."

She knew his work. His abstract paintings, beautiful patterns, and subtle textures, all about the surface had a good market in San Francisco. "Definitely Bay Area influence in your work, Esteban. Diebenkorn, the patterns, the colors, the lines, very California with an energy that's Latin American. Are you living here now?"

"Everyone calls me Lobo." He gave her one kiss, Colombian-style and nodded. "Yes, I'm in Bogotá. My family lives in the northwest where my father has limestone mines."

Lobo surprised her. A background of study abroad, family of landowners, and a career as an international artist was unusual. Most artists she met in South America struggled like Mateo. "Is the northwest emerald country?"

"Emeralds are in the east near Chivor. That area is very dangerous—more dangerous than Medellin or Cali, drug country. Foreigners traveling in the east are there to buy emeralds, and the bad guys know it."

Peril loomed everywhere, it seemed. "Is anywhere in Colombia safe?" She lifted her eyebrows.

"Sure. Of course. Would you like to visit the northwest part of the country? Interesting cultures inhabited the area for centuries. Sometimes father's men find artifacts when they work in the fields."

Enrique had no reaction to this description of what might be illegal. He didn't object or add any information, mostly he seemed disinterested in the topic.

She turned to Lobo. "Artifacts? I might have a client."

"The *gauqueros* find graves, sometimes they have mummies, clay figures, and pots. Sometimes gold artifacts. Many things like clay whistles from over two thousand years ago."

Maybe if the objects were found on your own land, you owned them like in the United Kingdom. She'd need to ask someone who knew more.

"That's curious. Pre-Colombian whistles?"

"Security devices. Some cultures used them to notify guards on the mountain tops that a friend was coming. Hollow figures in clay, each with a unique sound, repeated as a signal."

By now Enrique had begun a conversation with another guest. She hadn't come to deal in pre-Colombian objects, a subject that required serious study, especially about the laws. "My client wrote a monograph and included photos of little gold bells. He said ancient cultures placed them on tree branches above the graves to sing to the dead souls." She'd imagined a breeze sent from the heavens that was from Nick to ring the little bell, sending them his love.

"Beautiful idea, no? The bells are more difficult to find, but I own some I can show you. Would you like to see the whistles? You can buy those. My father's men can bring objects to my studio. Then you could see my paintings, too."

"Now? Tonight?" The weariness of a day that had begun in California dragged on her energy.

"You'll be busy all week once the fair opens. Me, too."

That was true. Unexpected events, like Enrique's dinner appeared on her schedule, and the business plan demanded she take advantage of the network opportunities. "I'll ask Mateo if he wants to leave. We haven't eaten."

"If he doesn't want to come, I'll take you in my car. Eat something now, not much food at my place." Lobo went to borrow Enrique's phone to set up a meeting.

This was crazy, just what she'd said she wouldn't do. Going somewhere strange with someone she barely knew at one in the morning, what was wrong with her? Fear of missing out, desperation to make every peso she could.

Across the crowded room, Mateo laughed, enjoying the company of the curator with the trendy haircut and European-styled glasses. Mateo promoted more than his paintings; she was certain. The curator remained aloof, which apparently made her more attractive because he seemed eager.

"I'm going to Lobo's studio to look at artifacts. Want to come?"

"No." Mateo answered without taking his eyes off the curator.

"It's okay. Lobo said we could go in his car."

Mateo whipped his head around, turned his attention toward her with a serious scowl. "What? Don't go. Stay at the party. A little longer, we'll go back together."

Before she could explain her plan, a handsome man approached and grabbed her. He twirled her around and almost knocked her off her feet. "I've missed you."

She couldn't see his face, but his *abrazo*, his fragrance and his voice told her everything she needed to know, even after all these years.

"David Martinez." She pushed him back, enough to view his face and shook her head in disbelief. "What are you doing here?"

"Heard you were coming to Bogotá, and I would not have missed seeing you for anything." He squeezed her again. "I am posted here, at the embassy."

She pushed David away and returned to Mateo who waited patiently. "Meet Mateo Lugano, one of the artists in my gallery. We're exhibiting his art and others at FIART."

Mateo shook David's hand and had that expectant look like he wanted more information.

"Graduate school together at Stanford." She pointed to David and back to herself.

Mateo lost his worried look. He abandoned his laser attention on the curator to listen to David.

"Colleagues and . . . more." David smiled.

Ugh. She did not need David bringing up the past, a past she'd buried from everyone. "I'm an old married lady now with a couple of kids."

"Widowed. Heard about Nick. Sorry about your loss." He reached to hug her again, but she turned and moved a step in the opposite direction.

David stood up taller as if to regain his dignity and establish dominance over her. No surprise with that either.

She didn't have the energy to handle him, and she searched the room for Lobo. "I'm leaving now. Perhaps we'll see you at the fair." She could not allow unnecessary distractions, especially ones like David.

David tried to take her hand, but she shifted her purse to that hand and avoided him. Instead, he took a hold of her arm and steered her toward a chair in the corner. "I'm not letting you leave Colombia without at least having dinner with me. When are you free?"

"The fair demands so much of my time, and my schedule after the fair closes is packed too."

Mateo had followed them and asked, "Didn't you want to leave together? Our driver's waiting."

David held his hand up like a traffic cop. "I've got an embassy car that will drive her to the hotel, completely safe."

She hated that David spoke as though she wasn't present. Lobo wanted her time too. If she left with Mateo, she'd get to sleep faster.

This was not the place or the moment to have a confrontation with David who was playing top dog. If David disclosed anything about their past in school or about Chile, it would ruin the new life she'd built. She needed to isolate him from everyone else.

She turned to Mateo. "You take our hotel car. I'll be fine."

Mateo scanned the room and asked, "What about Lobo?"

"Can't do that tonight. My only plan is to get some rest before the fair opens tomorrow."

David interrupted. "Break your plans. How often do you get to see me? Let's catch up."

Too tired to fight, she resigned herself to staying. "We could chat for a minute. The buffet looks great, and I'm starved." Maybe she could use a plate of food here to check off the 'have dinner with me' box and avoid David for the rest of the fair. "Let me change my appointment with the artist."

Lobo chatted with a musician who was on a break and quickly stopped his conversation when she approached. "A former worker from father's mines has antiquities to show you. At my place, in thirty minutes?"

"Something has come up." She motioned toward David, who waited for her in the corner. "Could I postpone for a day? See the artifacts tomorrow? I really do want to see them and, of course, see your paintings too."

"I will try to meet the men and rearrange. I'll see you at the opening party tomorrow night and let you know."

It was almost two a.m. in Bogotá, late in California too. Twenty-four hours was not enough for every opportunity. Sometimes sleep was optional, but not for her, not after the challenges of this day. Exhaustion had taken over.

A waiter came to her rescue and offered to bring her a plate of food from the buffet. Eating wouldn't spare her from having to talk to David, but she'd keep him from talking with anyone else. David reminded her how glad she was to have married Nick, built a life with him, even for the short time they'd had together.

David went on and on about his successes in the foreign service. She nodded and sampled the food on her plate, saying nothing.

"I'm the Political Attaché posted here in Bogotá. A very busy embassy." He hadn't changed, same self-congratulatory David.

She picked up her fork, pretending not to notice his attempt to impress her. She finished a bite of empanada, toyed with a fried plantain, and admired the caviar garnish on top. Enrique and Helena had outdone themselves with a sophisticated taste of Colombia that would satisfy this fastidious crowd.

David rambled on about the status of people they'd known at school and in Santiago.

She placed her empty plate on a tray a waiter held out. Without a mouthful of food as an excuse to be silent, she asked about Bogotá and kept David away from the topic of 'them.' Her academic persona kicked in and mined him for information. "What about the chaotic political groups, Mr. Political Attaché?"

He leaned over to whisper. "Not here. You never know who is about to stab you, metaphorically, of course."

David's comment didn't sound like a metaphor.

A waiter interrupted them with a tray of ceviche in shot glasses that looked delicious. She took one and tasted. When David asked her about her art gallery, she motioned she was unable to answer with her mouth full of fish. When she'd finished chewing, she asked, "What else is happening in your life? Wife? Family?"

"Since you left me, gorgeous, there has been no other."

Whatever charm he once had fell flat with her. Maybe he was never charming.

He laughed a hearty chortle, probably induced by a champagne buzz. With David, you never knew, could never quite scratch under the surface to find the substance, if there was substance.

Nick on the other hand, was all substance. Rock of the earth solid. Honest, hard-working, kind and . . . boring. No joie de vivre in him. But didn't matter, she remembered how their opposite personalities resulted in joy enough for her. A memory of a day driving up the California coast in his old car came back. No air conditioning in that old Ford, she'd pleaded with him to stop by the beach to cool down. Before he could turn the engine off, she opened her door and ran into the surf, clothes and all. He ran after her, leaving his shoes on the shore, grabbed her from the waves and made sure she hadn't lost her mind.

They laughed, splashing water with a freedom that now seemed so distant. Later, she'd used her hair dryer on the wet cards and the money from his wallet. He forgave her madness, but he never embraced the idea that spontaneity could beat a careful approach to life. They'd settled on a balance between the two, a balance that had shifted now without its rock.

David waved his hand in front of her. "Hello? Where did you go?

"My husband was a great guy. Wish you could have met him."

He nodded and squeezed her hand. She didn't withdraw this time.

"Sorry you lost him." He let go of her hand and fumbled with his tie. "I've missed you. Great memories of us, our adventures in Chile. Remember when we went to Peru together, hiked the Inca trail? The sunrise at Machu Picchu. Did you forget how great it was?"

"I remember, but then—"

"Then what? Allende was dead." His tone turned. "You knew what you'd signed on for."

"No way that I agreed to be an accomplice." She wasn't going to go there, not here, not now. "No matter, that's behind me, over. Forgotten."

Fatigue returned, making her weak, almost dizzy. The ugly memory added to her stress. "I'm tired, to my bones tired. Can we leave now?"

"I've got to stay until the ambassador departs. Protocol, you remember. But the embassy driver can take you to your hotel. Are you okay with that?"

Okay? She preferred to go alone.

"Tequendama, right? Everyone stays there, military owns it."

The military running a hotel? More surprises.

Enrique chatted with other guests across the room. She waved at him and mouthed thank you with a smile.

Outside, she walked with David to the embassy car, passing the hotel driver who smoked with some other drivers.
David closed the door and waved good-bye. She collapsed
on the leather seat, resting her head on the far window. She
sighed, grateful for a secure ride and a respite from the buzz
of people and parties.

CHAPTER 7

THE EMBASSY DRIVER SAT BEHIND a glass partition of a limo, even though David called it his embassy car. Whether the glass screen protected the driver from the passengers or the other way around, was not clear. David had given the limo driver instructions, but no introductions, no names. Ally didn't hear a response from the driver nor see his face, and now she rode behind a guy as stiff as one of those mannequins in a car safety test.

She rested her head against the window, slumping onto the leather seat and then sitting up trying to find a comfortable position for her tired body. She poured a glass of ice water from the tiny fridge. Crystal bottles of premium Scotch and brandy sat on a shelf that protected them from flying around the limo. If the U.S. Government used tax dollars, including hers, to pay for this, maybe she should take a bottle or drink a glass.

The nameless driver retraced their arrival route through the exit she renamed the Brandenburg gate. Scary dogs showed their teeth to the guard holding their leashes. Outside of the Ponce compound, they drove on until a checkpoint appeared. She didn't recognize it as the place they had stopped. The embassy driver ignored the military type guys and just drove around. A chase car followed their limo per embassy procedure for certain level foreign service officers. Apparently, David's rank now earned him this perk. At the Santiago embassy, they were expendable staff and rode in taxis or friends' cars.

Stunning mansions lined the road of the neighborhood they now drove through. Living in Bogotá, with obvious wealth, would invite betrayal. Who could you really trust? Constant worry about personal security had to hover over anyone with money.

The Bogotá neighborhoods, rich and poor, held tight to their secrets. At night, all seemed peaceful, but monsters lurked. As they proceeded deeper into the city, their limo parade passed places documented in press photos, places with mass shootings, singular assassinations of targeted officials by motorcyclists, bombings and attacks on the police by drug cartels, with bad guys plotting or sneaking around in the dark cave of crime. Hard to imagine in what seemed so peaceful in the dark.

Pablo Escobar from the Medellín cartel personified a paradox, a ruthless villain slaughtering hundreds but a people's hero, helping the poor of his beloved Medellín. Add to the toxic mix the fights between the FARC guerrillas looking to take over the government, the military, paramilitaries, anti-drug forces, former U.S. military turned private contractors, contra this and that—not to mention the campaign to avoid extradition to U.S. prisons, where no bribe could save you. Colombians and Americans gave up trying to understand who the good guys were.

David Martinez in Bogotá seemed a peculiar addition to the noxious soup. No accident for sure. The last time she'd seen him was when she'd fled Santiago in 1973. She'd worked for the Art in Embassies Program, where she'd been assigned to Santiago. She closed her eyes to forget the painful memories, stories she'd buried so deep that she'd never even told Nick. Seeing David forced her to remember.

The Art in Embassies Program, a great idea initiated by President Kennedy, failed in its purpose. Ambassadors chose what their tastes dictated. They all had . . . well, kindly said, limited judgment in art. It was a rare ambassador that had spent time understanding art. Being rich or a high-level bureaucrat did not translate into sophistication or good taste.

Occasionally an embassy requested works by Roy Litchenstein or Rosenquist, although even those could be pretty and decorative. It pained her that artists who put their souls into original work and could have benefitted from the attention, rarely received the opportunity to exhibit in embassies.

The odd thing about the Santiago project was that Ambassador Franklin wanted the pieces installed at the Chilean Presidential Palace. Some type of friendship gesture to President Allende. The U.S. Government disagreed with Allende's policy to nationalize banks, copper mines and other business ventures owned by U.S. corporations. The U.S. poured money into Chile to get someone other than Allende elected.

Allende was right to fight for the Chileans to own their country's resources. Like her, some foreign service folks had cheered for Allende and the Chileans. Quietly.

She had never placed art outside American-owned buildings in any foreign city. Too much risk to the lender, in this case, a small museum. She objected, and then did as the ambassador directed. The thirty-foot ceilings in the corridors of the Moneda Palace would make the paintings appear like postage stamps. They were wrong for the space.

The cultural attaché had scheduled the install on a specific day and time when they had a security team to go with her. Usually, installers were hired to help, but not this time. Another staffer pointed out the guards' briefcases contained automatic weapons. That's what guards do. The art wasn't that valuable, unlikely to be stolen, but the station chief had his reasons, and these decisions were beyond her pay grade.

When they arrived at the palace, the U.S. guards disappeared. When she'd hung all but three paintings, two guards came running back into the central hall. Each grabbed one of her arms, swinging her off her feet like a lantern. They rushed toward the side entry where the van was parked. Protesting, sputtering, she was helpless to protect the unhung paintings and complete the final paperwork.

A radio in the van reported that the Chilean military was marching on the Moneda Palace, a coup in progress the radio screamed. She sat stunned during the return trip; no words existed to express her shock.

After that, like waking from a bad dream, she lost track of the sequence of events. But she did remember sitting in her office, trying to fit the puzzle pieces into place.

David Martinez opened her office door and presented a newspaper showing the palace being taken over by the military.

"All non-essential American personnel are ordered out of Chile. That includes you."

He sounded triumphant and arrogant, like he was essential, and she was not. She and art were not.

"What about the art? Those works are loans from a U.S. museum. It's my job to protect them."

"People will pack up all the works and get them back to the museum. Unless . . . " He stopped as though he hadn't thought about what happened next.

"Unless what?"

"Things get bad, really bad." He paused, searched for the words, and continued with the one thing that mattered. "Rumors are, well, you know rumors, that Allende committed suicide."

Allende had a lot of enemies, but suicide? Assassinating him would have been crazy. She wiped away tears with a tissue from her desk.

David squirmed. He'd never known what to do with her tears.

When she returned to California, sleep became impossible. She reviewed the details in her head, like still frames from a noir film. She could not bring herself to listen to the Congressional hearings and the lies being told.

When State ordered her to another post, somewhere in Scandinavia, she applied for disability leave. No one questioned the claim, and she vowed never to return to that world.

THE LIMO PULLED INTO THE NEON-LIT porte cochére of the Tequendama. She quickened her step to the entrance, requested her key, and hurried to the elevator. Her exhausted body craved a bed and decent sleep.

She put the key in her hotel room door, opened it, and plumes of cigar smoke escaped into the hallway. She coughed and then gagged at the stench.

David Martinez reclined on the bed in the middle of the clothing she had strewn across the two twin beds. His head rested on her pillow, his shoes on her bedspread.

"What the hell are you doing here?" Confused and nervous, she took the clothes off the bed and threw them into the closet.

David chuckled.

She grabbed his cigar, threw it out the open window. "All my clothes will smell like your stinky smoke."

"Have a glass of wine, a great bottle from Chile to chill a bit." He laughed at his own bad joke.

Now the smoke was coming out of her ears. "Not interested. I need sleep."

"I'm not here to hit on you. I'm here to discuss business."

She pulled on his arm. "Leave, just leave."

He stood, pulled his arm away, and poured another glass of wine.

She waved her hand and pointed at the door.

Instead, he sat down. "Sorry to intrude, especially so late, but those parties are not a place to talk. We need you to do something for us."

She stared at him, pursed her lips. "Not interested. Not in those games anymore." She folded her arms over her chest. "This art fair is essential for me to recover financially, so much invested, and so much on the line—the gallery, the staff, my kids. I've got to focus on selling art."

"That's what we're asking of you—to sell some art."

She scowled but waited, wondering if she was too quick to judge.

"We have a painting we need you to sell to raise some cash for some . . . ah, projects. You could make a good commission." She paused, waiting, rolling her finger asking for details.

"It's a Ponce."

David with a painting like that? No way. "A Ponce? A fake?" This better be good.

"It's legit. We need you to sell it at auction."

Nothing made sense in her exhausted brain. People did not make art deals at three in the morning, sitting on hotel beds. Well, maybe people did, but she didn't. A good Ponce painting could net millions in commissions for her. But something besides the cigar didn't smell right.

David kept going. "We want a public record of the sale, but no connection to us. Submit it as 'Anonymous. Private Collection.' Happens all the time in auction catalogues."

That was enough to send her running. "Look, my reputation depends on accurate information—provenance, history of ownership, and legitimate attribution. Not to mention a proven owner with paperwork and bank accounts to send the proceeds. Can you provide that?"

He pulled out another cigar and held it unlit between his lips, like a pacifier.

She shook her head, wanting to end this now.

He returned the cigar to his pocket.

Why weren't they using Ponce's main dealer in London? Didn't make sense and perhaps whoever was behind this was counting on her naiveté, or the Agency didn't have assets in the art world. Maybe she was their only connection, someone who'd worked with them once.

"Ownership, David? The proceeds? Who gets them?"

He stood, like he realized his time was up. "Can't tell you. The bank accounts are clean, and the painting is authentic. Sell the damn thing. Tell the auction house to wire the proceeds to the account we give you, less your ten percent, you'll make more than the whole silly art fair. You can arrange to have the painting shipped to the auction house from here."

"You had many character flaws at Stanford and in Chile, but I didn't ever imagine you'd end up selling stolen art."

He raised his voice and his arms. "Nonsense. Not stolen." He gave her that stern look she remembered from Santiago. "Your government, your country needs your help. Don't you want Colombian violence to end?"

She howled at the absurdity of the claim. "How does a painting help with . . . ?"

Before she'd finished asking the question, the answer became clear, like a cartoon lightbulb turning on. The money was for something the U.S. wanted off the books. Congress had refused to fund something U.S. operatives wanted. Dirty money.

Without waiting for an answer, she grabbed his arm and dragged him toward the door.

"The answer is no, no, and NO. Get out of here." She managed to get the door open with the other hand. "Let me sleep."

He turned, reached to embrace her. She escaped and shoved him into the hallway, wine glass and all. She turned the bolt and added the chain to secure the door.

David's little project contained a mine field of problems. She knew it. No amount of money or financial desperation could lure her into being part of it.

Hotel security was worthless. She'd complain in the morning, even if the result would be the same. What did David say — owned by the military? She lifted the desk chair, carried it across the room to jam it underneath the doorknob.

She pulled her black dress over her head, tossed it onto the other bed and grabbed the flannel nightgown made for a mom. She kissed the photo of the kids, slid between the sheets, and hid herself under the duvet as though the bed cover could protect her.

DAY 2

CHAPTER 8

MORNING ARRIVED, LIKE NO TIME HAD passed. One cup of coffee was not enough, a whole pot, gallons and gallons of coffee wouldn't be enough to face the challenges of opening day. She needed to get the last crate delivered as soon as possible. They'd need to unpack the art and install it, maybe move other pieces around, then get the wall labels up, clean the booth and be ready to receive the VIPs at the private reception. The opening party brought the best collectors and was her shot at making the most sales.

She checked her watch to see what time it was in California. The kids were still sleeping, and she'd need to try later, maybe tonight. She left the room to find the shuttle to the fair.

After a short ride, she got out and walked into a mostly empty convention center. Jake Klingman, a dealer from Guatemala and not her favorite person, worked to set up the booth that was next to hers. Mateo had arrived and was installing the McGraws from the one crate they'd received.

He blew her a kiss from the top of the ladder. "You're going to be feliz, Roba-cop."

She groaned at the nickname he'd assigned her after the cult film hero who always tries to do right and get justice. Or maybe it was because Robocop's robot body was always falling apart.

"The only thing that will make me happy now is more coffee." She sat her things on the chair.

He shook his head. "What about the second crate? In our storage closet? Would that put a smile on your tired face?"

She couldn't believe what he said. "Here? Yes, yes." She turned, leaped three giant steps to the door of the closet-sized storeroom. An unopened crate sat next to the other one that they'd unpacked yesterday. She managed a coffee-deprived grin and went back to where Mateo was climbing down the ladder.

She lifted her palm to high five him. "That's great. A worry I can let go of."

"Do you want me to open it now?" Mateo pulled out the electric screwdriver.

"No time. It'll make a mess. We can't clean it up before the VIPs get here. Maybe there'll be time before the opening party to open it and hang a few large paintings." They'd need the crated works to refill the walls if they sold well at the opening party. She didn't know what to expect. "Tomorrow we can rehang everything."

She and Mateo maneuvered the ladder out of the booth into the aisle for the install crew to retrieve.

"Ally. Ally." A familiar voice came from behind her. And like a recurring bad dream, David walked down the aisle toward her. "Good morning." He reached to give her a kiss on the cheek.

She turned her head. "Our conversation from last night is over. If you're here to pressure me, don't waste your time. Or, frankly my time, time I don't have. The answer will be the same."

David mumbled something of an apology and then added, "I wanted to alert you. Some things are already in motion."

She scrunched her forehead. "Then, un-motion them. I want no part of whatever you're cooking up."

He didn't react, not even with his involuntary eyebrow twitch.

She shook her head with a forceful no.

Sounds of police sirens outside interrupted her. The screeching added to the crescendo of sounds filling the convention center.

David turned toward the entrance. "The ambassador and President Gaviria. Come, let me introduce you."

She stiffened but complied and walked with him toward the entrance. David was doing his job and she wouldn't embarrass him or the embassy, but she heard that sucking sound pulling her into that foreign service prestige trap.

"Greetings, Martinez. Been enjoying the art?"

David shook the ambassador's hand and poked her in the back to push her forward. "Ambassador, I'd like to introduce Allison Blake, a gallery owner from California."

"Ms. Blake. From San Diego, formerly with State in the art program. Frankie Brown, the cultural attaché briefed me."

She nodded, and understood what 'briefed' signified.

"You're exhibiting paintings by García Márquez . . . "

Oh jeez. She stumbled. "Ah, ah, ah. Yes, a California artist did a series of paintings inspired by García Márquez's novel *One-Hundred Years of Solitude*."

Informing him, without making things more awkward, she lowered her voice to discretely correct his error. She'd danced this tango when she worked in the foreign service, trying to make every representative of her country look good.

"Right, the author." McKenzie looked away. "Frankie said you'd invited Márquez to come to the fair."

"I wrote to the cultural attaché, but apparently, García Márquez is unavailable."

"Well, there's a surprise for you. He's right behind me in the president's limo. At the embassy reception, Márquez asked about you and the paintings."

Whoa! García Márquez asked about her. Was arriving, any minute. "I . . . am stunned." Panic distracted her from what the ambassador said next.

She steadied herself and searched for graceful words to leave them. "Excuse me, Ambassador. If he's arriving, I need to go back to our exhibit booth to prepare a welcome for this wonderful *author.*"

She backed away toward her booth, as if in deference, having been semi-successful in walking the thin line between educating him and disagreeing with him.

"Ally, wait." David followed her. "Can you meet me tonight at the opening party? Or maybe breakfast tomorrow?"

"Isn't that too public for the Agency?"

"We'll have breakfast—two old classmates. In the Tequendama restaurant."

"Not tomorrow—I may need to rehang the booth with art from a crate that arrived late."

Ambassador McKenzie had joined them and overheard her decline David's invitation.

She looked at David's forlorn face and didn't want to make problems for him. If she put him off closer to the end of the fair, there'd be no chance she could do what he asked. "Maybe on Saturday, day after tomorrow. Let me confirm."

"I understand. I'll meet you in the hotel lobby."

She nodded and hurried to her booth, passing a Japanese gallery exhibiting a Picasso painting, a bold move in a city full of crime. Two guards, useless if someone was determined to take the artwork, stood at the entrance of the booth which looked like a Shinto shrine. To steal such a recognizable painting, a fool's mistake. The work could not be displayed with the whole world, including Interpol knowing it was stolen. Every dealer checked such things.

Yet, this did occur with collectors who obsessed about certain art objects and had the wealth to make it happen.

Like Munch's *The Scream*, a famous theft of an iconic work stolen by either stupid thieves who'd learned there was no buyer or clever ones who contracted with an uber wealthy buyer who just wanted it, even if he could only view it in a secret vault.

She made a mental note to meet the Japanese dealer and see this Picasso before the fair was over.

Cheering and clapping interrupted the quiet buzz of the hall. The noise converted into a roar like Madonna had arrived. She stretched her neck to peer down the aisle, expecting to see President Gaviria.

Gabriel García Márquez entered the hall to adoring fans. Colombia got it right, even with all its problems. The author, a true treasure, received and deserved more recognition than top politicians, self-important ambassadors. How could you not love a people for whom a writer was a superstar?

She took long strides to outpace the VIP group and arrive at her booth before they did. DeLoss McGraw's *One-Hundred Years of Solitude Series*, inspired by Márquez's novel, made connections between the Colombian's writings and William Faulkner's writings. The works resembled Joseph Cornell's assemblages. An artwork about borrowed ideas, also borrowed ideas.

Her anxious persona, that voice in her head, took over. Maybe the little encaustic boxes with collages made from sentences clipped from both authors' novels would offend this great writer. To suggest that Márquez borrowed . . . and yet, no one was pure, without influence.

She got to the booth and found Mateo had switched into an ill-fitting suit jacket. He'd ditched the tie most dealers wore for a turtleneck and recovered his art mojo, a bit like a dealer, a badly dressed one. He looked relieved to see her, and she was happy to see him.

"You disappeared again."

"Sorry. Just met the U.S. ambassador who is coming any minute with the president."

"President Bush?"

"No Gaviria. President of Colombia."

"Did he seem afraid?"

"Why would you say that? There's an army of guards and press. Did you hear something? Have there been threats?"

On a normal day, she preferred not to know about her artists' networks. Idealistic young people in South America walked a razor's edge between responsible dissent and rebellion. With very real consequences of disappearance and death, like in Argentina, they played with fire for a great cause. There was not a studio she visited without a poster of Che. Contemporary art became an expression of angry defiance, if not overt revolt, in artists' studios.

Mateo grew up during the Uruguayan dictatorship of the 1970s and '80s when painting certain subjects, like an evil general with blood dripping from his mouth and naked from the waist down, could cost an artist his freedom or even his life. A *Los Angeles Times* critic compared Mateo to Georg Grosz, the painter who challenged the German industrialists supporting Hitler with ugly portraits of grotesque figures.

Mateo took a deep breath and answered, "Anyone who tries to stop Colombian drug dealers has a target on his back. Narcos control this country. Only the FARC wants Colombia for the people."

A noisy group rounded the corner and came toward them. She held her hand up to Mateo to stop talking. "Shh. Here comes the VIP parade."

A gaggle of journalists shuffled down the aisle toward their booth, with an attractive man at the center that she recognized as the Colombian president from posters around the city.

Ambassador MacKenzie guided the president toward her, and she reached out her hand, thinking air kissing was not protocol. The ambassador made a brief introduction mentioning her background and her art gallery. He got it right, and maybe she had David to thank for that.

Gaviria was charming. She shared the story about Santi's dinner with the Colombian education delegation at the United Nations in New York. She also mentioned Santi a couple of times as a great lover of Colombia. He nodded but didn't comment, except to ask what type of art she represented.

Ambassador McKenzie beamed. He did not need to apologize for her lack of knowledge or education. Or her network, something she'd spent decades trying to build along with a reputation for honesty and transparency. Despite her misgivings about her government's policies, she would never be critical in public or embarrass her country. Those conversations were for private discussions, in that sense she thought of country just like family.

The Ambassador shared what she preferred to avoid. "Allison worked in our Art in Embassies program in Santiago."

Hearing the ambassador's words darkened her mood and her sentiments toward her country. She'd managed to run from the Chilean ordeal, avoided thinking about being used in an assassination, and had succeeded in burying that experience. David and the Ambassador's entourage brought the nightmare back.

"Did you enjoy Chile, Mrs. Blake?" Gaviria, still holding the hand she gave him to shake, looked into her eyes and appeared genuine in his interest.

Say something, something neutral. "A beautiful country with excellent wines."

"Colombia has wine, too." He motioned to the complimentary bottle Maripaz left on the desk. Gaviria walked from painting to painting reading the labels on the McGraw gouaches, images of *Coronel Buendia* and his adventures from Márquez's book. Surely the president did not see any political advantage to this exchange unless he'd heard about Allende, read her file too. Geez. Maybe he thought she'd come to assassinate him.

Mateo shook Gaviria's hand. "*Buena suerte.*"

Good luck? The press corps erupted in nervous laughter. Gaviria responded with a forlorn smirk, a tacit admission of his impossible challenge to control the violence in his country.

McKenzie scowled at Mateo and moved on with the entourage to the next booth.

Ally turned to Mateo. "What was that? Luck to a president dealing with drug thugs? Black humor, don't you think? Urgh."

"The only thing I could think to say." He lied. "Don't you think he needs luck? Apparently, the journalists do."

Mateo rolled his eyes and leaned his head toward a handsome gentleman in a tweed jacket with a turtleneck, reading glasses on the end of his nose, studying the paintings. She approached him with the butterflies of a teenage groupie.

"Señor Márquez." She offered her hand.

He kissed her hand. No air kiss, a real kiss. "*Encantado.*"

"We're thrilled that you're able to be here. May I offer you some wine?"

"I'm not feeling so well, no indulging myself. But please go ahead." He paused. "I'd like to see this art."

She pointed at a vertical painting of a colorful figure. "This California artist interprets Macondo and El Coronel in his work. His art embraces Colombia's vibrant culture, described in your book."

He came closer. "Fascinating work."

"These collages have texts from your novels compared to texts from William Faulkner." She removed the encaustic box from the wall. "The artist sees a connection."

Paper scraps of text from his book and artist sketches covered the glass-enclosed surface.

Márquez adjusted his glasses, studied the words. He smiled and looked up, "So . . . what happens is I forget. I forget what I wrote." He laughed, and she laughed. "I barely recognize it in translation."

His eyes sparkled with life despite well-earned weary lines surrounding them. No matter the political affronts he'd suffered, there were also grooves that recorded many moments of laughter. His face mapped the history and spirit of Latin America.

He returned the painting to her, and she offered it back to him. "The artist, DeLoss McGraw asked me to make a gift of this small painting to you."

"How generous. Thank you, what a pleasure." He looked closely at the work and then at her. "I want to give you a gift too. When do you leave?" He looked to one of his assistants, waiting at the edge of the booth, holding back a whole group of fans following him. Being close to him brought national pride and wisdom, hope to people of all stations.

She regrouped to respond, "Sunday. We leave late Sunday."

Márquez motioned to the assistant, and asked her to gather Allison's contact information.

Ally had another thought and asked, "Perhaps a simple thing you could do, it would be a great gift for me. I've heard you don't sign autographs. May I ask you anyway? Would you sign this old copy of *One Hundred Years of Solitude?*" She'd brought this Spanish version in case someone asked about the translated lines in McGraw's paintings.

He took the tattered book with the coffee stains on the cover from her student days into his hands.

Márquez turned it over again and again. His eyes filled with emotion. "Where did you get this?"

Was he offended by her careless treatment of his famous book bought over twenty years ago?

"Madrid, 1967. I was a student at the university there." She shifted from one foot to another while he examined the book, even reading the copyright page.

Finally, he spoke. "This is a very special edition. Printed by Editorial Sudamericana in Buenos Aires. Political issues with Cuba, my friend Fidel, dominated the news and my life. Kept me out of the United States for years. When the print run was shipped from Buenos Aires to Colombia, the Colombian government impounded all the books and . . . " That sad look returned. ". . . destroyed the entire shipment."

She gasped and stayed silent, considering the loss of precious books, this masterwork. The idea that any books, however famous, well-written or not, could be destroyed, disgusted her.

He spoke in a quiet voice absent the rage she felt. "Some copies got out of Argentina, mostly to Madrid. This is the first time I have held this paperback edition in my hands in many years. Can you imagine my joy to learn it survived and made this journey back to Colombia?" He lifted his reading glasses off his forehead, stowed them in his jacket pocket and focused his eyes on hers. "You've made me happy twice in a few minutes." He smiled and searched his other pocket for a pen, which his assistant produced like handing an instrument to a surgeon.

Márquez, a writer without a pen, that was something she'd remember.

He scribbled on the title page of her book, closed it, and handed it back to her with a pensive look. After he returned his glasses to his pocket, he took her hand and kissed it. "A pleasure I will not forget. If I can do anything, anything at all to help you while you're here, take my private number." He nodded to the assistant, and she handed her a business card with a handwritten phone number.

Ally tucked the card into her pocket, although she would never ask a favor of her new friend, unless she was beyond desperate.

He picked up the McGraw painting, studied it, and whispered. "Like Colombia, many layers, joy and tragedy, always rich with life." He kissed her hand again and said, "Colombia is more than what you see. Look beyond the headlines, and you will find love and dignity."

No words could match his, but she hoped he saw the affection and gratitude in her eyes.

He moved on, a little unsteady, taking the crowd with him.

She opened the book where he'd drawn a sketch of a flower, and read,

Una linda flor. Gabriel

Gabriel. Not Gabo, not García Márquez, just Gabriel. She clutched the book and closed her eyes. "What a fine human being. Latin men, got to love them."

"Does that apply to me too?" Mateo took the book from her and read the inscription.

"Are you jealous of García Márquez giving me his attention?"

And who wouldn't be jealous? In five minutes, she'd met the president of a country who would rule for a minute and a beloved author whose works would live for all time. The burden David tried to unload on her, the stress he'd added, evaporated. She'd be Gabriel's *flor* in this garden of weeds.

She returned to the work of the art fair until two guys, not art types, wandered by. Márquez's comment on books being impounded in customs, a great author with friends and connections had no power to prevent the destruction of his art. How would she get rid of David and his preposterous scheme?

Mateo clicked his fingers in front of her face. "We got work to do." He took her hand and walked her toward the storage closet. "The VIPs are gone. Let's open the other crate before the party people arrive."

CHAPTER 9

A FEW STRAGGLERS, WHO'D BROKEN away from the entourage, wandered the aisles. The politicians, the VIPs, their handlers, and journalists moved toward the exit. A quiet interlude settled over the convention center.

Mateo pulled the heavy crate from the storeroom closet that she'd paid extra to have constructed inside their booth. A room with a door that locked provided secure space for additional inventory to replace what had been sold. The room was a tiny, flimsy affair that any determined criminal could get into with little more than a sneeze. However, untoward movements and noise would bring security guards, and they could stop a thief. And there was no way to carry an artwork out of a fair without a fist full of documentation.

She stood on the other side of the second crate and pushed while Mateo pulled. Once the crate was out of the storage closet, it could be placed flat on the carpet. The big crate left very little floor space for anyone to move around the booth.

In her garage at home, crates left over from art shipments piled up. Those empty wooden boxes represented the gallery's successes, because the art they'd contained had found a home. Empty crates got repurposed as imaginative toys for Mikey and Claire like a boat with a sail constructed of a broom stick and a bed sheet. Mikey named himself captain and directed Claire to be the first mate, even though she was older. Ally considered saying maybe the oldest, regardless of sex, should be the captain. Nick had disagreed. "Don't mess with happy kids, they'll find their way," he'd said.

She missed him, missed them, missed the four of them together. The family photo now had two empty chairs, but in four days, she'd be home filling her spot.

Mateo waved at her. "Screws are out. Can you help lift the lid?"

The wood was heavy. The inside was a mess, disturbed and unrecognizable from the carefully packed container she remembered from two weeks ago. The paper wrappings had been hastily replaced around one canvas, another paper was torn and the bubble wrap — essential to protect the works from friction scratches — was missing altogether. "This crate's . . . not the way we shipped it."

There was something else.

The shipped crate had been full, and with all the bubble packing missing, it should have been partially empty. But it was full as though something extra had been added.

Mateo lifted a couple of badly wrapped paintings. "Customs guys! In Montevideo, we receive containers like this. Claim they're looking for contraband, but I think it's stuff to steal, easy to sell, an electric screwdriver, but not art."

"Let's do a quick inventory, check against the bill of lading." She went to her bag and found the document that listed the paintings. She cringed, recalling some of the most expensive and saleable pieces, certain revenue for the fair, should be in this crate. "If we do the inventory together, it'll go faster."

Mateo unwrapped each work. She checked it off the list, and together they set the artwork against the wall. He got halfway into the box and stopped at the fourth painting. "This one is not on the list. I don't need to check."

She didn't look up from trying to organize her papers. "We need to check the list anyway."

Mateo cleared his throat to get her attention. "Will you just look?"

She stopped searching in her briefcase and turned around. "What the heck?" She grabbed the chair to steady herself. "No, definitely not on the list."

Mateo placed a large Ponce painting with the iconic emaciated figures against the wall. The brash colors called out "look at me" to anyone passing by.

This could not be happening. "Quick. Turn the canvas to the wall before anyone sees it."

Mateo shrugged his shoulders and complied. "Where did it come from?" Mateo checked the lid for marks that identified the container as part of their shipment. "So?"

Damn David.

"I have an idea how this happened, but I need to be sure. Better you don't know. Hide it in the storeroom for now."

He lifted the painting so no one could see the front and walked it back into the closet area, where he rewrapped it in brown paper.

Mateo returned to the crate with several paintings still inside. "What do you want me to do with these?"

"We don't have time before guests arrive. Finish unwrapping the others, clean up the mess. Please, hurry. The big collector crowd is coming soon." She needed to find David and get to the bottom of this.

"Couldn't you sell that Ponce to the big shot collector crowd? *Mucha plata.*" He rubbed his fingers together and smiled.

"Not ours to sell. I need to find out what this is, who it belongs to, how it got into our crate." She started to leave and stopped. "Please don't mention this, not to anyone. I can trust you, right?"

He winked. Always lighthearted with a sense of humor in contrast to her high anxiety level of emotion. She valued having him as a side kick.

She buzzed up, down, and around the aisles in search of any of those crew cut guys with the earpieces that had to be Agency guys. She'd ask them for David's whereabouts, even though the guards probably wouldn't tell her.

The bastard. He'd stuck her with the Ponce, probably what he meant by "some things in motion." He pulled her in, despite her insistence that she wanted no part of his dark money scheme. Now it would not be so easy to get rid of that high-profile painting. Damn him.

Ambassador MacKenzie's entourage had stalled at the booth of another New York dealer. Not Santi, someone else. They'd been introduced at Enrique's dinner, but she couldn't remember the gallery owner's name. She was wary of asking people she didn't know if they'd seen David. Never breach or breathe information until you verify and verify again, who is in the circle of trust. At this point, her circle of trust had shrunk to a few names.

She passed Enrique's booth, where he chatted with a client. She waved, tried to smile, and he nodded in her direction. She couldn't ask him anything, although of the people at the fair, after Mateo and Santi, she did trust Enrique. No real reason, maybe intuition, a sixth sense that he was authentic, honest in ways others were not.

After circling all the aisles, she arrived at her booth with no more information than when she'd left. The crate was back in the closet and the booth looked ready for the opening with a few of the higher priced works on the wall. Mateo was amazing.

Mateo sat at the desk and sketched a drawing in a notebook. "Where did you go?"

"On a futile mission. I still don't know anything about that Ponce painting."

"You mean paintings . . . Ponce paintings."

At first, the plural didn't register. "What?"

Mateo set down his notebook and got up. "There's two. Two Ponces—I hid them both back inside the crate."

Shit. What has David done?

CHAPTER 10

TWO GUYS, OUT OF PLACE IN DEMEANOR and dress, lurked in the areas around their booth. Private security for the fair, possibly. She had no way to be certain they weren't David's guys or something else.

She couldn't ask them where David was, even though she needed answers and soon. David's scheme made it likely he knew the whole story. But where was he now?

Mateo couldn't be told about this, or he would be caught in the web without escape. Anyone else would be trapped, used, and discarded, just like she was in Santiago. Until she developed a plan, the only option was to sell her art, be an art dealer, stick with the goal of coming to an art fair in a friggin' war zone. Maybe she'd just leave the Ponces behind in her booth and let David deal with them or send a truck with the paintings to his office at the embassy. But that would involve a lot of people, and the last thing she wanted was more people thinking she was associated with this crazy idea.

Mateo folded his arms across his chest and lifted his eyebrows in that expectant mode, aka 'explanation required.'

She'd try her best. "I need your patience and trust. Your loyalty. Can you do that?"

He drew her close and hugged her, the kindest, most understanding thing he could have done. Tears were forming, but she willed them to stop. Now was no time to be weak.

A parade of men dressed in Saville Row suits and smelling of cologne wandered the hallways between the booths. Colombians, for certain, and collectors or want-to-be collectors. The women on their arms looked like models walking the runways of the spring collections, draped in what they'd acquired during a stop at Bulgari for some 'trinkets.' Each man had at least one, one man had three. Interesting.

With aplomb, a useful attitude to crowd out real emotions, she smiled, hand outstretched, greeting collectors who made it their business to get to the fair before everyone else. They wanted access to the best pieces at the best prices.

She straightened the papers on the desk, mindless work to distract her in a lull between collectors visiting the booth.

The damn stolen, seized, or whatever, paintings were ten steps from where she sat. A plan, smarter than the pressure David was using, a plan that only an experienced art dealer could execute might beat them at their game and provide a way out.

David didn't want her to sell the Ponces in Bogotá; he wanted them sold at auction, a very public venue, with a catalogue record of the sale. It didn't make sense if they had been stolen. She needed to, no, she *must*, return the Ponces to David's realm like a game of hot potato. Unless . . . what? Unless she didn't return them. Unless she did something else.

"Mateo, you put the Ponces back in the crate, right? Don't mention them to anyone."

He looked up and then down at her. "You already told me that. Are they fakes?"

She rolled her eyes and played along. "No. We need to return them to the owner."

Potential clients wandered into the booth. She and Mateo smiled graciously, greeting them, urging them all to sign the guest book. Contact information was the key to future sales, building a client base for the long game so she continued to get sales after the fair. These contacts would keep her busy on the phone when the San Diego gallery waited forlorn and silent, without clients' happy chatter and without sales.

Mateo talked with a couple about Morini. He didn't like the work of his countryman, but he behaved professionally, praising his painterly skill.

She moved to the area where they'd hung five or six new paintings.

Mateo approached with the couple following behind. "Los Señores Galván. Meet our gallery owner Allison Blake."

Señor Galván, natty in a crisp shirt, diamond cufflinks, and an expensive tie, took her outstretched hand and kissed it. He noticed Nick's ring and smiled.

That wedding band eliminated a lot of complicated scenarios and made her feel protected from awkward advances, even without a husband to back it up. She liked the connection the ring gave her to Nick, to that good life, a comfort she craved, especially now.

"This artist's paintings were at Christie's auction in New York."

Ah yes, the auctions, her biggest competition for Morinis' collectors. A Buenos Aires gallery put works of living artists like Morini in auctions to pump up the prices. Many collectors didn't realize bidders organized by the dealer would bid up the prices. She avoided these tactics unless she had to step in with a bid to protect her artist's work from not being sold in front of the world. No buyers. The dreaded pass.

Her gallery could be the beneficiary of someone's pricing games, but she had ethics. Her conscience got in the way of gouging collectors with pumped up prices. Integrity is a choice of sacrificing profit in exchange for a good night's sleep.

She couldn't know if the Galváns were savvy about auction games. All she could do was represent the truth. "These particular works are being shown for the first time in Bogotá."

"Ms. Blake, paintings on your price sheet are marked sold. Is that what the red dot means? If we're the first here at the opening, how is that possible?"

"Let me explain. At the LA Art Fair, we sold everything we had. Several collectors asked for the first right of refusal on the next group of new paintings and provided a deposit for the privilege. They've been waiting, some as much as a year. We had photographs before the paintings were ever shipped to the U.S. Those collectors chose from the photos."

"Bad luck for us."

"But there's good luck for you. Yesterday, Mateo brought several works from the artist's studio in Montevideo. I don't even have photographs yet. Your reward for coming to the opening is that you are the first to view them. Would you like me to get them out?"

He glanced at his wife, who smiled her approval.

Ally had danced this dance so many times. Certain collectors want first choice, special access to works before anyone else. Many dealers offer a series of lies, ones that always failed in this gossipy art world. If a painting was presented as a new work, a ten-year old date on the back of the canvas could not be explained. Collectors knew each other, compared prices and details about their holdings. It happened. She'd been ripped off early in her career and learned to ask the right questions. Experienced now, dealers and artists knew to be straight with her.

She invited the Galváns to follow her into the crowded storeroom. The Ponces were hidden deep in the crate to eliminate the chance the Galváns or anyone else might inquire about them. The couple flipped through the four new Morini works, pausing at one, talking about it, touching work and all the things that developed toward a sense of ownership by the collector.

"Could we take these into the light?"

She called to Mateo. "Please help me put these up on the wall with good lighting."

He gave her that I-told-you-so look. Earlier, he had wanted to take down the sold works with the red dots and hang these new works. She knew better. Red sold dots made people want what they could not have and showed activity for their artists to new retail clients like the Galváns.

She waited in silence, her best sales tool, for them to consider the works and give her a sign. Before they spoke, she knew they would buy the one on the far left.

The couple exchanged a glance. She fought the desire to speak, not an easy task for her.

"Can you get them to Panama?"

Proceeding with the assumption they were buying the painting she would give them no time to reconsider or overthink the decision they did not yet know they had made.

"Several choices. The international shipper could crate it and ship it. Or we could have it removed from the stretchers, roll it in a tube for you to take with you."

As she was speaking, someone was watching her. Galván answered, but she was distracted.

"Pardon me, which one did you prefer?"

He responded that they would take these fresh Morinis that Mateo brought from Montevideo with them on the plane, saving the customs, and avoiding a written record of what they were doing with their money. She sat down with Galván, wrote up an invoice, and gave him the bank information to transfer the funds. He instructed his assistant, the curator who followed behind them, to make the phone call to the banker. Certain people reached their bankers at ten at night, but it was banking hours somewhere in the world and for some, the bank was always open.

Mrs. Galván spoke up for the first time. "I like the table with the rancho scene too. Very amusing. Reminds me of my father's place in the country. Can we have both?"

"Well, hmm. I wanted to keep some new ones for other collectors. I would prefer to limit one painting per client, and you are already taking two."

Saying no meant saying yes and would close the sale on two more paintings. She might have felt guilty for being so manipulative, using a classic dealer technique, if she wasn't so desperate.

Galván said nothing. He knew the power of silence too. With everything pressing on her, she gave up the dance and went for her straight-forward approach. "I think you'll be loyal collectors of Morini's work and perhaps other artists in the gallery." She motioned toward Mateo with a nod and continued. "Adding Mateo's work like this small painting to your collection will establish you as a collector with a good eye, not just an admirer of popular, high-priced works."

Never give something without asking for something in return, and what she wanted after selling the Morinis was a sale for Mateo. An everyday example were clients who wanted a discount; she would ask them to pay cash to save the five percent or more credit card fees on the gallery's transactions. She could then pass that discount to the clients. The Galváns were paying cash anyway.

Galván understood. He nodded, committing to more purchases without saying so.

The couple studied a small Mateo painting. "We could hang it in the children's playroom. It's not expensive."

"Calculate the costs of the two Morini paintings and this small—sorry what was the artist's name?"

"Mateo Lugano." She scribbled an amount on the page.

He conferred with his assistant and gave the nod. "Here is a cash deposit to hold the paintings." He handed her $6000

USD. "The remainder of the funds will be in your account tomorrow. Friday."

Galván did not quibble on the price, for which she was grateful. This sale moved along the pathway toward the numbers she needed to make this trip work, pay the expenses, pay the artists for their paintings, and earn enough money to pay her debts back home.

"While we wait to receive the wire transfer, Mateo will remove the stretcher bars. Please come to the booth before you leave Bogotá on Sunday, and the paintings will be ready to pick up."

Señora Galván, who had not said more than ten words, smiled as they departed. He patted his face with his monogrammed handkerchief, neatly folded it into his suit coat pocket. Irish linen, at least $100 each. He probably had boxes of them.

Ally scanned the aisles for David, or his out-of-place friends.

Mateo stood and twisted his head around his neck trying get out the kinks from hanging and unhanging works. "So, we will need to un-stretch those works that couple bought, the ones I just stretched?"

She nodded. Un-stretching canvases, taking out all those staples was a miserable job, but he'd be happy to have sold a little painting.

He heaved a sigh and headed to the back room. He'd rather be painting his own works than un-stretching someone else's paintings. He disappeared to the storeroom looking for tools in the first crate.

Scanning the dwindling crowd, she did not see the man who watched her earlier. She escaped into the little storeroom where Mateo had removed his jacket.

He pulled back the brown paper covering the painting and a quick view of a corner told her enough.

She asked, "What else is in here? Is that it?"

Mateo flipped through the canvases he'd unloaded. "Large McGraw works, Morini paintings, and some catalogues."

She checked the bill of lading. "It's correct, except for these two Ponces, which were added after we got here."

Mateo studied her face and asked, "What are you going to do with them?"

"I need to figure out how this mistake happened. Did you see that guy with the black shirt and tie standing just outside the booth?"

"Maybe—I don't know. Is he a client?"

"Don't think he looked like a collector or dealer. Just keep your eye out for strange characters. Report anything to me."

"Shit. Roba-cop, what are you into? CIA?" He smirked in that irritating way.

He pushed her buttons; how could she be upset with him when she kept him purposely clueless? He knew nothing of Chile or the past she'd hoped David would not divulge.

Colombians and many other Latin Americans tended to be from a different planet when it came to personal security. Fatalism with a shrug of helplessness was the coping mechanism to deal with the random violence that came with the acceptance that cartels controlled Colombia.

She had managed to kill that worry during the opening. Now that everyone had left, the worry about what David had gotten her into returned. David and these black shirt goons could not be allowed to distract her from making sales and achieving her goal. She had gotten off to a good start and would not be pulled into their dirty money quicksand.

CHAPTER 11

THE EXHIBITION HALL PLUNGED FROM its high energy crescendo to the melancholy lull of an event in its waning moments of opening day. Ally rolled her head around her neck then shook her arms to release the stress and distract herself from how much her feet hurt. Sitting, resting her whole body, and sipping cold water provided a luxury in this moment that was better than drinking fine champagne in an exclusive Paris salon. Mental stress relief usually came from sales, but this time it was different. David, who had not appeared all day, had dumped the Ponces into her crate, she was certain. Until she found him and demanded he undo this, she'd be fixated on how to extract herself from this web, including hiring a truck and returning the paintings to David's office. She'd love to see the look on his face. Until she understood who and what was behind this, she'd wait to make any moves.

Exhaustion came over her at closing every day of an art fair. Regardless, there'd be no break. Her forty-year-old body yearned to flop on a bed and sleep, but another exhibitor party waited. She could skip it and instead rest.

She lowered her head and pressed her throbbing temples with her thumbs. The sucking sound of being drawn into the dark games being played around her took over her pounding head. She knew the art world, but this . . . this was different than Santiago. In Chile, she had been young and naïve. They tricked her.

No more games. Like the saying, fool me once shame on you, fool me twice . . . She had to protect herself.

"Are you going to the club?" Mateo, one of those twenty-somethings, who loved the parties, couldn't wait to leave, go out drinking and dancing.

She shook her head. "I've been 'dancing' all day. *Agotada.* I'm spent."

The two Ponces paintings haunted her. She needed quiet time, away from people and parties, to devise a plan. First, she could unload the paintings, get rid of David and his pals. The first part might be easy. If she couldn't get David to take the works back, she'd use her skill selling artwork. But she'd need to disassociate herself and her gallery from the sale. Moving millions around was not easy, and it was still tempting to just deliver them anywhere out of her booth and let David deal with it. But she had to know more before she did anything.

Second, she needed to get rid of the operatives behind this forever, but she feared that she might never be rid of them. She'd never forgotten what these people were capable of after Santiago. She believed she'd succeeded in purging them from her life. Years had passed and the dark hole of slick and sleazy covert operations reappeared, now, at this time when she was most vulnerable. She shuddered at the thought that was precisely why they'd picked her.

"Come on. You can find the energy. I've seen you do it many times." Mateo did a little dance around the booth to music in his head.

She lingered on her troubles. A flash of an idea, some help she needed, was right here at the fair. "I'm going to Enrique's booth. Be back in ten."

Mateo stopped dancing and asked, "Minutes or hours?"

She was already walking toward Enrique's and craning her neck to look for David. The guy had flaws. Didn't they all? David had always been smart, one of the best at Stanford. And he had been kind to her once. But then this, this was different from what happened in Chile. He had to be desperate to mix her into his Colombian mission. His job required a walk on the razor's edge. She might pity him, but she would not help him.

Shipping the Ponces to a U.S. auction house, as David had asked, could not happen. Paperwork, even on duty-free original art would be required by Colombia and U.S. Customs. Visions of the customs morass, bribing people and all the rest, was not something she'd do even on legitimate works. The paintings had to be returned to David's people, or failing that, she'd unload the paintings one step ahead of the Agency guys. Then she'd need something more to seal the deal to make them stay away forever.

The lights dimmed as she made her way to Enrique's both. The crevice between her eyebrows, the one that created an intense, menacing look on her face, formed again. She relaxed her brow to release the lines and return a pleasant or at least, a neutral appearance before she found Enrique. Smiling might help.

Enrique stood on a chair, rearranging his booth's artworks. He scowled and considered what painting to hang where to maximize sales at an expensive art fair. They all did it.

"Enrique, *buen día*, Coronel Buendía."

He climbed off the chair and laughed. "Maybe I am the coronel: live to fight on, conquer another day of art fair madness until you stand in front of the firing squad."

She turned her head away from Enrique to hide her fear of facing a firing squad of David's thugs if she failed to cooperate. She turned back to Enrique and said, "Nah. You're a reasonable man who played my hero with the missing crates. Thank you for helping me."

She gave him two air kisses and half a hug, hoping if the spooky looking guy was anywhere around, he'd be bored with this nothing-to-see-here moment.

"The crate was already on its way to you. I didn't do a thing."

She nodded without responding. The crate's detour and delivery had been directed by David's people or his associates. Maybe David hadn't added the Ponces to her shipment. But then other operatives, connected to him, who knew about her background, had done it. Holding the multi-million dollar works created a burden she couldn't easily undo with something like a consignment to another dealer or sending them back to customs since they were inside the crate. She could complain, but she already knew the customs people would be unresponsive. David's clever associates, devious and effective, had compromised her, left her only with the option to do what they wanted.

"How was the opening?" Enrique said with a look that expected a detailed reply. What he was really asking in a polite way was how many sales did she make.

"A good collector bought a couple of Morini's works." She almost mentioned the collector's name. "From Panama, I believe. I was hoping to get more sales for the *One Hundred Years Series,* because those works connect to Colombia."

"I heard Márquez came to see you, even autographed a book. He never does that. You're the buzz of the fair."

She laughed and the respite from worry felt good. "I was thrilled to meet him. If I didn't need to earn money, I'd go home happy now."

But she wasn't happy, not at all. Couldn't think about sales or anything until she solved the Ponce problem.

He rolled down his sleeves and put on his jacket. "How is everything else?"

"May I ask for your discrete opinion? Do you have ten minutes?"

He chuckled. "Might be the last few minutes before I collapse."

His laughter took away tension. "We can hold each other up."

Much of the good business in art fairs was between dealers. Like a grand game of musical chairs, trading and selling, dealers worked with other dealers. The fair hummed, somebody, somewhere had a client for anything and everything. If they all worked together using their network, everyone could succeed. There was no grand plan, like bees in a hive, they buzzed, and at the end, a dealer or dealers might be left with art that had no buyer. It happened.

She and Enrique walked to her booth, past catering trays filled with empty wine glasses and crumpled napkins. Waiters hopped about like black and white penguins, retrieving the inelegant remains of a gala.

Her booth looked stunning, glowing with color from McGraw's works.

Mateo offered his hand to Enrique. "Great party at your apartment. Thanks, man."

"My pleasure."

She wanted to move privately and quickly to ask what she wanted from Enrique. "We are going to the storeroom to discuss those paintings. Can you cover out here?"

She stared at Mateo, sending a silent message that she didn't want any interruptions.

Mateo nodded and walked toward the other end of the booth.

She and Enrique entered the storeroom, and she closed the door. It was the first time she been able to unwrap and fully study the Ponces. She pulled the wrapping paper off one canvas, revealing an image of a thin woman sitting at a table eating dinner with a cat at her oversized feet. Black and white tiles covered the floor and window curtains waved in the breeze like a Matisse painting. The second Ponce was an image of thin man with the same iconic feet riding a bicycle. Amusing. Not bad paintings as these things go.

Enrique covered his mouth to smother a gasp. He strained his neck and held his chin in his hand.

"Do you think they're authentic?"

After a long delay, he spoke. "Where did you get these?" And then he quickly added, "Wait, don't answer. I don't want to know." His voice quavered.

This reaction was not like the polished gallery owner she knew. She shifted her stance in the cramped space. "Are they Ponces?"

"Let me check. My father-in-law adds special hidden marks that will tell me for certain. But I cannot show them to you."

She nodded. "Should I leave?"

"No need. The paintings are either very real or very good fakes. May I?"

He turned each painting around to the back looking for something very specific.

He returned the painting to the front side and nodded. "They're authentic."

Multi-million dollar works sitting on the floor of a closet with a lock that any teenager could open.

His hand shook as he adjusted the second painting to stand next to the first one. "There's a bigger problem. It's ah, ah . . . well I'm not certain, would need to check, but it's . . ."

She waited without probing and then could wait no more. "What? What's wrong?"

He leaned over to whisper. "These paintings belonged to *Pablo Escobar.*"

No!

Enrique reached out to keep her from falling.

"Don't mention this to anyone, so dangerous. How did you come to have these works?"

She thought for a minute about what she might share with him, and then answered, "Can't really say much."

"I understand." He stopped and returned to his previous advice. "Don't answer, don't say anything to anyone."

Escobar! Just the name, linked to her, her family, to her children. Damn, David. She now had two giant secrets.

Enrique was the only person she could trust with this. "It's risky to have them here. Should we get them out of here?"

"Did you show them to anyone?"

"Only Mateo."

"Tell him, your lives depend on silence. I'll do some research, quietly, discretely, and . . . quickly to find out what I can."

She reached for a water bottle and swallowed big gulps. Murdering David had not been part of her plan, but now she was considering it.

Enrique reached over and rubbed her shoulder. "Are you going to the *Art Connections* party?"

Aye, how do these fellas do this? "No, no—too tired. And this, the stress. I'll grab a taxi to the hotel, I suppose."

"No taxis—not safe. Come with me, and I'll drop you at the hotel." They left the closet, and she locked it. Enrique added, "Let me gather my things."

"I'll close up and meet at your booth."

Mateo interrupted her thoughts, now filled with giant worries, and he put two bottles of water on the table. He pulled up a chair and sat with an expectant look on his face.

"I'd rather be back in Montevideo working. Not having to put up with this art fair circus." Just like Mateo to bury what he really wanted to know by talking about something else.

"You've been a huge help. Thank you." She pulled out the receipt and showed him the invoice for the painting Galván had purchased.

Mateo tried but failed to suppress his relief. "Thanks." He smiled and chortled like some huge burden was off him.

Perhaps the sale earned enough money to pay his back rent or something.

He recovered to his smart-ass self to scoff at another artist. "Seriously, Morini's work. How can they like it? I should prostitute myself to make paintings that sell. Copy Morini's work."

"Forget about other artists. Collectors are attracted to different styles. You'll find the audience that loves you. Art fairs are not your world. Your creative planet is your studio, and this crazy art biz is mine."

He laughed, cheered a bit by the idea of one sure sale and three days to sell more artworks.

She shook her head and doodled squiggles on a paper pad. Moving ahead with an incomplete, not well-thought-out strategy was not her style. But his comment about copying other works sparked an idea, a random puzzle piece, without a place in the whole, yet. A pre-emptive move that, even if abandoned later, could keep alternative pathways open.

CHAPTER 12

ENRIQUE WAITED IN HIS BOOTH TO give her a ride to her hotel before he went on to the *Art Connections* party.

"Ready to leave?" he asked.

She scanned the walls of his booth, admired his installation. "What great artists you represent." She studied a drawing of a nude male by Caballero, an extraordinary draftsman, a piece rendered in the classic style. "Frances Bacon's influence?"

"Unfortunately for Colombia, Caballero resides in Paris. A gay man here has a tough life, could be ostracized, even imprisoned. Europe is so much more open-minded. No one was buying the *grandes* like Caballero at the opening. Everyone wants Ponce."

She changed the subject. "How's Helena?"

He picked up his briefcase and sighed, looked away and placed his hand on his forehead, brushing his thick hair to the side. "Marriage is complicated." He nodded toward the wedding band on her finger.

She twisted the ring and considered if, or how, to tell him. Either she got pity or pity combined with the 'you're still young' remark. She preferred to talk about anything but Nick's death.

"Nick died. Unexpectedly in June from a ventricular fibrillation. Almost always a fatal cardiac emergency. He didn't have a chance." She sighed. "I keep the ring because — well, I just do."

He squeezed her hand and gave her a hug. "So sorry about that. I didn't know." He squeezed her hand again.

She gulped a big breath to steady herself but preferred not to speak.

After a long silence, Enrique said, "I hope you are not offended, but in some ways, Helena is dead to me too. My marriage, my finances, my whole life are up in the air. Our economic situation will get solved or get worse depending on Ponce's generosity. His high society contacts are the clients I need. Helena, she's impatient for the gallery, for me to succeed. I'm desperate."

He paused to catch his breath after the words came rushing out. Instead of leaving, he sank into a modernist chair, an impractical but arty touch to his booth.

She sat next to him putting both elbows on the desk, focusing her eyes and attention on him. He ran his fingers through his thick graying hair and sipped on a water bottle. When at home, he probably drank his water from a crystal goblet, one the maid would bring on a silver tray. Even the maid, Helena's childhood nanny, belonged to her.

He deserved support, but Ally needed it too. "I understand desperation. Yes."

His lip trembled. Even with Latin culture's macho imperative, Latin men had no problem showing emotion. "Allison," he shook his head, swallowed, and sighed her name as if asking for forgiveness. "Let's leave. This place and our troubles. The *Art Connections* party started an hour ago."

"I've no energy to party."

He had to show up, he was on the Fair Advisory Board. Maya, the editor and owner of the first English language Latin

American art magazine, *Art Connections*, would be expecting him. The two of them, Maya and Enrique had created the idea of FIART. They wanted the art world to buzz about the great Bogotá market.

The party was a must-show for him and really, she should make an appearance too since the party was to celebrate the art dealers. "Okay I'll go, but for a short while."

"Thanks." He picked up her hand in his and held it.

She didn't withdraw her hand, not wanting to reject him in his vulnerable state, and at the same time, hoping this gesture meant nothing. She did care about him and now she needed him too—he had the contacts and the expertise and most important, she could trust him with the Ponce deal if they could make it happen. She could trust him because he needed secrecy too.

He responded in a whisper. "I made a discreet inquiry to confirm what I suspected about your paintings."

"Let's talk in the car." He gathered the papers on the table and swept them with one motion into his briefcase.

The lights in the hall flashed, signaling for everyone to exit. Most of the booths had already emptied. Enrique stretched his neck to see if anyone was nearby. He took her arm, making it clear she was not alone. It had been a while since a man had cared for and wanted to protect her.

They had to walk through the same exit tunnel to the parking garage she'd visited yesterday. She rotated her head from side to side surveying the musty concrete structure. A chill made her shiver.

Enrique noticed. "I've made you paranoid about things. You're safe with me."

Was anyone safe in Colombia? "Nothing to do with you. A habit from being alone. I make certain there is no one following me."

"Why would you be followed? No one knows you have those paintings."

She couldn't wait until they reached the car. "Well, not no one. Tell me what you learned?"

He leaned close to her ear and whispered. "It's confirmed. Those paintings were seized from Escobar's remote estate. He fled, leaving all the trappings when the army pursued him. I doubt his lieutenants knew or cared about paintings. They had mountains of cash to hide."

She bit her lip. The Ponces had belonged to Escobar and that fact changed a dirty money deal into a potentially lethal proposition. Those paintings connected the U.S. Government or their 'advisors' to the Colombian army or the paramilitaries chasing Escobar on behalf of the government. The cash would have been a better seizure, but maybe the Colombians got that. The U.S. would not want the press in either country to expose their involvement in a raid on foreign soil. They selected her as their naïve foil.

Like a half-finished painting, the picture was becoming clearer as more information was added, but it remained incomplete.

"Shh. Wait until we're in the car," Enrique said as he pulled out the key to his car.

They got into an old Mercedes. German cars were imported and driven only by the very rich in South America.

"It's Ponce's old one, gets a new one every year. Collectors think I am doing well to own this car." He chuckled at his clients' banal measures of success. "Now tell me how you got the paintings."

"I can't tell you much, except with this new information, the problem got more dangerous for me. And you; you may be better off not knowing. I need to think."

He nodded in agreement. "I'm here for you. Maybe I can help."

"Life is hard for you—me too."

He nodded but said nothing, concentrating on driving the car up the narrow ramp and exiting the garage to a street filled with cars. "Damn traffic." Enrique slammed on the brakes jerking her forward. He banged his fist on the steering wheel, rattling his Tiffany bracelet against his Rolex watch. "Can't even drive two blocks. Maya will be upset if I am super late for her party. I should be greeting the art dealers."

The traffic moved forward a bit. "I'm glad you encouraged me to attend this fair and help create excitement for Bogotá's art scene. You're an important part of that," she said.

Enrique took the first exit out of the traffic onto a dark side street in a maneuver that threw her toward the window. He headed the opposite direction around the traffic to get to Tu y Yo, the hot club in Bogotá.

"Back to the paintings. Everyone expects me to sell Ponce's work, but 'Papi' won't help or go around his dealer to give me any paintings. I've much better artists in my gallery than Ponce. Wealthy Colombians don't have the courage to put their money on my unproven artists. It's about staying with the elite, being in the club, to drop names."

"Exhibit your artists in the United States, maybe at my gallery. I have similar problems in San Diego, but we are more open—the California spirit. I'm grateful for some collectors who know and buy what they love."

He nodded. "You have some challenging artists too."

"I have to like an artist's work to sell it." She could never represent the same ol' seascapes even though she could sell truck loads. "Mateo, for example, original and provocative. In a few years, his collectors will be amazed at his success. However, I am struggling to pay the bills, just like you."

"I cannot ask Helena for any support. I've got to figure this out." He rested his head on the steering wheel, waiting for the light to turn green. He raised his head. "What are you going to do with those Ponces?"

They stared at each other.

"What can I do?" She paused to assess how much to share with him, whether to include him to execute a plan together. If Enrique slipped and told the wrong person . . . she couldn't imagine what might happen. Trusting him was everything, and she couldn't be certain of anything except that Enrique was the only option available.

She moved forward and turned to him. "Maybe there's an opportunity for you, for us. Not sure . . . well . . . perhaps we could make some decent money." She tucked her hair behind her ears and paused.

She said it before she changed her mind. "Could you or someone else flip the Ponces?"

He turned his head from the traffic in front of them, swerving the Mercedes.

"You're joking right? Ponces. Easy. But the trail to Escobar. Madre, this cannot be leaked."

"Agreed. Could you find that buyer? One that would share the need for absolute discretion?"

"Possibly. I couldn't survive in Bogotá as Ponce's son-in-law without keeping secrets. We need an opportunist who wants to hide some cash in those paintings."

"Could be dangerous."

"A collector could grab these now, and then when Escobar is dead, when his cartel is dissolved or also dead—and that's inevitable—the collector can do whatever he wants."

"The buyer would need to wait years, maybe more, before moving them. Or if they kill Escobar. Meanwhile total silence would be required."

"Big collectors everywhere, even South America, don't want anyone knowing their finances. Not just for taxes, for everything—where their money comes from is not a question they want to answer. Only fools brag about what they have."

"Their fears will work to our advantage." An exit plan began to take shape.

"Their fears and ours too? You understand the risks."

"More than you can know. Let me think about this." *Better you don't know.* "Talk to me about something besides violence."

Not everyone in Colombia was a narco dealer. Colombian families wanted the same things she wanted—for her kids to have good schools, grow up healthy, and yes, to be safe. She made a mental note to call Claire and Mikey at the first opportunity.

CHAPTER 13

SECURITY GUARDS, POSITIONED AT the club's entrance, questioned the guests. Enrique ignored the line and tossed the keys to the valet without stopping to be checked off the list. A Mercedes owner in Colombia could do that. He guided her past the crowd with the aplomb of someone who belonged.

She wondered if the silk top and pants from the opening event would work as party dress too. The cashmere shawl she'd tucked in her bag protected her now from the chill of the evening air.

Inside the club, a blast of hot air hit her, and she no longer needed the shawl. She tied it around her waist so she could move around the party and use her hands to carry her drink. The club throbbed with bass sounds from the DJ's mix. Pulsating rhythms changed the lighting, rotating the colors between the yellow, blue, and red of the Colombian flag. The colors bounced off a six-foot-high ice sculpture of the *Art Connections* logo displayed in the middle of the dance floor.

Enrique turned to her with a smug smile and shouted over the crowd. "A better party than I expected. Headline: FIART TRANSFORMS THE GLOBAL COGNOSCENTI'S OPINION OF BOGOTÁ. Art diplomacy." They laughed.

The noise got louder and instead of answering she raised her hand with a half-hearted congratulations, wishing she had the quiet of her hotel room. The new information about Escobar terrified her; she needed to peel back the layers to learn the truth about how those paintings got to her booth and what David knew.

The ambience resembled a hip club in Berlin, Madrid, or London. They made their way through sweating bodies on the dance floor toward the bar. Enrique nudged her ahead of him toward an open seat next to three youngish girls in sequined dresses.

"Let's drink to our business deal, the deal that will free us from financial worries."

Free of one type of worry only to land in a treacherous vice of a whole underworld.

He raised his tumbler of Scotch to clink her glass of Campari in a toast to their success. As she tipped the glass to her lips and stared through the bottom, David Martinez's face appeared, magnified and distorted like a fun house mirror. She'd found him.

He mouthed inaudible words over the music.

She peered at him through the glass, his head visible, floating in her Campari. Then she remembered the warnings. She slammed her glass down and spit what she still had in her mouth back into the glass. She beckoned the bartender to bring a beer—an unopened bottle, please, she added. One swallow of drugged Campari couldn't have done that much harm it seemed. Whatever, it was too late now.

The crowd had carried Enrique away, downstream toward a giant bar where his head bobbed above the dance floor. She was glad he'd left, because David made his way toward her, motioned, and mouthed words for her to come toward him. Seeing no easy route to get to him, she remained at the bar, waving at him to sit by her.

He made it to her and lifted her off the stool, marching them both toward a flight of stairs despite her protests. A steroid-fit man stood guard by a sign that read VIP Lounge.

As much as she wanted to get the information about the paintings, she didn't like the way he was controlling her. She pulled away from him.

David bowed with a grand sweep of his arm, giving her some space to go ahead up the stairs. At the top, he guided her to a corner banquette, a spot where an adulterous couple might conceal themselves in the darkness and no one could eavesdrop on conversations.

The noise subsided a bit. She could wait no longer. "I've been looking for you all day. Where have you been? What are those paintings doing in my crate?"

"Which question do you want me to answer first?"

Annoyed, she waited for him to respond.

"Ok. At work. I've been at work. I can't spend my day at an art fair. And I know you already know the answer to the question about the paintings."

Her face got hot, and she wanted to choke him. "I never agreed to your scheme, this whatever you call it, mission, assignment."

He looked distressed and stammered. "True, you did not. I tried to stop it but—"

She interrupted and wanted to scream at him for assuming she'd help. "You put me in a bad situation. Take the Ponces to some other dealer. Get me out of this."

David mumbled, strange and detached.

Useless waste of time to attempt a conversation with him, exact an explanation about those paintings. Maybe he'd had too much to drink. Good sense didn't enter the rage that consumed her now. She'd learned who owned the paintings and that increased the risk.

He seemed weak and exposed, to *what* she didn't know, and he reeked of desperation. If he'd even tried to stop the paintings from coming into her orbit when she refused to play the game, he'd failed. She peered at him and said nothing.

He placed his pathetic head on her shoulder and whispered. "I'm not drunk. Just play along with me." He touched her hand, gently. "I want to explain what happened. I will get you out of this."

She stared at him assessing the surreal situation and then returned to the hot anger rising like a thermometer in the desert. These guys were all loose cannons, leadership shifted by the hour, and no one had control. She knew it and sober or drunk, he knew it too.

Tears collected in his eyes. He leaned toward her ear. "Stay with me, let's help each other. It could have been different for us. Something special, us, once."

She pushed his head off her shoulder and sat straight upright.

He moaned. Moaned!

"You're drunk. Incoherent. Useless."

"I'm sober enough to know there's an intelligent woman, a partner to get us both out of this."

She moved to the chair across from the couch, wondering how his problem had become hers. No useful conversation, about them, their history, their future—their non-future or most important how to end this nightmare was happening at this party. Not possible.

He tried anyway. "I could always talk with you about the work, about this crazy life, the life of being a captive of our own government. I can't exit; you get that."

"You're smart, could have been a professor, led a research team. When we graduated, the whole world wanted Hispanic professionals to parade around to prove the promise of diversity and equal chances. Everyone in the program thought you'd be the first hired."

"I was the first hired—by State."

"Not State. The Agency, the same criminals you're still with."

"Top people. Not just Stanford. Harvard, Yale, the best and brightest. You'd be shocked, generations of important families. Former presidents." Now he sounded sober.

"Shock me. What quality people?"

"Jerry Jackson," he said in a barely audible voice.

She could not ignore that comment. "The chair of our program was a spy? The Agency trusted a book-informed WASP-y academic who rarely set foot in Latin America and couldn't speak Spanish?"

"Jackson was a leader of a whole field. State was always on the phone to him to get his opinion." Of course, David defended the Neanderthal academic.

"No wonder the government gets Latin American strategy wrong. The guy didn't even speak Spanish. Cringe-worthy every time he said Peru—PAY-RUH."

Jackson had brought in only two women to satisfy gender quotas. He was shocked when she took top honors the first year and hired her as a research assistant. At first, she had been flattered until she learned he only wanted to use her. He celebrated a major money grant that he claimed as his own even though she wrote every word. The dean poured a glass of champagne for Jackson and treated her like she was invisible. She promised herself she'd not be used again. But then Santiago and Allende happened. And now again, Bogotá.

She and David enjoyed campus life as students, working, studying, and hanging out with friends. It surprised no one that they became a couple. No one, but Jackson.

Jackson was livid. He refused to write her a reference for a position when she graduated, the support that was expected and required for every graduate student from a prestigious program. She moved on and found her own job. She joined

State with the art history faculty recommendation and a stellar score on the Foreign Service Exam.

David stroked her arm and pulled her back on the couch next to him. "I have never loved anyone like I loved you."

She was not going there, she was done. The Ponce thing was the last straw, and she was stuck depending on a vulnerable guy who had limited self-control, the emotional IQ of a twenty-year-old.

A photographer wandered by, snapped a photo of them. She waved the guy off. She did not want an image of her and him in anyone's camera. The flash made David open his eyes. He shook his head like he was back in the land of the conscious.

"What happened to us?"

She shot him an angry look, surprised he couldn't remember that she'd left him for cheating on her. "You tell me."

"Nothing happened with Cheryl. She was all over me, but nothing, *nada*, happened."

Her stylish silk pants had lost their elegance, the 'look' turned frumpy, hair wilting, makeup smudged, needing a shower from this cigarette-smelling club. Disabling fatigue overwhelmed her. It was not productive to stay here and talk about what happened decades ago when she wanted to know what was happening tomorrow with those paintings.

Across the room, Enrique chatted at the smaller and more civilized VIP bar. She leapt from the couch to ask his help, but David grabbed her arm with the response time of a fully functioning brain.

"No us. No spook games. Nothing."

She pulled back, trying to regain control and hide her fear. She pushed his hand away and focused on his now alert face. "I'm leaving. But if you can comprehend anything, get those paintings out of my booth. First thing tomorrow."

"We're still on for Saturday morning breakfast. The hotel lobby, right?"

She nodded in agreement, a ruse to escape him in this moment.

She walked toward Enrique, who chatted with a dealer from Toronto. Before she got there someone tapped her on the shoulder.

Mateo, his face sweaty and flushed from alcohol and dancing. "Nice party."

"Aren't you tired? I'm exhausted."

He didn't answer the question and instead pressed her. "What are you going to do with those Ponces? Big cash to pay the bills and fly me up to San Diego for another exhibition."

"Don't ask that. You must . . . Do not mention those." She planted her eyes on his with a piercing stare. Another useless effort to communicate with the semi-conscious.

He ignored her gravitas. "They're still bad art, get rid of them."

She nodded. Elements of a plan whirled around her own alcohol addled brain. "So, you think it's easy to paint a Ponce?"

"Could do it in my sleep. Simple."

"Want to bet on that? Try it?"

"Try what?"

"Make a copy of each canvas, in the next two days. If you win the bet, I'll get you an outstanding payment from the collector who wants the copies." The dark lighting and noisy atmosphere of the club became her friend, in this moment when she waffled between whether she was deceiving or protecting him.

"Seriously?" He was laughing. "I'll need money for supplies and make some sketches from the originals."

"Use the Polaroid camera to photograph them. Be discrete— maybe get to the convention center early before the fair opens. Best if no one sees the originals."

Seeds of a plan began to come together. David was useless, and now that he'd tricked her and involved her in his dirty scheme, she'd need to find her own way out.

The scent of some income sobered Mateo up, and he shifted to his art business persona. "I'll need a place to paint. Unless you want me to do it in the hotel."

That would be too risky. "No. Not the hotel."

Lobo appeared at her side and greeted them. "Hip party, no? Are you having fun?"

She answered with the upbeat script used at every art fair no matter what trouble weighed on her. "Great to be here. Bogotá has created a fantastic welcome for us."

"We're going to the studio to see the artifacts, right?"

She'd forgotten. "Yes, of course. I want to see your paintings too."

Lobo could help with something else and going to see these things was the least she could do. "Also, could I ask you a favor?"

She looked at Mateo and raised her voice above the noise so that both Mateo and Lobo could hear her. "Are you using your studio this week? If it's available, Mateo would like to paint there, a commission for a client. Could I rent the studio from you?"

Lobo shrugged and nodded. "I'm gone to the fair all week, helping cover my Bogotá gallery. Mateo can use the studio. No need to pay rent."

Mateo shook his hand and thanked him.

"I'll give Ally the key, and she can give it to you tomorrow."

She thanked Lobo for the studio and picked up her cashmere shawl to leave with him.

She waved at Enrique, deep in conversation across the room and pantomimed that she was leaving with Lobo. He waved back seeming to understand. Enrique must have thought Lobo was trustworthy or he'd have stopped her. Unless Enrique was drunk too.

People jammed the pathway to the exit. Lobo took her hand and navigated through the sweaty multitudes.

He flagged a black town car amid a sea of limos and signaled the driver to come toward the club entrance where they waited.

"Fancy ride for an artist." Her knowledge of Lobo's background had gaps including where his money came from, but there was money. His painting prices couldn't bring in this type of cash.

"Cars are cheap. Taxis are not safe. Only way to escort a lady is with a car and driver."

CHAPTER 14

LOBO SAT NEXT TO HER IN THE BACK seat with their legs and shoulders touching. She hugged the car door, longing for a friend like Santi or Mateo, even the guards at the club who stood at the ready near the club entrance.

American clubs had security to protect patrons from other patrons, those who drank or drugged too much. In Colombia, security protected patrons from violence outside the club that might occur on any street, at any moment without provocation.

"Is security like this everywhere in Colombia? Nowhere is safe?"

"Violence is part of our lives. Everyone is related to someone or knows someone who has been kidnapped or murdered. One degree of separation. We live with the illusion that we can control this and protect ourselves. The truth: if they want to kill you, they will."

No need to ask Lobo to clarify who "they" was. They were in her circle now, becoming more threatening with each bit of information she added to the puzzle. She said a silent prayer for her children and for their mom. They needed their mom.

"Drug cartels fighting each other and anyone in their way."

"Started out like that until the rebels, the FARC got involved with drugs. They were advocates for rural peasants."

He reached for some cold bottles in the center console. "Would you like some water?"

She shook her head. "The FARC are the good guys?"

"Not really. At first, when the military moved in, the priests, young teachers, and lawyers fled into the *montañas*. The government hunted them, and the FARC needed weapons to defend themselves. To get the cash for arms, they started their own drug farms."

Drugs to buy guns. A story that permeated the history of this region, maybe most of Latin America, and elsewhere in the world. Now art to buy guns.

They rode in silence. Lobo's lively eyes and smooth face gave him a magnetic presence. He looked seventeen but was more like twenty-seven. A bright young kid on the doorstep of a stellar career as a painter, he would age fast trying to survive in this place.

Another thing was different about him. He hadn't spoken much about his paintings. Most young artists would crave a chance to have a couple of hours alone with an American gallery owner.

Lobo broke the silence. "I'd love you to see my work."

She laughed to herself. So, he wasn't different after all. "After I see the artifacts, maybe we will have time. I promise I'll come back before the fair ends, and we will do something together in California."

She paused and added, "I've got so many pressing deadlines here. Mateo's commission must be completed before the fair ends so the collector can take the works with him."

Lobo thought for a minute. "I've got some quick drying acrylics if Mateo wants to use them."

"Perfect. What the collector wants is very specific, and I'm sure it will work out." She was satisfied with that honest explanation, although using the term 'collector' to describe herself was a bit shifty.

The driver exited the highway, entered a dark tunnel of a neighborhood, no streetlights, no moon to light the way. The narrow bumpy streets, cobblestones from centuries ago. Eerie silence filled the air.

Lobo pointed to a row of old colonial houses. *"La Candelaria*—Old Town, built in the 1500s, well before the days of Simón Bolívar."

Nice digs for an artist! Fancy car, impressive house. His paintings didn't sell for that much. Mystery money always caught her attention. The art business had taught her: stay away from money that doesn't have an obvious source.

"My family had this place for hundreds of years . . . so free rent for a starving artist."

Odd that Lobo explained without her asking him. Maybe he'd been asked about this paradox before. Combined with what he'd described about his father's mining operation when she'd met him, perhaps the money made sense. But he smiled, and his blue eyes made him an attractive fellow she could see charming collectors at an exhibition. She abandoned other probing questions leaving them to be asked another time.

The driver stopped in front of an ancient adobe, two stories high with rough-hewn poles and hand-applied stucco. Authentic rustic architecture copied by Southern California's ubiquitous strip malls was still familiar to her from California's historic missions.

Lobo took a giant key from a locked box and opened a ten-foot heavy door that closed behind them with a boom. The sound of it echoed throughout the entry and beyond.

A staircase rose in front of a dark patio with a ceiling that opened to the night sky. Lobo flipped the switch of a single light bulb hanging above the foyer. The place smelled of smoke with a touch of mildew and wood polish from centuries of use. He led the way up the creaky staircase.

"Is this an artist's colony?"

"No, just me. Lots of people crash here. Sometimes my father comes from the *estancia* in the north to handle business in the capital."

At the top of the stairs, Lobo opened another door with a modern key and motioned her to enter a hallway that led to a sitting room where time had stopped four hundred years ago. Early colonial furniture and artifacts filled the room from the tile floors to the heavy beams in the ceiling.

"Charming." It could have been a setting from García Márquez's *Love in the Time of Cholera*. On the table, a framed photo showed Lobo with President Gaviria, celebrities, and other glitterati. Another photo showed Lobo with two men in suits, one with a very familiar face.

"Is that David Martinez?" For an American, he'd gotten around in Bogotá.

"Yes, with the U.S. ambassador. I saw you talking to David at the party."

"We studied at graduate school together, Stanford—a million years ago." She hid her concern. If Lobo was part of David's conspiracy, that would be a problem, a big problem.

"David's the political attaché to your embassy here."

"I know." She twisted the strap on her purse, looking around the room. "How do you know him?"

Before he answered, the antique door knocker echoed up the staircase.

"José and the *guaqueros* are here with the artifacts. Make yourself comfortable." He left to answer the door.

She regretted asking him if Mateo could use his studio. Would Lobo discover what Mateo was doing in the studio? And tell David? The only other option was a hotel owned by the military. Nothing could be secret at the Tequendama.

She wandered around studying objects in the vitrines. The vast pre-Colombian collection in this room must have been assembled over generations. There were simply not that many objects available now. Even with big money, some artifacts never made it to market, at least not the legitimate market. This room held hundreds of objects in a dozen cases and cabinets. She'd never seen so many except in the Museo de Oro pre-Colombian collection.

Colonial antiques were part of the collection too. A silver saddle rested on a stand made for it in the corner, an extraordinary colonial piece that would weigh down the strongest horse. In the dim light, she examined religious paintings from the colonial era. An exceptional example from the School of Cusco, a Madonna with a gold crown and a gold cape covering her garments sparkled even in dim light. Gold. Not gold-leaf or gold paint. Solid gold. A work like that, cleaned of centuries of dust and grime would be a treasured addition to any museum collection.

A hand carved secretary desk, inlaid with mother of pearl, displayed hundreds of pre-Colombian pots, statues, and tools. On one shelf was a locked glass cabinet with dozens of intricate gold pieces shaped like bells, birds, frogs, and other creatures.

Lobo surprised her from behind. "Those bells are the ones placed over a grave to ring as a signal from the spirit of the soul buried below. Very valuable—made from pure gold. Tiarona culture."

"So sweet in a sad way. A lovely gesture—I'd like eternal sleep with those little bells ringing above. Beautiful."

She didn't mention Nick to Lobo who'd never met him. Melancholy swept over her. Nick might have smiled at the idea of those bells back in the days when death seemed distant. She yearned for him to be here now or even in San Diego to seek his advice and the wisdom he always seemed to provide.

She'd hid the Santiago Allende history from Nick, better he knew nothing of this dark world, some unknown danger might come to him if he knew, if he had known. Now, she questioned whether she would have even told him about

David and the Ponces. Threats had materialized without Nick here to protect their babies, to protect her. But this was bigger than Nick. He wouldn't have been able to do anything.

She turned to see three men in peasant pants and saggy shirts standing behind Lobo.

"Meet José Maria, Rubén, and Pablo."

She offered her hand to the humble men. They didn't move as if they weren't used to shaking hands and nodded instead. Pablo did respond after an awkward moment. He took her hand in his limp hand and cast his eyes downward. All three men carried lumpy cloth sacks.

Lobo pulled out chairs for everyone to sit at a heavy wooden table. The three opened their bags and unwrapped newspapers from objects. One by one, they placed them onto the table. A musty smell of dirt and age filled the room as puffs of dust escaped when they tossed the newspapers to the floor.

The complex pre-Colombian cultures, unfamiliar to her, had a wide range of styles. A dozen figures formed from clay into priests and warrior type men and women still had specks of paint color and were displayed for her to select what she wanted. She'd never seen anything like this.

Lobo turned on another lamp, which did little to provide enough light to study the objects in detail. He pulled the light closer to the table.

Lobo picked up one figure and brought it to his lips. "Whistles. Blow into them like this."

An ancient sound, that touched her soul, came from the clay figure. Lobo picked up another and blew a higher pitched sound.

She examined the figure of a squat female with a large headdress. The clay woman had a patina of age that was hard to describe, part smoke and a gritty texture that comes with being buried. The face was well-formed, perhaps it was a real person, not just an artist's imagination. She ran her fingers over the lips, the nose and eyes trying to reach across time to know her. Her ears had holes in the ear lobes. Maybe they once held earplugs, gold perhaps. There were smaller holes in the top of the headdress and a large hole in the bottom revealed the figure was mostly hollow.

"Blow into the bottom." Lobo showed her again with a third figure. Another different sound, something primeval from a distant time and place, eerie and comforting at the same time, escaped from the simple clay object.

She blew air through the figure in her hands. The whistle sounded mellow and deep unlike the high pitched one Lobo had blown into.

With one finger, he covered the hole and pulsed out a Morse code type sequence.

"Each whistle has a different sound, used for rituals and security to identify who was coming across the mountains. Ancient Colombian alarm systems."

She laughed. Even centuries ago, people near this place were looking over their shoulders, protecting themselves from unseen enemies, just like she was, and maybe Lobo too. "Where did they find them?"

"In the fields near my father's mines. They poke sticks into mounds, which often turn out to be graves. They remove—"

She raised her hand to stop him from talking, better not to know. She picked up a few more of the pieces and studied them in silence. Artifacts were not her expertise. She didn't know about authentication, legal or illegal exportation of antiquities. She had to trust Lobo.

"Can I take these out of Colombia without a permit?"

"Probably impossible to get a permit. But these are not patrimony requiring permits. They're very common, in hotel gift shops, marketplaces."

Lobo sounded informed, but she wasn't sure, and she had no time to do her own research.

"Are they really old or made last week?" She asked in English, hoping the *guaqueros* would not understand. But she didn't wait for the answer. "What's the price?"

"Maybe $25 each." Lobo answered.

At that price, they couldn't be real. If she were asked at customs, she'd tell them they were copies, and they probably were. If they turned out to be real, she could make some money on them, make her collector do the homework and get the permits. She shook her head. If they weren't pastiche as she suspected, and her collector could authenticate them, she'd insist they do the right thing. Return them or whatever the authorities required them to do.

Too tired to negotiate, she gave Lobo $200 for eight whistles, hoping it was enough. The men wrapped up the hollow clay people and put them in a shopping bag. The old clock chimed three times.

"Do they ever find any of those little gold bells? I would love to have one for myself."

Lobo asked them a few questions and then turned to her. "No, the bells are already stolen from discovered graves. Perhaps in an undiscovered grave."

She nodded. "If they ever locate one, I might be interested, depending on the price." A bell with its gentle sound from a distant place and a distant past was a luxury she couldn't afford, but she embraced the idea as a connection to Nick. A replica would not be the same, not like an ancient bell that had been ringing for millennia to reach some after-life place.

Extreme fatigue came over her and like an addict looking for a sleep fix, she wanted to collapse as soon as she could. "Lobo, thank you. Tomorrow's a busy day, with lots of sales, we hope." She raised her crossed fingers. "I must leave, to sleep."

She stood and Lobo jumped up. "Do you have time to see my paintings?"

Ugh. She just couldn't. "Another time? Bring photos to the booth tomorrow, and we'll begin there. I promise you we will do something in San Diego."

"Of course. Thanks."

She was glad he didn't push her to look at paintings at this late hour. "Could you deliver the whistles to our booth at the fair? It will be easier to pack them with our art." She yawned, even though she tried not to. "Oh, and would you connect with Mateo about using the studio? Thank you."

"Sure, I'll try to find him in the morning, but in case we don't connect, take this and leave it for him at the hotel." He reached in his pocket and gave her a key to the box that held the ancient key to the big door. "I'll walk you to the car."

They stepped onto the cobblestones damp from the nighttime mist and entered an atmosphere filled with whispers from history.

She would have preferred to drive herself as she always did in California. But here at this hour in this neighborhood with its creepy silence, she needed the driver's protection, unless that was an illusion too.

Lobo whistled, only this time with two fingers in his mouth. The town car came around the corner from an unseen parking spot. The artist opened the door, kissed her on both cheeks, and then put his arms around her, hugging her tight, lingering a little too long. He practically lifted her tired body into the back seat. "Lobo, you have been so helpful. Thank you." She mumbled additional forgettable words and wondered what all that hugging was about.

He told the driver to take her to the hotel. The driver didn't answer or if he did, she didn't hear him. They drove into the blackness.

CHAPTER 15

THE TEQUENDAMA DOORMAN NUDGED her with "Señora, señora" and woke her to consciousness. He commented something about four in the morning and offered his arm to steady her semi-awake body out of the car toward the entrance. Still in a fog, not sure if she'd been asleep or in an alcohol stupor, she walked slowly toward the elevator. Then she returned to the front desk to ask for her key and a paper and pen.

She scribbled a note to Mateo. If he followed the plan, he would be gone before she got up. She wrote, "Here's the key to Lobo's studio and money for supplies. Go to the fair tomorrow early, sketch what you need and then take the day to make the paintings. I'll cover the booth." She sealed the envelope and told the clerk to deliver it to Mateo's room.

The clerk handed her the key and another envelope with nothing written on it. She made her way to the elevator, half-asleep, and opened the envelope while she rode to the ninth floor. It contained one sheet, a fax of a photograph. The dim light in the elevator made it hard to understand what the image was.

Her two kids walking up the steps to their school. Shit. What bastards!

In the foreground was a man's wristwatch with today's date showing on the dial. She was going to kill David. He had to put a stop to whoever was involved in this.

She marched with fury out of the elevator, breaking into a run to get to her door and start making calls. She unlocked the door.

Something, someone made a sound. She switched on the light ready to kick the balls off whoever was there, poke his eyes out with the key as she'd learned in self-defense class. She scanned the room in the bright light.

David Martinez, half asleep on the bed.

"You bastard!" She waved the paper at him. "What the hell is this?"

David sat up in the bed, mumbling, still drunk or drugged. "Ally. I'm glad you're here. Safe. It's so late."

She took both his shoulders, shook him, and pushed the paper in his face. "My kids. My precious kids."

He startled. Fully awake, he took the sheet and studied it. "Oh God. I told them not to even consider this. It was wrong, over the top, wrong."

"Don't play me. You got me into this. Without you, they would not know where I live, that I even had kids."

"The Agency knows. Their contractors, rogues."

"You are one of them."

"I don't control them, and now it's worse. I have little influence."

She had no words. Fury raged but murdering him would gain nothing now. She needed to rescue Claire and Mikey. "You dragged me into this art deal after I told you no a hundred different ways. I wanted no part of it. I worked years to put that Chile experience out of my life. Seems I can't shake the stench and now my kids—God, David, do you people have no boundaries?"

"You don't get it. If you don't sell those paintings, you'll be signing my death sentence."

"Don't dump that guilt on me. No way this is my fault."

He dragged her into the bathroom. She sank to the floor, her face wet with tears.

He slumped down on the floor beside her. "At least, now you have to listen to me," he said in a voice more focused.

"God knows who else is listening too. My room is bugged, isn't it?"

"This isn't a spy novel, Ally. But you're right. They're listening."

He reached for the shower handle and turned on a crescendo of water. Putting his finger to his lips, he uttered "Shh."

When she tried to stand and leave, he grabbed her and pulled her back. He held her there on the floor.

She gave him a dark look but nodded her cooperation.

He relaxed his hand and removed it. "Listen. Just listen. Hear the facts."

She glared at him and mouthed the word, "Talk."

"The FARC, pathetic communists want to take over the country. They've morphed into narco-terrorists, killing whoever looks cross-eyed at them to get money for weapons."

That fit with what Lobo had said.

He continued, "A special government police force was created to deal with them. They sent undercover folks to train them." He turned on the bathroom fan to create more noise.

"They? Ex-Marines, former Special Forces faking they are something else in Colombia?" She thought of the crew cut guy hanging out near her booth.

"Contract advisers who don't engage."

"So, they're 'advisors.'" She flicked her fingers with the air quote marks. "How many times have I heard this before? Scandalous U.S. actions in Latin America. Protect U.S. moneyed interests with our military working undercover on foreign soil. Free corporate security like in Chile, right?"

He rolled his eyes and ignored her rant. "Colombian police couldn't shut down the FARC. Tactics were thwarted by snitches who took bribes and goons from the cartels. *Plata o plomo?*"

"Pay or get shot. Right?" She continued listening. She wanted to learn as much as she could, anything might help her understand how to get her family out of this.

"Look I don't control the Medellín guys or their former associates who now hate Pablo, want him dead."

"Listen to yourself? You and the Agency are doing the same thing. Coerce loyalty from me through fear. But my kids? Geez, David." She elbowed him aside in order to leave the bathroom and get to a phone to call California.

"Let me finish." He stood in the way and blocked her. "Some escaped with their lives when Escobar blamed them or their families for snitching. These guys are joining with paramilitaries who share the same goal. Kill Escobar."

She could not believe he'd gotten her into this. Now he needed to get her out. "Does it matter? Slaughter in the street funded by our tax dollars, our government. A fake moral purpose. Right now, all I care about is getting the hell out of Colombia. Getting home ASAP. You should too."

He dried his face from all the moisture. "The ambassador told Gaviria to stop the killing."

She scoffed at his words. "Gaviria doesn't control anything. They murdered his mentor."

His eye twitched, that thing he did when his anxiety hit the roof. "You're right. We're losing control."

Well, at least he owned that he wasn't running the show. "Let me guess, you need untraceable money—money from the paintings—for weapons to murder people." She moved closer to the door.

"To kill a murderer and save this country from turning into a narco-state alliance between the cartels and the FARC."

"You don't need to do this. Find another way. Congress would probably give you the money, fake an account for supplies. Ask them for money."

"DEA and DOD account for every nickel."

"No one wins this way. Keep me out of these little boy games."

"What about me, Ally? Do I matter to you?"

Only the sound of the water running in the shower could be heard. She broke the silence with a whisper. "I did, once, care about you. I care that you don't get killed."

He pulled her closer, his heart pounding on top of hers.

Fatigue and emotion overwhelmed her. She could neither resist nor react.

He leaned toward her ear and continued to whisper.

"I need the money to buy out the thugs, or they will reveal the U.S. role in this. I'm being squeezed, extorted too. I want to protect you and your children. Help me."

He should have left his government job, got out when she did.

Out? Ha. She was, not 'out' either, still caught in their web. Can anyone exterminate these cockroaches?

"The Agency will have me killed, pretend they never heard of me. A story I went rogue or some accident." His posture sunk to despondent, a hopelessness with no way forward. "Then there'll be no one there for you."

They were on the precipice. "If you get them the money, will it end?"

They both knew the answer.

He sat on the edge of the bathtub, turned off the shower, put his wet head in his hands. She opened a towel and placed it on his head, sat beside him, dripping wet with a towel wrapped around her shoulders.

"*Una linda flor.*" He kissed her forehead adding Márquez's words from the autographed book that David had seen at the fair. "I'm sorry."

She closed her eyes at the nearness of him, wishing she could erase the last two days, return to California, and find some other way to earn money. She leaned against the wall exhausted, wanted to escape to anywhere but here. She pulled the towel over her head to hide from the world.

He stood and heaved a sigh. The sound of the hotel room door closing broke her out of her daze.

She rushed to the door, still dressed in her black silk blouse and pants, opened the door a crack, looked down the hall, and saw David at the elevator.

She covered her wet clothes with her cashmere shawl, grabbed her room key, and raced after him. She cared about him—not for him—what happened to him. Maybe together they could figure a way out, and perhaps she could trust him with the fragments of the plan she was developing.

The elevator door was closing, but she put her hand in the door to force it open.

David looked up. "Go back. To your room. Lock the door."

She pushed her way into the elevator before the door pinged and closed on its way to the garage.

David shook his head. "You're right I shouldn't have involved you. Go back."

"I can't forgive you for that. But we've got to figure this out, for you and me. I have some ideas. Let's go to the restaurant for coffee, away from your cohorts who are listening to what I am saying."

He nodded, but before he could push the elevator button to the lobby, the doors opened into the garage. Two men jumped from behind a column next to the elevator and grabbed David. He struggled to free himself, but they tied his hands and covered his head with a black hood.

She froze.

She pounded the button again and again to close the door. Before it closed, one of the men grabbed her, pulled her out of the elevator, and dragged her toward a van.

She kicked and bit him. He covered her mouth with one hand to stop her screaming. She couldn't see David anywhere.

The thug opened the van's rear door, covered her mouth with tape, and grabbed a rope. He tied her hands and wrapped the rope around her arms. With another black hood, he covered her head and tossed her onto the back seat. The door lock clicked.

Voices. Voices, arguing in English.

David's voice, definitely him. At first, muffled, then clearer. She strained to understand.

"What game are you *gringos* playing?" The second voice, a heavy accent, continued. "Free Colombia, what a joke. Shit man, you'll get us killed by Escobar's guys. We need you to get that money from the art girl."

"If you eliminate me, you'll get nothing. If you hurt her, you'll get nothing." David's words came with an unfamiliar tremor.

"You want us Colombians doing your work, but for nothing. Get our money, cabrón. And then we'll kill Escobar."

She recognized that voice too, from where, where?

"We've almost had him a few times." David's voice sounded stronger.

The bully countered. "We follow orders."

She couldn't tell who these guys were—and who was issuing the orders. American ex-military, Colombian mercenaries, Agency contractors, rogues? Good guys/ bad guys. Did it matter?

"Bosses ordered you to take care of this."

David's vulnerability was palpable. She didn't want him to die. She struggled against the ropes to free herself.

Another voice, a different gruff voice with a heavy Spanish accent chimed in. "Not here. Take him."

A scuffle began, glass breaking, punches being thrown. Shots, gun shots.

Silence. Footsteps.

Couldn't breathe. She wanted to disappear.

The van door opened. The engine started. Tires squealed and the force of the speeding van threw her onto the floor of the back seat.

DAY 3

CHAPTER 16

A BITING WIND BLEW THROUGH A SEPARATION in the boards of what had to be a shack. The cold meant she was somewhere in the mountains, but she had no way to know. A blindfold kept her from discovering more. Her wrists, rubbed raw, were cuffed to a metal headboard.

Gasping. The tape covered her mouth and part of her nose, making it hard to breathe. Fighting, struggling, futile efforts that resulted in more exhaustion. Fury combined with fear and a throbbing head. Her back hurt from sitting, and she wiggled to lower her body onto the mattress with squeaky springs.

What did they want? She had no money. The Cartier watch Nick had given her weighed on her wrist, but they hadn't taken it. They weren't thieves.

They must know that she'd seen them in the hotel garage. They blindfolded her so she wouldn't know where they'd taken her. Maybe they also knew in the tussle she would not remember anything except David being taken, the shouting and then the gun shots. Oh geez, the gun shots.

Colombia. Coming here was a disaster. Dying here . . . not an option. Her precious children, those babies required that she survive.

Be smart, think it through, figure it out.

Who were these guys? Where were her compatriots, the good guys? She needed someone she could trust, because having her own back wouldn't get her out alive. Her tears made the blindfold wet and even more constricting.

Voices.

Voices, closer.

Sucking in the sobs, she willed her tears to stop. Don't show weakness. She repeated the words, imagining herself stronger and braver.

The sound of a key rattled in a lock.

Heavy boots tromped on a creaky floor. They came closer. Sweat and cigar breath smells made her turn her head away, disgusted.

A hand fondled her breast. He growled.

She squirmed, trying to escape his touch and withdraw as far as the handcuffs attached to the bed allowed.

He chuckled at his prey struggling in the trap.

More footsteps.

"*Pendejo.*" A different voice—a familiar voice. Maybe the leader.

A slap, a howl.

Someone, something struck the cigar smoker who fell on top of her. She struggled to move from under the weight of him and get him off her.

Cigar smoker stumbled up, squeezing her breast as he pushed off her. Footsteps running toward them.

The other guy grabbed her hair. "*Gringa puta.* I keep you safe. You Americans come to Colombia, think you own, control us. You know nothing."

He yanked her hair and pulled her face toward him. He spit and drops of saliva sprayed onto her cheeks and forehead. In this moment, she was grateful for the blindfold and tape over her mouth.

He pulled her hair and banged her head against the metal bed frame. And then straddled over her.

Do something, anything.

She lifted her leg and landed her knee into his groin, connecting and hurting him good.

He jumped away. "*Puta*, bitch!"

He grabbed her hair and banged her head against the metal bed, again.

SHE OPENED HER EYES INTO THE darkness of the blindfold. No telling how long she'd been out, but light came through a small crimp in the cloth covering her eyes. Daylight. Her head throbbed and she tried to touch the spot to assess the size of the swelling, but her hands remained cuffed to the headboard.

Dampness and cold filled the room. She gasped for air. Moving awkwardly, she wriggled to a seated position. Springs in the old bed squeaked as she tried to steady herself pushing with her legs.

Footsteps, loud, tromped closer, more than one person, she felt certain.

Voices. The muffled voice of the man who hit her was talking. The door opened.

The men approached the bed, stood close enough to hit her again. She turned her head and recoiled toward the wall where she'd balanced her shoulder against the rough boards.

"Take off the blindfold and the tape."

The words spoken by an American. Her head pounded, dizzy.

Even in the darkened room, the light burned her eyes. She closed and then reopened them slowly to squint at the man before her. A shaved head, like an American military man.

She adjusted her position on the bed and pain from her cuffed and chafed wrists shot through her hands.

He just stared and said nothing.

"Uncuff her."

Cigar-smelling guy reached for her arms, leaning over her, lingering longer than he needed. An erection grew against her torso, and she squirmed to escape him.

He fiddled with the key to the cuffs to linger there, but finally her hands were free. She reached up, slapped him, and scooted away.

He raised his hand to slap her back.

The American grabbed his arm and stopped him. "Get out of here."

The guy glowered at her but complied and slumped out the door.

She tried but couldn't stand.

None of the scruffy strangers looked familiar. Her memory was fuzzy, but she didn't remember any of them from the incident in the garage. But perhaps one of them had taken or shot David.

The American surveyed the room, looked at the men staring at her and ordered them out.

Cigar mouth and the other men obeyed him and left the two of them in the room alone.

She sobbed quietly in premature relief.

The American sat next to her on the bed. "I should have a clean handkerchief to offer you, but I don't."

A kidnapper that was concerned her face was covered in tears, shocked her. After what she'd been through, nearly raped, a large bump on the back of her head where the guy had banged it against the headboard, and stuck in a shack in God knows where, he's worried about a handkerchief. Seriously.

He ripped the tape from her mouth.

She yelped, winced, involuntary tears streamed from the pain, but she could speak.

"Are you a hostage too?" That was stupid. The guy was giving orders, not taking them.

"Who are you? What do you want with me?"

He could have been the one who murdered David, but in this shack, he was all she had.

"They took you. Wasn't supposed to happen."

"But it did happen. Where am I? Can you get me out of here?" She was ranting. That wouldn't help. Slow down, choose your words carefully to find a way out of this.

"They. . . we need you." He sounded like a lousy actor reading a script.

She leaned her hand on the rickety bed to steady herself. Strength and more important, her wits began to return. "Who is we? They, whoever they are, beat me and nearly raped me."

He recoiled at the mention of 'rape.' This reaction separated him from them, though their connection, their alliance or whatever they were to each other remained unclear. "They've been following you, listening to you in your hotel room. You and David. They know he failed to convince you to sell the Ponce paintings."

Flashes of David's struggle in the garage reminded her that he was in peril too. "Is David okay? Did they shoot him?"

The American paused before answering. "He's not the guy for this job. He was reassigned."

A lie, she could tell when he looked away. "Reassigned like to the cemetery?" David had been telling the truth about the jeopardy he faced. If she'd trusted him, she'd have reacted differently.

The American didn't answer her question, but she'd learned something important. They knew everything she'd been doing, at least everything she'd told David before they'd used the bathroom as a conference room. But not the plan, they couldn't know her plan.

David didn't know about Mateo's copies either and couldn't know about the deal with Enrique for the Ponce originals. She racked her brain to remember what she said in her hotel room or on the hotel phone. All the other conversations were in the noisy club with David, Lobo, and Mateo. Regardless, she needed to know what the goons knew. And David, she needed to know what happened to him.

"What was the job he was supposed to do?"

"Don't be coy. David told you. Those paintings from Escobar, seizures by the Colombian military. Sell them and get us the money. That's all. Just do it."

She could just agree and for a second, she thought she should. But experience told her giving them what they wanted might mean the end of her. "Who is *we*? Does the U.S. do business in little shacks with blindfolds and handcuffs?" She felt an urge to shove him and run.

He didn't flinch at her words. "Nothing to do with government. I'm my own man." He tried to sound outraged at the suggestion, but she wasn't buying it. He pretended to be too insulted.

"Who's heading this mission? Who pays you?" Lessons from Santiago. Survival depended on information, understanding motivation and players in positions. And most important who was in control.

"Doesn't matter. I have an assignment to get the cash out of those paintings. If you want to live, you need to cooperate." Ok, from clean handkerchief to tough guy, a killer maybe.

She clung to her boldness and pluck, although her emotions eroded them. A tear slid down her cheek. She blinked the tears away before he noticed and breathed to steel herself.

He turned his head from her face. "Calm down."

"Calm? I'm a hostage here." Screaming the words, she lost control. She gagged, turned her head to vomit in a small bucket by the bed. The dizziness and nausea only made her weaker.

He steadied her by her shoulders as she bent over the bucket. When the retching stopped, she wiped her mouth on the pillow and rested her head in her hands. A Colombian guard pushed the door open with the barrel of his rifle, peered in, leaving the door ajar.

"You're right. Not supposed to happen like this." He shook his head and appeared a bit angry. "Let's start over. I'm Mark Bingham. We're on the same side, same background."

Did he mean Chile? Everyone had seen her file. He was too young to know more details beyond the lies in the file.

"You don't know me at all. And you don't know the truth of my background."

He stood and lifted himself to his full height. "I do know this: these guys aren't messing around. You need to agree to do what they ask."

"If David, an old friend, couldn't convince me to be part of your dirty scheme, why would I sell those paintings for you? Screw you."

His face looked like he was ready to shout something in response. He lifted his hand like he was about to hit her and then lowered it. He sputtered, summoned control and said nothing. Regardless, he showed her what he was capable of.

The guard spoke up. "*Todo bién?*"

Mark motioned him to close the door and appeared embarrassed.

She glared at him. She sat taller to breathe, to regain some strength and to control her thoughts. She needed to organize an exit strategy. Doing what they wanted, export and sell Escobar's paintings at auction presented huge problems for her. Things like her reputation, her relations with other dealers, and that they wouldn't stop with one deal. But she'd survive and that mattered most right now.

If she let them believe she was with them or was considering it, they might agree to take her back to Bogotá.

"Look I'm sorry, very sorry you are in this situation. We know you need money. How much? Call it a commission?"

"Get me the hell out of here, back to Bogotá, and then we can talk."

"Not a lot of time for talking. The Medellín cartel is close to controlling the country, running a narco-state with Pablo at the helm. We must stop them. Too many groups, Delta Force, CIA, DEA, FARC, the whole alphabet is fragmenting control of the country."

"What a bureaucratic word jumble. Where are the good guys, Mark?"

"Yeah, that's a question. Maybe you, maybe you're the only good person. As a private citizen, you can fly under the radar without calling attention to the U.S. Government. Get this painting deal done and leave."

"I'm an art dealer, yes with distance from this, from all of you. I know if I give in and do what you ask, I'll get sucked back in." That was a mistake. She shouldn't share anything with a guy who could not be trusted.

"David failed. I won't." He took a newspaper clipping from his shirt pocket and laid it in front of her. In the photo, four ragged guys in camouflage pointed guns at school children standing in a circle. In the middle of the circle, a boy, not much older than Claire, knelt on the ground. A soldier had a sword at his neck.

She didn't see a frightened Colombian boy. She saw Claire and Mikey. Claire and Mikey!

Mark appeared to be disturbed by the photo. "Same age as my kid brother. Those are Medellín drug cartel guys, trying to coerce the kid's parents into keeping their mouths shut. I keep it to remember why I'm doing this."

He seemed sincere, but she was not convinced. The dizziness returned, and her head spiraled. She grabbed the headboard to steady herself.

He offered her a water bottle. "Drink. The altitude—it's 9000 feet—will dehydrate you in no time."

A few sips of water soothed the rawness in her dry throat and then she swallowed more in large gulps.

Mark took the bottle back. "Get those paintings to the auction. Your bank account will be filled, maybe a million or two if you play your cards right. You'll go home and I'll go home too."

That was the biggest lie. He was too young to know that once you are in, there's no way out. The money was tempting to take care of her family, but not this way, not if the money she'd earn went to buy weapons and kill more kids for a different side of the crazy conflict.

His hair was thin for a young man. He was in good shape, smelled sweaty, a familiar musky smell. He loved his kid brother, that was not an act. Maybe he wanted what she wanted: to survive, protect the people he loved, and be left alone to live his life.

She had to find out. "You don't have to do this."

He didn't react for a long minute. Then he shook his head but still said nothing.

The vision of freeing herself, escaping this shack, evaporated. Maybe he was thinking what she was thinking. Once they had what they wanted they wouldn't need either of them. She knew too much. She'd be dead either way.

Sitting upright, drawing strength, and trying to assess Mark's inner thoughts, she tried her legs to stand. Up off the bed, she took a step and then another.

Mark finally spoke. "These guys don't negotiate. You know too much. I know too much."

She sat back down and kept trying. "I'll figure it out. Take me back to the hotel. The proposal requires detailed planning, or it will blow up."

Mark looked pleased. "If you agree to sell the art, we'll leave for the hotel now."

Doubts clouded the way forward. He didn't control the thugs in the other room and things could change in a minute, like they did with David. No one was calling the shots, at least no one she could count on. Having no leader to negotiate with was the worst possible scenario.

She needed the sales pitch of her life, a pitch to sell Mark on joining Team Ally and abandon whoever was paying him. Her instincts said change tactics. Mark had left the photo on the bed to remind her. Arguing with him would not get her freedom. She understood more than she had with David, but important gaps remained.

He asked again. "Send the paintings to the auction."

It wasn't a question. "What're those Ponces worth? Eight million or so each?" She made up the numbers and suspected they'd be higher.

"More. New record sales for the artist. It'll be worth the trouble—say typical dealer ten-twenty percent for handling it?" He waited for her reaction and continued. "The auction house will wire the money to a safe bank account. Untraceable to you or to us."

She asked, "How would I get any commission? It's too risky. Too many missing pieces. I can't have any connection to this."

Mark must have sensed progress in his goal, just as she'd hoped. "Let's get you some food. Clear your head." He left her alone and she searched the room. She tried one window and found it locked.

Before she'd tried the other window, Mark arrived with a bowl of dingy soup and a piece of bread. He shoved a wooden box closer to the bed and set the soup, the bread, and water on it. She nibbled at the crust and took a long drink of water to wash down the dry bread.

After she felt stronger, she realized it was best to agree, make them need her. For now. But if she arranged the auction sale, once the paintings were in New York and the money in their special bank account then they wouldn't need her. That's the part where the plan fell apart. There'd be no commission coming her way. They'd eliminate her unless she had leverage, protection. She made a mental list of options, tactics, strategies.

David was . . . she couldn't be sure . . . possibly dead. Mark had replaced David, and like a surreal painting, the images changed with the viewer's juxtaposition.

She finished the bottle of water. Hydrated, mind in gear, she resolved to get back to Bogotá. Then get the hell out of Colombia and back home.

If she agreed to sell the paintings, Mark said he'd drive her back to Bogotá, but would the thugs in the other room agree to let her go? Mark was a stranger. She didn't know what motivated him nor trust that he'd take her to safety. The thugs had kidnapped her, with or without orders. Maybe they were renegades who did whatever they wanted.

Time was running out. She needed daylight if she was going to escape and find her way out of here. And she needed a foolproof plan.

Maybe she could find a road and go straight to the airport. That couldn't work. No money, no passport.

Abandoning the art and Mateo just when she'd begun to implement an exit plan that could get her away from them forever was not smart. Running would leave her vulnerable still. Like Mark said, she knew too much. Well, this gal knew more than they thought she did.

The grey area between refusing and agreeing had kept her alive, bought some time. Her head throbbed, pounded out a rhythm that set a cadence. She paced a few steps in one direction, marched with determination in the other until her legs strengthened and her mind cleared.

"I need to pee."

"No bathroom in here. Got to go outside in the woods."

CHAPTER 17

A GUARD SHE HADN'T SEEN GRIPPED her arm and guided her to a larger room with a small coal stove in the corner. The room was cold despite the stove's glowing fire. The air smelled musty and rotten.

The guard pushed her roughly through the shack past a worn plank that served as a door locked with a padlock and out into the forest. She took note of everything along the way—every detail mattered as it might save her life.

When she got outside, a shock of sunlight shining between the forest trees hit her eyes, causing her to stumble on the uneven doorstep. The guard grabbed her arm, but she twisted it away from him. A clearing surrounded the shack and the forest beyond was thick with trees. High mountains rose above the tree line and a cliff dropped off below. Her watch, the one Nick had given her, read 3:00 p.m., but the sun shone like mid-day this close to the equator. The air felt cooler than inside the shack with some breeze blowing through a thick forest.

The leader, the guy who slapped her unconscious, someone whose voice she would not forget, shouted "José!"

"*Sí, mi jefe.*" The cigar smoker who had fondled her came running. He took orders to take her into the woods to pee. Anyone else would have been better than this José.

José smirked, perhaps at the prospect of raping her alone in the woods. He had been beaten once by his jefe and a scream from her would shut down any attempt by him. At least, she hoped it would stop him.

The barrel of his gun poked her back pushing her forward into the trees and making her cringe away from him. She staggered, noting the details of the kidnapper's hideout including a rusted car parked in the dirt along with a newish Range Rover that had to be Mark's. The plates weren't visible, probably U.S. owned but with Colombian plates for security. Mark wouldn't be so stupid as to have diplomatic plates.

Four guys smoking puros, one must have been the driver, leaned against the Range Rover. The other car, the rusted one, looked like it hadn't been moved in a decade. Escape by stealing a car appeared to be impossible.

Her pace slowed to a crawl and José noticed. *"Rápido. Muévete, perra."*

Being called a bitch meant nothing. Walking into the forest, shivering from cold, she stopped to tie her shawl on her shoulders.

A gravel driveway headed into the distance, but she could not see where the road led. No car noise either, only the chatter of birds. Dense trees with high canopies grew in the surrounding forest, but they were unusual trees. The bark peeled off in sheets like birch trees revealing red trunks covered with dark stripes, like a sunburned tiger.

Yes, tigerwood—the tree that provided the wood for the paneling in the hotel bar.

Santi had told them more about tigerwood. She wished she'd paid more attention, something from the bar conversation. This had to be that tree with the striped wood.

Fuzzy memories came together. Tigerwood endangered in Colombia. Hard to find. Some on the coast and one other place, a place five miles from Bogotá. That was it. Five miles—not so far. She trusted Santi had been right, but not her ability to identify trees.

Rotating her eyes, searching. Running downhill on foot was her only option.

Horny José poked her in the back with the AK whatever, moving her along, muttering for her to hurry up.

The other men laughing and talking, exaggerated their sexual exploits with preposterous lies, just like men on a coffee break at a real job. Two of them were thirty feet away, where the flat landscape around the cabin dropped off abruptly. Horny poked her toward the path part way down the cliff. She moved forward, sliding on the slope, until he shouted, "*Alto.*"

She stopped, angled her eyes back, peeking at the shack up the hill behind her. A large tigerwood tree hugged the edge with its ancient roots dangling in the open space where the cliff had eroded away.

Horny motioned to her with the rifle. He pointed the rifle toward the tree and called it a toilet.

"*Privacia. Por favor.* Please turn around." Give me privacy, privacy to run.

Not happening. "Heh, heh, heh." He chuckled staring at her. Three teeth were missing, the remaining ones were stained from years of cigar smoking. He pointed to the Cartier watch on her wrist and held out his palm.

She pointed to the watch and pointed her finger downhill. He didn't respond, but she saw an opening. He wanted Nick's watch, the most precious thing she owned. He hinted at something so important it could save her life . . . *Horny José had a price.*

Possibilities flew in and out of her mind until a plan settled. Personal price, something she understood, her world, one where every sale, every collector, every artist negotiation demanded she measure her opposition's price. This deal had one opportunity to hit the number out of the gate. One or done.

The clasp on her watch stuck. She fumbled, ripped the fastener, until it released. She held the watch out, and he smiled at the prize.

He reached to take the watch, but she grabbed his fingers and squeezed before he could. Her eyes met his surprised look. In a laser stare, she searched for a soul.

Oh God, let him have a daughter, a sister, a mother — someone, a sense of humanity in this sleazy thug?

In a breathless whisper, still locked onto his eyes, she gasped a plea. "*Ayudáme.*"

He was not laughing now. Not smirking, not now.

Silence, seconds into an eternity . . . she could not breathe, nor move — frozen.

A reaction. Did he move?

Yes. He did it again.

His pocked-marked chin moved. He lifted it a third time toward her hand.

What did he want? The emerald ring on her right hand. He wanted the ring. Emeralds — something he understood.

The two-carat faux emerald ring she'd bought in Rio, a souvenir of little value, was stuck on her swollen finger. She pulled, pulled again. It loosened. She held it out to him with the watch.

He grabbed for it, but again she closed her hand before he could take it.

She waited to learn more about the wordless bargain she'd made with this devil.

"Let me go?"

He nodded, and she released the watch and the ring into his grasp. He shoved the treasures into his boot.

She looked back uphill to see the chatty guy group, drinking something from a shared bottle, leaning on the car, thirty yards away from the cliff edge where she and Horny stopped.

Horny handed her a heavy eight-inch rock and pointed to his head. "*Fuerte.*"

He wanted her to hit him, hard. She didn't bargain for that. Violence was not in her repertoire. A rock that size could kill him. He wasn't a good person, but still . . .

In the distance, the other men, now probably drunk, roared with laughter at some joke.

Their laughter caught Horny's attention too, and he shook with nervousness. "*Rápido. Rápido.*"

In one motion, without more thinking, with all her force, she hit him with the jagged rock.

He fell to the ground.

She released the rock, slid down the embankment holding the tree's dangling root to avoid rolling down the steep slope. Her position below the cliff provided a last glance at José's body slumped onto the exposed roots of the tree trunk.

The root provided a ten-foot lifeline, until it ran out. Her feet couldn't get traction in the loose soil. She attempted to get stable footing, but continued sliding, then falling.

Falling, now tumbling, over and over.

Branches cracked, scratched her arms and face, as she rolled down the hillside. Rocks, more branches, falling, until she stopped on a wide flat ledge, an outcrop on the slope.

Disoriented, about thirty yards below where she'd left Horny, she jumped to her feet and felt scratches and bruises on her legs. Arms, head, bones—a quick inventory to confirm all survived intact.

Damn slippery soled shoes. She kicked them off, shoved them in her belt. Her California hot sand tested feet might be tough enough to survive the rough brush on the forest floor.

She took off running, wincing with each step, pain she had to endure to gain secure footholds.

Men shouted from the cliff above. No one appeared, but flashes of being back in the shack ramped up her running. She kept going, didn't look back but kept her eyes scanning the surrounding forest for an escape route.

Men yelled now, fighting with each other, wrestling on the ground. The scuffle sounds stopped.

"*Jefe, la puta me pegó.*" Horny's voice trembled as he said she'd hit him, blaming her for his injury and her escape. His plan worked.

For a minute until more shouting came. "*Mira, un reloj, jefe un reloj.*" Another voice hollered.

They'd found her things, the bribe she'd given José in his boot.

Move. Anywhere. Downhill.

Trees and branches swept back and made snapping sounds as they broke off with contact. She skipped over fallen trees in her path or went around them, running always downhill.

A commotion, more voices. Horny José begged, then cried out. Punches, a gunshot, but Horny continued to howl, escalating to screams as the beating continued.

They'd be coming fast when they finished with him, and she wasn't sure how far she could get before they caught up.

Hide, hide. Now.

A rock, a stump, something. Only trees and bushes.

A felled log on the hillside below caught her eye. She slid down, hurdled over the log like a running back, hitting the ground next to it. She rolled under it. She pushed to get lower, squeezing her body to be smaller, under the log. This mother tree had to absorb her, consume her, make her invisible, become one with her.

Voices closer, branches cracking and snapping . . . had they seen her?

She scraped debris and dirt from underneath her body to make more space to crawl under the log. The ground under her began to crumble. A mound of mulch collapsed, and she slipped into a hole.

A soft crevasse at the bottom of the hole opened wider with the weight of her body, and she fell farther into a cave.

Pitch black, the hole smelled like decaying leaves and worse. She lifted her head, removed some dirt and branches, and created a small opening by removing debris above her head. A streak of light large enough to enable her to see came through the top of the cave.

The voices came closer. She'd dared not sneeze, cough, breathe.

Noise, heart beating, pounding, so loud they must hear it.

Branches breaking from footsteps, coming closer. The footsteps stopped on top of her.

They stopped, right above her.

Please God, please, make them move on. Every hair on her body stood at attention, frozen along with the rest of her.

More footsteps arrived. They stopped and remained above her. Wood pieces drifted down weakening the ground. If the ground caved in, she'd be found. Closing her eyes, she begged to be transported away, beamed away from this nightmare.

The small cave had a dirt wall behind her that supported her body. She explored the walls with tiny movements of her hands, like reading braille in the limited light.

A hard round object was not ten inches from her face. When she touched the deep depressions, she recognized the shape—a skull.

She held back a scream. Overwhelmed with dizziness, she struggled to remain alert. She squinted in the darkness and continued touching the skull that was covered in a linen cloth rotting away, exposing eye sockets. Nasty long hair remained attached to the bony head. She pushed against the dirt wall, separating her face an inch more from the thing.

The men remained above her and spoke in muffled tones. They speculated on which way she could have gone. Any movement, any sound would be a death sentence. This grave could become her grave. Never to be found, buried, eaten by worms like the skeleton. Her children abandoned by their mother who disappeared in Colombia.

The sound of peeing came from above. Urine drained into the hole and onto her head.

CHAPTER 18

A MAN SHOUTED, "BOSS, SHE'S NOT HERE." Footsteps moved away from the log above her, and the voices trailed the footsteps.

"*Idiotas. Búscala.*" Find her, the leader commanded. Many feet stumbled, branches breaking, until the sounds disappeared.

She released a slow, inaudible sigh and struggled to inhale. At first, gasping in whispered gulps, she breathed in a measured, slow rhythm to steady herself. She lifted one arm just enough to use her shawl to wipe the urine from her face and head. Her legs and arms cramped in pain. Still, she dared not move more.

Were they gone? Did they all leave? Did one stay behind? She listened.

Time passed, maybe an hour. Frozen minutes merged with the challenge of remaining silent and rigid. The small shaft of light dimmed. She tried to see her watch, find its luminous dial, but there was nothing on her wrist. This precious memento of Nick was gone, in the hands of thugs to be fenced in some marketplace for a fraction of its value.

Her chin dropped onto her chest. Exhaustion sapped her strength and sadness eroded her will to escape. The sides of the cave's earthen walls squeezed her body. Her legs twitched because of her semi-crouched position, without space to move her arms upward. Part of her was so exhausted by the struggle, she wanted to die here, in this hole. With a deep sigh, she drew upon an internal ferocity she'd come to know over this last year.

She squirmed and considered that she might be stuck. Her bare foot touched something hard buried in the earth below. She probed with her toe to assess the object about the size of a grapefruit. The object had holes in it just like the other one.

Another skull in this grave, a mass grave. How many people had they kidnapped and killed? This small skull, maybe an infant, was buried under her feet. What monsters kill babies? Those monsters in the shack.

She stared at the adult skull that had emerged from the shadows in front of her face. With her arms pinned by her sides, she moved her hands a few inches and discovered the sides of the broken jar that had held this adult body.

These were not the remains of kidnap victims but bodies of native peoples in an ancient grave. She'd seen these jars in museums. Indigenous people buried their dead in a crouched position in large clay jars. Mothers were buried with their infants. Sometimes they died together in childbirth, or the baby was sacrificed to go to the next world with its mother. Sad. But these practical people realized that a baby starving to death, with no mother to feed it, was no kindness. A practice that her culture could never accept, but a reminder that if she disappeared, her children would have no one to care for them.

A connection with this dead mother and her baby touched her heart. This maternal grave had protected her and hidden her from the kidnappers. She'd need to dig deep to find the energy and resolve to make it out of here and repay their gift. An adrenaline rush flowed into her body with the roar of a tidal wave.

One arm up across her chest, she lifted the other one over her head, extending it up as high as possible, she wiggled higher. Then she rested and did it again. Reaching upward for an exit from the grave, she heard a noise and stopped. In the dark, she felt something hard and cold hanging from branches above her. She waved her hand, felt another object and another that made a gentle, tinkling sound.

Bells. Tairona bells like the ones she'd admired in Lobo's cabinet. She pulled three little bells into her hand, curling her fingers around them, and stuffing them into her bra. She felt the metal on her skin, near her heart.

She braced her foot against the side of the jar holding the mother's corpse. She wedged her own body higher up the side of the hole. Pushing with one foot, balancing with her hand, she was able to inch her body up the sides of the small grave toward the top. She repeated the move like climbing a chimney. Pushing, grabbing with her free hand, the bottom of the fallen tree appeared. Determination and grit propelled her upward when her strength failed. Bits of rotting wood crumbled into her eyes. She moved her hand slowly around the edge of the top of the hole, hoping it would not disintegrate. Her arms trembled with muscles losing the strength to keep her wedged between the dirt walls.

Struggling for something to grab, she found a root. She pulled hard, and it was solid. She exhaled a huge sigh and pulled on the root using all her strength. Bracing her legs against the dirt walls, she expelled herself from the grave, headfirst, into the fading daylight.

She rolled away from the opening onto a bed of mulch. Lying there hidden by the log, she lifted her head, keeping it low to look around and listen. The blue sky revealed it was not as late as she thought. Twilight, the time between day and night, when you could imagine the curve of the earth was magical. Light and dark visible at the same time, it was a moment to cross from one world to another.

Even with this special light, she couldn't see an escape route to find help. Trees, bushes, and fallen debris covered the ground down the mountain. The bottom had to be below somewhere, but she could see only forest.

She grabbed the ends of her shawl, tied them around her waist, and secured them with a knot. Her kids helped her pack it, and Claire had said, "Let this shawl hug you, Mommy." She gave herself that hug and sent a silent message of love and hope that she was returning to protect them.

She rose on her knees to peek above the log. Hearing nothing, and knowing uphill was the shack and the guards, downhill was the direction where the thugs would be searching for her. She could not see nor hear them. Above was certain death, the only way out had to be downhill through the forest until a clearing, a house, a road, something would appear.

Then she heard it: Music—cumbia rhythms, the same music they'd danced to in New York. Where was it coming from? There was nothing ahead—nothing but mounds, uneven terrain, and trees. The sounds persisted and came from below.

Screech. Screech. Gears grinding against each other came through the forest. A car. No. A truck, maybe a bus. Brakes squealed and the sounds stopped. A road had to be nearby.

She ran, dodging bushes and small trees and cutting her feet with every footfall. She lifted the shawl's edge and pulled it close to her body to cut the cold wind. The chance to catch a ride kept her going, running, searching for an opening in the forest.

The sounds of the cumbia came closer. Still in the distance, but closer and closer.

As though a door had opened, the brush disappeared, and she stood at the top of a six-foot embankment. At the bottom, a road hugged the side of the mountain.

She slid down the mound on her bare feet, grabbing at small brush to slow her descent. The level ground stopped her slide next to the pavement. A road twisted, turned, and wrapped around the mountain like the path on a child's gameboard. Several switchbacks in the distance, she spotted a red and yellow bus. Its rickety chassis creaked down the hillside barely staying on the narrow road. It would arrive in a minute or two. She hid below the shoulder behind a bush where she could avoid being spotted if the kidnappers were searching here.

She was a mess with leaves and twigs in her hair, dirt on her black pants and blouse, and scratches on her aching feet. Her appearance would give her away. She took her blouse out, covering her leather belt with the designer clasp where her shoes were still stuffed. She untied and wrapped the cashmere shawl, now soiled with dirt from the hole, over her head and shoulders like the ruanas women in the streets and marketplaces wore.

The colorful bus rounded the corner. Triangular soccer banners hung from the plastic guard above the windshield. She ran barefoot across the road clutching the shawl, keeping her head down and waved at the driver. With screeching brakes, the driver pulled to a stop. She kept her eyes down and said nothing.

The driver pulled on a hinged handle to open the door from his purple vinyl seat. She grabbed a bar, pulled herself and one leg up onto the step like she was decades older. She limped toward a seat in the back of the bus.

"*Billete*," hollered the driver. She had no money to pay for a ticket.

She couldn't utter a word or risk that her accent might expose her as an American in this place where no one trusted anyone. Anyone would give her up for the price of a meal and she hoped that her black clothes and her grubby look made her into just another peasant, a widowed peasant.

Think, think. Something, some way to pay. She felt her wedding ring, but it's value would reveal her as someone other than a poor grubby peasant from these hills.

She turned around to react to the driver and felt something move near her heart. She reached into her blouse, encircled her fingers around the little objects. Drawing her hand from the blouse as though she were retrieving money for the driver, she held out one bell in her open palm, then turned her palm down, releasing the bell into the driver's hand. He studied it. She lifted her eyes and saw the recognition on the driver's face. He would know, as any Colombian would, the precious value of what she had given him. He said nothing, put the treasure in his own pocket.

In a second motion, his hand pulled the metal handle to close the door and with the other hand, he turned the steering wheel toward the road.

She spotted an aisle seat in the third row and sat down before the motion of the bus threw her to the floor. The seat tilted as though springs were missing. The corpulent flesh of the woman seated next to her spread onto her side of the seat. The woman's bare feet lay spread all flat, crusted with dirt, on the broken boards of the bus floor. She looked down to see the state of her own feet. They were in bad shape after the run through the forest, but she had a bigger problem than dirty, bleeding feet.

Dante's Inferno.

Dante's Inferno, the absurd name of the polish color she'd chosen at the salon, screamed red from her toenails. She flexed her toes toward her soles like a geisha with bound feet and then tucked her feet under the broken seat.

The bus rumbled down the mountain into the darkening valley below.

CHAPTER 19

THE BUS PULLED UP TO THE CURB and screeched to a halt next to the bustle of a Bogotá marketplace. The driver announced this was his final stop, end of the line. A dozen bodies rushed from the back of the bus to the exit before the driver had even opened the door.

The woman in the seat next to her had not bathed in a while, but the same could be said about Ally. She smelled her own body and got a swift reminder of where she'd been. The woman squeezed her large body over her and stepped on her bare foot. Ally winced and swallowed a yelp, not wanting to call attention to herself. She stood to limp toward the door and exited onto the pavement.

In the distance, a silhouette of skyscrapers lit the evening sky, and perhaps one of them was the Tequendama Hotel. A crush of people, scurrying in different directions, ignored the wooden stalls lit by bare bulbs hanging from a tangle of electrical cords. The marketplace crowd had no patience for someone standing in their way, admiring the city view. They jostled and shoved her like she wasn't there, unable to move forward, a fish swimming against a human current. She ducked between two stalls to get out of the stream and find her bearings.

The market stalls were simple affairs. One sold children's underwear, another offered all things plastic from buckets to wash basins, purses, and even shoes in a riot of colors that turned the dingy stand into a kaleidoscope. The evening breeze rustled the clear tarpaulin that protected the goods from an unexpected rain shower and brought smells that included an odd mix of burnt toast, body odor, sweat, and dirt.

She pushed forward flowing with the crowd, moving fast, but avoiding attention. Buses had to be nearby to serve the marketplace, and taxis also, any transport to get her to a safe place.

A delectable odor came from a simmering pot of *ajiaco* stew. Every day the cook would add to the leftover *ajiaco* that Colombians rave about and argue over where one can find the best version of the dish. There was a large metal pan inverted to form a dome with cakes grilling, giving off a nutty smoke.

There was an empty chair next to the bubbling pot. She'd only eaten stale bread in the last twenty-four hours, and she was hungry. But she was penniless.

Busy merchants, getting the last sales out of the day, paid her no attention. The little black Chanel flats dug into her stomach, still stuck in the waistband of her pants. She took out her favorite shoes, a special splurge when the gallery had had a good month and slipped her bloody feet into them.

She considered heading straight to the airport before they found her to catch a plane out of Bogotá, to anywhere outside of Colombia. Without her passport, money, and decent clothes, she couldn't leave. Maybe she could sneak through the garage of the hotel and avoid the lobby. She shuddered at the memory of the scene of her abduction. She had no room key. Everyone could get into her room but her.

The reality remained: the men extorting her wouldn't stop trying to find her whether she sold those paintings or not. If she did what they wanted, they'd want to get rid of her. Plans, flushed with fear, rolled in her head. She needed a scheme for an escape from Bogotá with a permanent end to them pursuing her. The plan needed irrevocable consequences for them if they threatened or harmed her or her family.

The hotel couldn't be far, somewhere in all those high-rise buildings glowing on the horizon. She headed down the street, away from the market. A large intersection ahead had a bus terminal on one side. A taxi could get her to the hotel where they'd know her, which could be a blessing and a curse.

Walking fast, looking around to be sure no one pursued her, she spotted the taxi stand across the street. She crossed and walked to the head of the line, considered reversing her disguise to get respect in the line instead of being a poor peasant who would be refused service. A man, a peasant himself, looked like he was about to object to her cutting in the line. Ally said in a low tone that she'd been robbed. A middle-class woman, maybe a merchant in the market, was standing beside her. The kind lady spoke up, urged her to go ahead and take the next taxi.

What kind people to care for a dirty woman with no money, a woman they'd assumed was one of them. She said little to avoid revealing her accent, just nodded and mumbled her sincere gratitude. She climbed into the taxi. The driver dove into the traffic to stop the angry horns of the cars he was blocking while he picked her up. She'd figure out how to pay once she arrived at the hotel.

"*Dónde va?*"

She mumbled, "Hotel Tequendama."

Even if he was surprised by her appearance and the disconnect of taking this customer to a five-star hotel, he said nothing and turned the taxi in the opposite direction. With her disheveled look, the driver would not target her for a robbery. Besides, at the Tequendama, he could pick up a wealthy fare.

The neon signs along the lively boulevard lit up the backseat. Her pants were torn and muddy. Her hair was littered with twigs from her shawl when she'd covered her head with it. She removed the twigs from her hair and used one to clean the dirt from her fingernails. She fluffed out her brown locks, removing more leaves and bits of whatever.

She could never pass as a hotel guest once she got out. If the doorman or the front desk clerk recognized her, they'd ask questions. The shawl slipped from her shoulders, and she tied it around her waist, turning it into a skirt. She wiggled out of her pants. The pants turned inside out with the seam showing and the two legs tied together turned into a deconstructed hobo bag. The new "purse" contained her only possessions of value, her leather belt and two little gold bells from the grave.

The taxis' rearview mirror projected her image and stopped her cold. Her frightful face, the eyes of a deranged woman met the driver's eyes. Frightened, *he* looked frightened. This taxista no doubt thought a mad woman sat in the back seat, a woman who wouldn't pay the fare or worse, rob him or kill him.

The taxista drove faster, darted in and out of traffic, through the streets in the direction of the high-rise buildings. She didn't have much time. They'd be looking for her everywhere by now, but maybe they'd believe she was still in the mountains. Finding the bus was a near miracle that neither she nor they would have expected. Whatever she did, stay or leave, she needed to move fast and smart.

The taxi pulled into the brightly lit entrance of the hotel with the security guys and their automatic weapons at the ready.

She opened the door. "A minute. I'll come right back." She didn't wait for an answer. The doorman held the door and stepped out of her way as she rushed through.

Well-dressed people chatted and moved in and out of the lobby. She scanned the room for suspicious characters.

"Tomás," she read the name tag as though the front desk clerk were an old friend.

"A problem. I left my purse at the fair." Lying was becoming easier.

"Yes, Mrs. Blake." He recognized her, and that was not a good thing.

"Could you pay the taxista waiting outside?"

"*No problema*." Tomás rang the bell three times in fast sequence to summon one of five bellmen standing nearby. He reached in the cash drawer, took out an envelope of cash, giving him a 50,000 peso bill, about $10 U.S. The bellman rushed out the door to take care of the taxi.

"I'll pay you in the morning." She wondered where she'd be tomorrow, or even tonight.

"No problem. We'll charge it to your hotel bill."

She was relieved. "May I have my hotel key, please?" Yes, please. Please hurry.

The clerk hesitated. "Yes señora, but there is a problem."

How did she go from *no problema* to *problema* in a few sentences?

"The manager has your key and would like to escort you to your room."

Her belief that she'd escaped the kidnappers evaporated. Were they here? Was the manager working with the thugs? The hotel was a military outpost. For a small price anyone could get her key, anyone but her. She had to stay calm, avoid revealing anything to these people she did not trust.

The manager came walking double time around the corner from the administrative offices. Ugh, the manager on duty, the guy with Puig cologne, smiled, showing his bad teeth. He sputtered on and on, something about how the maid had seen something, like he was trying to cover up something.

"The security people, they are worried."

He struggled with English, and she only understood every other word. At this point in the day from hell, her brain could not process two languages. She kept pace with his quick, brisk steps; the faster she got rid of him, the sooner she could leave the scene of her kidnapping.

He opened the door to her room, a room that had been destroyed.

She hid her shock. Her suitcases had been dumped, drawers pulled out and clothes thrown on the floor. He claimed intruders had tried to remove the entire safe in the closet, where she'd kept her passport, extra cash, and another credit card. Fortunately, they hadn't succeeded in opening the safe.

The manager prattled on about how the hotel tried to prevent such things, but they could not be responsible. Every guest had to lock the room, blah blah blah. "We can help you—certainly we will contact the authorities to recover what has been taken."

No authorities. No police, no authorities.

She started laughing—a big, hearty, full, open mouth laugh until tears filled her eyes. The little manager stammered and looked confused. He asked her if she wanted some water. And she laughed more.

Finally, she caught her breath. "Don't worry. There's no issue. This is the room of a very messy guest, rushing from one party to another, trying to find the right outfit. I thought the maid would hang things up for me, but apparently my messy ways scared her. Sorry I made you worry." She feigned embarrassment with giggles.

He paused for a long minute. Clearly, he didn't expect this and maybe didn't exactly believe it either. But he sighed and appeared relieved he wouldn't need to file reports or protect the hotel's reputation. Then he laughed too.

After a polite exchange, he offered to get the maid for her to help pick up the clutter.

"Thank you. I must change and leave immediately for the art fair. Once again, I'll be throwing things everywhere." She smiled, took his arm, and turned him around, sweeping him toward the door. "I'm late and need to hurry." She took her key from his hand and nudged him, muttering, out the door with her other hand.

She leaned her back against the locked door. She sank to the floor, frozen, too exhausted to move.

Kidnappers touching her things, the shack, the murder, the grave in the mountains, all of it overwhelmed her. And now she was in the place where it had begun. She sucked in her breath, unable to pause even for a minute to rest.

She stood on her wobbly, dirty legs. Priority one was to call home and find a way to protect her children. But she couldn't call here where the phones were bugged.

No time for emotion, she needed to find people who could help her, and they were at the fair.

CHAPTER 20

SHE THREW DOWN HER FILTHY CLOTHES, examined her scrapped and bruised body, and decided a shower was not optional. But she'd need to bathe fast. They'd be searching, thinking there was no way she could navigate the mountain terrain. Without money or transportation, she wouldn't be able to return to Bogotá. When they realized she wasn't anywhere near the shack, it would take them time to drive back to the city, and this hotel room would be the first place they'd look.

The antiquated metal shower blasted refreshing water onto her weary limbs. She turned each part of her back, then her shoulders, the left, then the right one toward the strongest spray. She lifted her head like a wilted plant drinking rainwater. The pulsating water pumped on the spot where the bump throbbed. She used the hotel shampoo on her knotted hair, rubbing out the grime from the grave, the grime of those who could put her in a grave. She scrubbed off more filth, and the dirt went down the drain with the water, but the emotional muck could not be so easily removed.

She needed to get on top of what unnerved her, she needed to regain focus. Her mental list of options no longer included heading straight to the airport. Assessing the pros and cons of each option, she weighed them. She was caught in the middle of leaderless gangsters and her own government. It didn't matter which of these enemies had destroyed her room, she had to beat them all.

The safest place was the art fair. A fast trip to check on her kids from a phone that wasn't bugged. Oh God, had they overheard her talk to the manager? Did they know she was back here? She picked up her pace.

At the fair, she'd complete the final bits of the plan, including getting the Ponce copies into the crate to ship to auction. Enrique could hide the real Ponces. Then, she'd get the hell out of Colombia. Fast as possible.

She had to elude them for at least another day. She could hide and sleep in Mateo's room. That meant coming back to the Tequendama. Ugh. Risky.

She turned off the water. Fleeing would just mean more running and hiding. She stepped out of the shower, surveyed the mess in the room as she dried herself, and gathered what was essential.

She threw only a few things into her duffle bag. It was better to leave the mess so if they returned, they'd assume she hadn't been here. She opened the safe, noticed scratch marks and the corner that was dented where they'd tried to remove it from the closet. She retrieved the cash, her passport, and some inexpensive but sentimental jewelry, gifts from birthdays past. She scraped the remaining contents from the desktop into her purse. She locked the safe even though it was empty. Let them waste time trying to get it open. She put on a statement piece of inexpensive jewelry. Appear normal, unflappable.

The fair shuttle pulled up to the hotel entrance. When she saw it, she exited the lobby, rushing and, without waiting for the driver to park, stepped on board. "Can we leave immediately?" She handed him five dollars. "I'm late to get back to my booth." She'd left her fair badge on the back of the booth's storeroom door; she showed him her passport and an invite to one of the exhibitor parties. He glanced at it but said nothing. It didn't matter because he turned the little van into the traffic toward the fair. He wove in and out, arriving at the convention center door in five minutes.

She dashed from the van, waving the passport and invitation at the guard as she passed him without her badge. So much for art fair security.

Mateo paced inside the booth, waiting around for her to show up. She greeted him Uruguayan-style with one kiss and asked, with feigned nonchalance, "How did the painting go?"

"Good, good. Where've you been?"

"An errand. I need to get to a phone. To the office." She did not intend to tell him about the kidnapping, nor about the kids. Nothing good could come from telling Mateo about the terror encircling her. "Did you bring the paintings back?"

"They're drying at Lobo's studio."

"Great. You finished them so fast."

"Lobo had equipment to project my sketches onto the canvas. With that, the work goes fast. The canvases will need tweaking tomorrow.

"If they're dry, can you bring them in the morning, early, early? Put them in the storeroom, please."

His face turned dark. "Something is very wrong. Talk to me."

He unfolded something from his pocket. "When I came early this morning to sketch and measure the paintings, I found this." His hand trembled as he handed her the paper, a rough fax of a blurred photo.

They'd sent a copy of the photo of Claire and Mikey on the school steps to the booth, too. Oh God. She had to get to the phone. Now.

Mateo's hand shook and his face was white. "Who sent this to you? I've been worried all day."

She didn't answer but left, walking toward the office. She turned back and said, "Cover the booth." She ran to the center's office, hoping it was still open and their phone functioning. She passed Enrique's booth and saw Santi from afar but looked straight ahead. She could not stop.

She opened the door to the office. "I need to make a—no, two, two calls to the U.S."

The typist continued pounding keys without looking up. Ally added, "As soon as I can."

The woman stopped typing and reacted with a concerned face, like she understood her urgency, perhaps a mother herself. "If you need privacy, you can use the director's office, but you must pay for the calls."

"Yes, good, the director's office. Charge calls to Allison Blake Gallery, the art fair account." She couldn't breathe, and she tried to hide her desperation from the unsuspecting clerk.

"You need to dial—"

"I know." She made her way to the office while the woman's words hung in the air. Before closing the door, Ally turned to the woman and said, "Thank you."

She called her sister first. Please God let her be home. Dawn had to help with what she desperately needed her to do.

"It's your sister. Can you hear me?"

"Well, hello to you too."

"Not now. I need you, need your help. I'm in Bogotá."

"What the hell? Why would anyone with a brain go there—they're killing each other."

"This is an emergency, please just listen. I need you to drive to the Denny's off the 5 near San Juan Capistrano. Do you know the place?"

"Sort of. I can find it. What's up? Need me to ship you the super breakfast meal?"

"Be serious. Please drive there and wait for Margarita and the kids." She lowered her voice and checked to see who might be listening on the other side of the door. "Take them to the cabin on Mount Baldy. Take Margarita too and keep them all there until I come home on Sunday. Can you do that?"

"Why?" Dawn demanded.

Ally considered lying, but her sister would sniff that out. "A long story. I'll explain when I get back. Bring enough to eat. Don't let anyone go to Baldy Village or play outside. Don't let strangers near any of you."

"My God, what have you gotten yourself into?" Dawn paused a second. "Okay, but you demand a lot."

"I appreciate it. I do. But now I've got to go, got to call Margarita. You have her number, right?"

The phone clicked off and she dialed, wishing it would be Nick on the other end.

"Margarita. *Es urgente.*" Spanish was faster, and she needed to be certain her faithful housekeeper understood every word.

"Where are Claire and Mikey?"

"At school."

Please God let it be true. She swallowed and took a long breath.

"Are there any strange cars parked by the house? Out on the street?"

Margi looked out the window and described a Chevy sedan, a conspicuous classic with a guy parked under the jacaranda tree across the street.

"Margi, I need you to follow my instructions, exactly as I tell you. Take the car and drive slowly so the man in the Chevy follows you to Vons grocery store. Park in the garage underneath and make sure the man sees you park."

She paused.

Margi's voice quivered, and she whispered, "*Sí.*"

Ally didn't want her to panic, but there was no time to mince words. "Go inside the store and then go out the other door by the taxis. Take a taxi back to the house, get Nick's old car, and go to the school to pick up Claire and Mikey. Tell the receptionist that Claire has a dentist appointment, and that their mom forgot to send a note."

"*Sí*, okay."

This loyal woman had had more than one adventure crossing the border after visiting her family. Margi could handle this, probably better than Dawn.

"Take Mikey's blanket and Claire's doll and their pajamas, maybe a change of clothes. You must hurry. Don't return to the house once you've left. Not for any reason. Drive north on the 5 to Denny's at the San Juan Capistrano exit. Do you know the place?"

"I have never been that far north." Margi paused and then added in a low voice, "There's an immigration check north of Oceanside."

Another checkpoint. Ally shook her head and let go of the worry they'd be detained. These spooks would never look in an immigration lock-up. Odd that the kids and Margi might be safer locked up in immigration secondary than in their own home.

"Sometimes the checkpoint is closed and no need to pull over. Take the emergency numbers with you in case you have a problem."

Margi answered with a voice that sounded unconvinced she'd be so lucky to hit the checkpoint when it was closed. "I don't know the Denny's."

"You can see the huge sign from the freeway. My sister will meet you there. Leave Nick's car parked in the Denny's lot. Dawn will drive you and the children to her cabin in the mountains. Tell the kids it is a fun trip their mom planned for them until she comes home on Sunday."

Unlike her sister, Margarita did not ask questions. And unlike her sister and despite her nervousness, Margi would do exactly what Ally asked

"When you arrive tell my sister to call—" She stopped mid-sentence. "No, wait, don't call. Don't call me unless it's a big emergency." Ally didn't elaborate on what a big emergency looked like and didn't want to carry that thought, like it was some bad karma to even think it.

"Yes, yes but . . ." Margi hesitated, her voice quivering.

"Strange, I know. My sister too, tell her not to call unless it's life threatening." There, she said it.

A phone had never been installed in the cabin. She couldn't call them once they'd left home. They'd risk discovery if they tried to call her from the little café in the village. She was on the move too and had no phone number to give them.

She thanked Margi and hung up.

Her children, her life, so far away and so vulnerable. Worry, worse than any fear she'd had when Nick died, consumed her now.

She'd done what she could, and now she'd put everything she had into finishing the plan and getting the hell out. She walked back to her booth, calm, greeting those she passed in the aisles as though all was well with the world.

Mateo thrummed his fingers on the desk's glass top. He said nothing but lifted his eyebrows over his bulging eyes in that 'explain yourself' expression.

Still reeling from the telephone conversation, she dropped her fake calm demeanor. "I know you want answers, but don't ask." She paused. "Please." She continued, "So the painting went well."

"I'll bring them tomorrow." He stood and came closer. "What is going on with you? That photo, something's wrong. Tell me."

She gulped and moved away from him. "Those calls, I took care of things." No one, not even Mateo could know where the kids were.

"You can tell me anything."

She tried to erase the anxiety from her face with a smirky wince. Mateo would not be asking if he could even guess what had happened to her in the last twenty-four hours. "We need to get back to business. Half the fair is over."

"Did we sell anything while I was away painting?"

She skipped his question. "I've asked a lot from you, but can I ask another favor? Can I sleep in your room tonight?"

Those raised eyebrows again.

"The plumbing in my room is broken." So much for not lying. Of course, the hotel would have changed her to another room. "The hotel is filled." One lie led to another. "I can sleep in a chair, the floor, whatever."

He laughed. "I didn't sleep there last night. Probably won't tonight either."

A normal reaction would have been to tease him about the trendy curator, but he probably painted all night to finish the copies. He was safer outside the hotel whatever he was doing. "We'll leave the fair together to get your key before you go off to party."

He smiled in that Cheshire cat kind of way. "Let's eat. Lobo's place has no food. I'm starved."

Then she remembered their agreement. "I suppose you think you'll win the bet that you couldn't finish them."

"I'll win. Maybe instead of money, you'll pay me with the story of whatever the hell is going on."

That was something. Mateo turning away money in exchange for information. "I'm starved too. First, I need to take something to Enrique. I'll be quick, be right back."

Mateo sighed and sank back into the chair.

Enrique looked surprised to see her and commented about her empty booth and her whereabouts all day. "I was worried. Where were you?"

He was thinking about the Escobar people who might look for the Ponces.

She couldn't share the kidnapping incident with Enrique. She trusted him, but couldn't expand on what he already knew creating more risk for him and for her. She ignored his question in favor of leaving the fair fast, hoping Mark Bingham and his friends hadn't left the mountains to search for her here. "Sorry to make you worry. I'm good but leaving the fair to eat. Mateo and I are hungry."

She kissed Enrique on one cheek. They embraced long enough for her to place the key to her booth's storeroom in his hand.

"Until tomorrow."

DAY 4

CHAPTER 21

THE ALARM SOUNDED. A DEEP DREAM, a dream so real and then poof, it ended. A surreal moment that erased the content and left only vague remnants, like scraps of paper scattered on the floor of memories of a family that no longer existed.

Morning arrived like no time had passed between hitting the pillow and the light coming through the ugly curtains. She patted the bedside table, feeling for her glasses. There was no table.

Memories surfaced, a repeating echo of a very alive Nick and two carefree children. Neither was real now. Her children were hidden away where only God could protect them. She said a silent prayer: Let none of this sordid world touch them. The only way to get through this day, until she could leave tomorrow and draw them into her arms, was to focus on executing the plan so that she could shield them forever and then forget this ever happened.

She sat up and surveyed her surroundings. Mateo's duffle and his dirty clothes littered the floor of a room that wasn't hers. Her sleep-fuzzy brain struggled to organize her next move. She stumbled to the bathroom, passing the undisturbed chair lodged under the doorknob next to the bedside table she'd moved in front of the door. She squinted swollen eyes to find her glasses by the contact case and looked at her wrist to check the time.

The nightmare of the last twenty-four hours returned. Horny Jose put the watch in his boot. He'd been beaten, shot, and maybe, was dead. What mattered more than the watch, more than anything, more than selling art, more than success for her artists, more than outing the U.S. operatives at their own game, was for her to survive and get out of Colombia.

The desk clock read 6:30 a.m., or 4:30 a.m. in California. She closed her eyes and imagined her children asleep, warm and safe, in the cabin's bunkbeds. Her lip trembled, and she exhaled a long sigh. She willed a protective aura around them and renewed her resolve to extract herself and her family from this mess not of her making.

David had invited her for breakfast at 7:30. But that was before the garage incident. Too dangerous to call him and the only way to know he was unharmed was to go and hope to meet him. Maybe he could get a message to her.

If he showed up, she'd appeal to him as a friend. Mark said David had resisted involving her, and most important, her kids. Perhaps he cared more about them than himself and was being coerced to use her. Last night she wanted to kill those people. Now she wanted to be smarter than them.

More information from David would help put the remainder of her escape plan in place. She hoped he would show up.

She rifled through her duffle and took out black outfit number three: a jersey dress. Wrinkles in the dress' synthetic fabric would shake out with ten minutes of hanging in a steamy bathroom. Plus, a quick rinse off in the shower would wake her up, sharpen her mind.

She lifted her face toward the shower head and stayed there to renew her physical energy and her emotional spirit. She left the water running to create more steam, exited the shower, and shook water from her face and hair. Zombie eyes stared back from the mirror. Make-up could not turn them into something that looked more . . . well, more human.

She organized papers, especially the invoices, made sure data was filled in after the rush of sales. She spun and whirled through the multi-task steps that had been practiced with the many hats she wore, only today she didn't need to dress, feed, and drive children to school.

She checked her calendar, yes, it was Saturday. No school today and no need to call the school and lie about where they were.

Her mind flipped between a to-do list at the art fair, and a list to elude that criminal world. The narco guys wanted the paintings and didn't care if they killed her to get them. The CIA, the DEA, groups that didn't even have an acronym yet, pursued her to get money out of the same paintings. She needed to pull off a plan that beat them both, stay one step ahead. But ahead of who? The identity of the shadow operatives remained as foggy as the mirror. She put on her lipstick, grabbed her duffle, and headed out the door.

The empty elevator gave her a chance to review what had been put in place and what was missing. Mateo hadn't returned to his room last night. Maybe he was waking up with the curator from the Wilson Institute. But if he did as she'd planned, he would have retrieved the dry copies of the Ponce paintings, brought them to the booth, and put them in the crate.

The hotel lobby was empty. She scanned the entrance and all the nooks, searching for and hoping to see David. There was a lone man polishing floors.

It was only 7:35 a.m. Five minutes late was not late, not a panic, not yet. David was a high-profile guy and killing him would create an international incident. They, the illusive they, worked against David and the U.S. people, and they knew they wouldn't get their money if he was gone. Her resistance to their plan, necessary to save herself, had both her and David in a precarious situation or worse. She had to say no to him, she could not do what David had asked. It didn't seem right though that he should pay the consequences.

She rested on a gilded Louis XIV chair in an alcove. The chair was so high that her feet didn't touch the floor, but its position enabled her to view the hotel entrance as well as who came and went from the restaurant and the elevator without being seen.

The lobby had an eclectic design. High ceilings, modern glass windows, French antiques. Modernism meets Marie Antoinette, and not in a good Philippe Starck kind of way. Strange choices for military hotel owners if that rumor was true. She filled her brain with this mental flotsam to push out her guilt about David and the worry that he wouldn't show. She kept her head turning on high alert for Mark and the creeps from the shack. No one came or went, not even a tourist had shown up in the empty lobby.

7:45 a.m. She needed coffee but saw no lobby to-go coffee service like most hotels have. In Latin America, consuming things to-go didn't exist, at least not in this neighborhood. Latin Americans of a certain class considered drinking or eating in a car or while walking on the street to be uncivilized behavior. More flotsam.

She got up from that French chair. Good ol' Puig cologne manager was at the desk reviewing receipts. He didn't look up.

"I am waiting for David Martinez from the American embassy. Do you know him?"

He averted his eyes to look at the entrance. "We've not seen him." He paused. "Traffic is terrible."

His shaking hands made him appear nervous and in turn, she felt it too. "When Mr. Martinez arrives, please tell him I'm in the restaurant."

She needed to make this quick, but desperation for coffee pushed her toward the aroma in the restaurant. She walked toward the archway entrance to get coffee and leave.

A chubby grey-haired woman in a polyester pants suit blocked her path.

"Allison, I'm Frankie Brown, cultural attaché from the embassy." She extended her hand. "We corresponded about García Márquez."

Frankie had recognized her, a reminder that State probably had photos of everyone posted on a board in a conference room. Frankie handed her a business card.

"I wanted to greet you at the opening but got held up. David Martinez mentioned you would be meeting for breakfast and asked me to join you."

In normal times, Ally would have been thrilled to have breakfast with a cultural attaché. She'd pitch some exhibits for her artists, work on collaborations with Colombian artists, seek grants and other joint projects. Not now. Not ever again. David didn't mention Frankie. She was lying.

"David's late. Have you heard from him?"

"In Bogotá, we expect late," Frankie answered, avoiding her eyes, and then recovered with everyone's excuse. "The traffic is terrible."

"I've heard. I need coffee." Ally motioned for Frankie to follow her.

Frankie discussed other things as they entered the restaurant.

They settled into a booth in an empty restaurant except for three American-looking men each sitting alone at different tables.

Maybe Frankie was part of the undefined 'team.' With her frumpy look, Frankie did not appear to be a polished Agency operative like the ones she'd been able to identify in Santiago, and she wasn't someone connected to the art and culture world.

"Tell me about meeting García Márquez." Frankie stopped talking and waited for a response.

Embarrassed, Ally muttered, "Sorry, what?"

"Tell me about Gabo. You'd written to the embassy about meeting him. I was so pleased he was able to attend the art fair and meet you."

"He was kind. He autographed my copy of *One Hundred Years of Solitude*." Small talk dominated the exchange with Frankie. Ally rifled through her purse to find her fair badge. The card with Gabo's personal assistant's number fell out when she pulled on her exhibitor's badge. She tucked the card safely into her wallet.

If she wanted her coffee and to see David, she'd have to endure this conversation. "Ms. Brown, how long have you been posted in Bogotá?" Ally rotated her head to survey the lobby, the still empty lobby. David was not here, more than Bogotá late. She held on to a hope he'd show.

Frankie rambled. "Gabo never gives autographs. Doesn't want to get mobbed by fans."

"How did you hear about Gabo coming to our booth at the Fair? You'd written me in California that he wasn't coming."

"News travels fast. The fair has its own news network: Booth to booth." Frankie laughed at her imagined cleverness. "Among the embassy group, it's our job to be well-informed about Americans in Colombia."

"Where's the coffee?" She looked for a waiter and checked the lobby at the same time. "I need to get to the fair soon."

"Coffee is an art in Colombia—no glass pots burning on a hot plate. Each cup a presentation of perfection."

Frankie continued with the meaningless orientation to Colombia. "I do like coffee strong. Strong but also fast."

Frankie's mission to distract her from David's absence and keep her in the hotel restaurant tested Ally's patience. Why was Frankie doing this?

At least no criminals could kidnap her while talking to a U.S. diplomat. She shook her head at this wrong thinking; the thugs had not been deterred in the hotel garage when she was with David.

The waiter arrived with a linen-covered silver tray, a small cup holding a thimble's worth of thick, black liquid. He placed it on the table and a small pitcher of steaming milk, a bowl of sugar cubes and a pair of silver tongs. Skipping the milk and sugar, she took a sip of the coffee. Strong, really, strong. She set the cup down and added the hot, never cold in the Hispanic world, milk to the coffee.

Frankie yapped away about artists, art fairs, tourist stuff, munching her *desayuno Americano* between words.

Ally took a plain looking piece of bread from a silver basket and covered it with *dulce de leche*, that sweet caramel-flavored spread. The sweetness cut the coffee brew, so strong her spoon could stand upright. She sipped and nibbled.

Out of patience, she interrupted Frankie's ramblings. "It's been an hour. David isn't coming."

"He might have gotten pulled into a meeting with the ambassador or something." Frankie tried to seem unconcerned, trying too hard to deflect Ally's concerns.

Frankie knew something, she was certain.

Ally asked, "How is David doing?"

"He's applied for a transfer back to Washington."

"When does he leave for Langley?"

Frankie stared, shocked at the mention of CIA headquarters. Frankie's position at the embassy was a front, just like David's was. Frankie and the whole embassy had abandoned David or if you believed her, David was abandoning them.

David was not coming, and she wouldn't find out anything from Frankie. Ally put her linen napkin on the table, gathered her purse and duffle bag. "Nice meeting you. Need to make calls back to California before I rush to the fair." She looked at Frankie and added, "Tell David we'll catch up later."

Frankie grabbed her arm and stopped her from standing. "Too early to call California, and the convention center isn't open yet. Keep me company while I finish my breakfast. Are you finding the art fair a good business opportunity?"

Frankie had been assigned to keep her there, now she was certain. She shrugged her arm away from Frankie's grasp; she wasn't going to be kidnapped again without a fight. "I'm leaving."

"If you need me, call the after-hours number." Frankie handed her a different card.

She took the card and walked toward the entrance. She grabbed the first shuttle to the fair, taking a seat in the empty bus near the driver. She would not return to the Tequendama.

She fumbled to put the card into her wallet and noticed something. The card Frankie had given her read: David Martinez. On the back side, a phone number was written in David's handwriting.

CHAPTER 22

ALLY ENTERED THE EXHIBITION HALL of the convention center with her heels clicking on the marble floor. Not a walk, a march. Fury at David for pulling her in, at the Frankies and the Marks who collaborated and enabled. At the stupid U.S. Government, yes, the whole government, thinking they could control every country in the world. Their clandestine handiwork and misuse of employees and private citizens like her to advance objectives outside official public policy was wrong and likely illegal.

Let it be. Let Colombia be Colombia. A policy that pretends to support self-determination with actions in which one country coerces another into the template of the more powerful one, is authoritarian dominance regardless of the aspirational labels they use.

The booths were a buzz of activity. If she hid in plain sight, no one could grab her.

"Allison Blake, *amiga guapa.*"

Jake Klingman, notorious for being a sleazy dealer, was the last person on the planet she wanted to see. He tried to buy up Morini's works before the fair, calling galleries in Buenos Aires, New York, and elsewhere comparing their prices to hers. If she sold to him, he'd flip the works and share his dealer discounts of thirty to forty percent with the collectors, undercutting the stable pricing system that she and other quality dealers tried to maintain. She kept the relationship pleasant, she had to. He controlled collectors with mega dollars, even if those dollars came from questionable sources.

Klingman stood between her and her booth, like a sentry.

"Good morning, Jake. We were so busy at the opening and then yesterday . . ." She didn't want to engage in that discussion. "Sorry I haven't had time to say hello."

Not knowing the Guatamalan kiss-hug ratio, she kissed him on one cheek. He'd been lurking and she'd avoided him, but she did notice the artworks he'd brought hadn't sold well. No red dots and Jake for certain would have been using, or overusing, red dots.

He placed his hands on both her shoulders, an inappropriate gesture from someone she barely knew. "I missed you all day yesterday. We should talk."

Of course, he'd noticed she was gone all day. Appear normal, business as usual. "Sure. We'll talk . . . when there is a lull in the traffic. No wasting time when there are clients in the aisles, right?"

Jake nodded but looked put out. He ambled back to his booth where he stood at attention to greet anyone who paused near one of his artist's paintings.

Mateo waited with his eyebrows lifted toward his forehead. "So, you decided to come to work today?" He swept his arm, gesturing at the walls of the booth unchanged from when they'd left for the *Art Connections* party on Thursday night. "Looks like nothing sold yesterday."

She forced a smile to avoid another conversation about where she was yesterday. A story about visiting a client's collection wouldn't fly, and she decided against lying, not again, not to Mateo.

"Ponce copies are next to the crate, as you ordered."
He saluted.

She shook her head at his usual sarcasm. "I'm amazed. It's impressive you finished."

"Making copies is how they teach art in Uruguay. I was damn good at it too. Could whip out a Vermeer in a day." He laughed and then turned serious. "There's a problem. Some things are missing, not in the crate or the storeroom."

Great. More bad news. "What's missing?"

Mateo walked to the storage closet and opened the door. "The original Ponces are gone. They were here last night. Do you think someone stole them?"

Not bad news, good news. Enrique followed through and picked up the original Ponces. She needed to get the originals out of their booth so no one could discover there were two sets of Ponces. Enrique didn't know about the copies, and she did not intend to tell him.

Her voice quavered as she told another untruth. "Returned them to the collector. Big mix up with his staff failing to tell me about putting them in our crates." She added, "He wanted the copies to hang in his home instead of the originals, which he'll keep in a vault for security reasons." A weak lie, beneath her, really, especially to someone she cared about. And Mateo was too smart to believe it.

Lies stacked upon lies would grow into monsters, but she had no choice.

Mateo stared at her face.

What could she say? She turned, hid her face and her shame, telling herself the less Mateo knew the safer he'd be. Her trust meter was on high alert, questioning everyone. Maybe if Mateo had more details, he could be on alert too, more eyes and ears to watch for unusual people. But if he knew more, spotted something or someone, he didn't have the experience or the tools to beat these guys.

She bit her lip and then asked him to show her the paintings.

The two of them squeezed into the tiny storeroom, and Mateo removed the paper that loosely covered the Ponce copies.

"Wow. You're amazing." To the untrained eye, there was no difference between these paintings and the originals in Enrique's booth. The way Mateo applied the paint, the shadows in the gaunt faces, the flesh tones of pink and beige were perfect. The colors matched the originals.

"Thank you."

"Thank you to *you* if the price is right." Mateo pulled a pencil from behind his ear and pantomimed summing up in his palm the dollars he'd earned.

"Bigger than you could imagine. You've got to add something to these first."

From her pocket, she pulled a small paper where she'd traced the markings from the back of the originals. She wasn't sure which ones Enrique searched for and so she copied them all. If they added them, anyone who knew to authenticate Ponces would be satisfied. Mateo could paint them well enough to pass a customs official if they even knew to look. Authenticators might also declare these paintings genuine works by Ponce.

Mateo took the paper, paused, and shook his head. "I believe in you and respect your ethics. But . . . but I gotta know. I deserve to know. Are you pulling me into something, something not good?"

Tell him, spill everything. He deserved to know, and she yearned to have a partner.

But knowing put him at risk. How could she explain to him, or even to herself, why she had crossed so many boundaries? Was there a greater good to justify how she'd drifted?

Survival. That was the only answer. She had to survive and make sure he did too.

He didn't wait for her answer. "You can't sell this shit as real, don't even try."

If all went according to plan, these paintings would disappear forever or better, they'd be destroyed. "No. Not selling them."

His face said he needed more.

"I am protecting you, us, from . . . it's dangerous. Can you trust me?"

He stared at the paper. The atmosphere filled with confusion, indecision, and uncertainty about what came next. She needed him to finish the markings, at least well-enough that a trained eye would believe the works were real Ponces.

An invisible clock ticked off seconds while she breathed in the paint smell from the fresh canvases. A million words came into her head, but he had to find his own answer. Silence created a space to allow him to visit what she had been to him, how she had believed in him, and how he had trusted her in the past.

He lifted his head and picked up a small brush he'd borrowed from Lobo's studio, squeezed out a bit of acrylic onto a palette made from discarded cardboard. He brushed a few strokes of paint on the back of the canvas to match the markings on the originals. Then he proceeded to do the same on the other canvas to match a separate paper she showed him.

She exhaled.

He stood back, studied the paper and the markings he'd copied. He set the paper with make-shift palette on the top of the crates and cleaned the brush with a rag, apparently satisfied with his work. "Dangerous? Why is making copies for a collector who owns the originals, dangerous?"

She bit her lip. His tone sounded bitter.

Before she could answer, he continued, softer. "I want to help you, but I don't know what's going on."

"I'm trying to keep us all safe. You, too."

"It doesn't matter. You can't sell these copies as originals. These paintings are twenty-percent smaller than the ones I copied."

She did not expect that, not from him. "What?"

He nodded. "It's what we do, routine for students and anyone making copies. Reducing the size by at least twenty percent eliminates any chance someone would accuse you of forgery." He nodded with a certain satisfaction, a pride that he knew something she didn't.

If the copies were next to each other, the size difference would be clear. Surely the auction house, if they arrived there, if her plan failed, would measure for the description in the catalogue. But if her plan worked the copies would never reach the auction house. The size difference did create a new worry.

The pause was long and uncomfortable. He blew on the paint to accelerate the drying.

Finally, she responded. "Okay. Fine. We've no choice but to use these smaller ones."

She'd preferred his sarcastic comments to this rebellion, but still he'd saved her with these smaller copies. She gave up explaining and squeezed his arm. "Thank you."

He responded with a stern expression. "How much do I get paid?"

Got to love Mateo, always trying to earn a living with his art. "If the Ponce paintings are so awful, copies can't be worth much, right?" She teased, restoring their usual banter, and then put on her serious look. "Besides the size, they're exact copies, right? No screwing around. Hidden sexual messages or something."

He shook his head. "Yes, exact copies. How much are they worth?"

"You'll be paid well, well-enough so you can stock more than cold water in your fridge." She searched his face to see if he was pleased. "No one can know you made copies. *No one.*"

Now the puzzle had all the pieces, and she had what was needed to leave Colombia except for a buyer for the Ponce originals. That piece was in Enrique's hands and she'd have to wait for him to get back to her.

Five grungy artists, portfolios in hand, stood in the aisle outside the booth. Artists always appeared on the Saturday of an art fair, trying to calculate what would impress her and convince her to add them to her gallery group. One wore a wide sixties-era tie, but the paint splatters on his shoes could not be disguised.

Saturday at art fairs was aspiring artists' day, when they could escape their day jobs and pursue what was in their hearts. They believed in their art and had courage, the guts to bare their souls for someone else to critique. For most there was less than no hope. She offered them the respect that came with giving her time to meet with them.

Her head hurt. Even the coffee at breakfast didn't revive paralyzed neurons. *Harta.* Such a good word in Spanish. She was *spent.*

The artist interview drill kept her in the open, away from forces that would blow her world to shards. Sitting in the public space, doing the work of a gallerist gnawed at her normal inclination to leap into problem solve mode, to act, to fight, to fix.

Smiling, she motioned to the first artist to have a seat and continued rotating her head, looking for suspicious lurkers. Seeing no one, she returned to the sketches the artist had laid out.

Naif painting, flat two-dimensional, Grandma Moses, untrained, it was everywhere, especially for tourists in the Caribbean. She asked the short fellow a few questions, feigning interest. He was untrained, from the countryside, up in the hills, never went to school. The man proved that the creative spirit made artists, not slick magazines nor the king makers of New York, London, and Basel.

She fished in her purse for the hotel business card and gave it to Jose, Juan—couldn't remember from two minutes ago. "At this hotel, they have similar paintings in the gift shop. Yours are better. Maybe they'll take some on consignment." The artist nodded, thanked her, and smiled.

A guy in a black windbreaker hovered near her booth. He turned toward her.

Mark Bingham. Oh geez.

Her public stealth game had ended. Her hand trembled as she shook the artist's hand to say good-bye.

A polite but dismissive greeting, a head nod maybe, to her former kidnapper, didn't exist. Mark must be confused, equivocating on this misguided mission otherwise why is he here? If she could get him alone, maybe she could convince him to do the right thing. Mark paced back and forth.

The next artist sat down and dropped his portfolio in his nervousness. She helped him pick up the drawings with one eye on the work and the other on Mark.

The artist made paintings that took on subjects ranging from landscapes to random abstract strokes of primary colors. She stopped at one and examined it. Two children, a girl and a boy, close to the ages of Claire and Mikey played in a field of flowers. "Tell me about these children."

The artist explained that those were his children that he'd left in a rural town near the coast to come to the city for work.

"Do they miss you?"

"I don't know, señora. There's no phone, but I miss them."

A silent bond connected her to this parent and their common plight. She lifted the painting to show Mark. "What do you think of this work? It's the artist's children, far away in another town. It could be anyone's children."

Mark nodded and scrunched his lips. He looked pissed.

She stood closer to Mark and whispered. "Shame on you, all of you. My kids! Who's behind this?"

"What about your kids? I don't understand." Mark turned whiter and walked away down the aisle.

Her hand trembled and the drawing shook. A mistake. Mark had nothing to do with the fax of her kids. So, who was behind this wicked ploy?

She returned to sit next to the artist. "I want to buy this piece for my own collection; a memento of Bogotá."

The artist glowed and said the drawing was fifty dollars. She paid this modest price. He thanked her multiple times and moved on.

A courier from the fair administration arrived to deliver an envelope. Mateo talked with a visitor, and she excused herself from the line of artists and went into the storeroom to open the envelope.

It contained a photo of a car, Nick's car, parked at the Denny's.

No! They've found them.

She crushed the paper against the storeroom wall. She wanted to leave, but to where? To do what?

Panic. She struggled to stave off the rush to flee Bogotá. If she was on a plane, she'd still be hours away from them. She couldn't warn them. She couldn't call them. She wobbled to her chair and sat down.

Her precious ones couldn't hide forever. She'd run before, ran from the Santiago mess. Now decades later, they'd pursued her here and extorted her to do their bidding. Running and hiding was a short-term strategy. She needed to stay the course and get rid of them forever.

With a clearer mind, she went over the situation.

Margarita had made it to the meeting place, the car proved that. Yes, the kids and Margarita had left with Dawn, the abandoned car proved that. The photo was not taken from a security camera, so the rogue bastards only found Nick's car, not Dawn's car. If they'd found the cabin, they would have faxed a photo of them there.

The Mt. Baldy property was hidden from the main road and required a hike half a mile up a hill from Baldy Village to get there. Only locals knew about the cabin. But if the thugs had satellites, surely the Americans did, and they could track a car to the Denny's.

They hadn't found them yet. She needed to move even faster, move on the chance they were searching for her sister's car, too.

Another artist sat down. She couldn't go on like nothing had happened. Just like these artists, she needed a mentor, a guide, someone to show the way out of this fiasco. No one was going to rush to her side and take her hand.

She excused herself from the growing line of artists and went in search of help.

CHAPTER 23

ENRIQUE REACHED TO REMOVE AN artwork from the wall and replace it with an unsold one. She set her bag down to help him straighten the painting.

She stood back and admired the work, trying to keep her emotions in check. "This piece will sell quickly." Barbara Gomez's works had gained steam in the market and deserved consideration for an exhibition in San Diego.

Enrique stopped to answer a question from the young woman covering the booth. Interns were helpful to a point, but she didn't use them. Their limited knowledge resulted in them taking more time than they saved. Ally couldn't hear the question, but Enrique's annoyed tone indicated it was something the girl should have known.

She waited for him to finish. The smell of dying flowers from the opening night party mixed with after-shave and coffee odors from the café made her nauseous. She covered her nose, glad she didn't have these strong smells in her booth.

Enrique finished speaking, brushed the hair out of his eyes, straightened his tie, and put on his jacket. He leaned his head toward his own storeroom. "The paintings are in my storeroom."

"Thanks. They're safer here." A bit of irony underlying that comment, because she also meant the undereducated staff could not recognize a million-dollar painting from a poster.

"Is it okay to talk here?" She leaned toward him.

"Definitely a good place to talk about paintings." He laughed. "We're going to do this deal."

She appreciated his effort to lighten the conversation. He'd overcome his depression about Helena and financial challenges.

Enrique knew more than anyone about the risks this venture presented. But Enrique didn't know about the threats to her children.

"Have you got a buyer? We need to move them fast."

Enrique rubbed his chin. "Possible buyers have occurred to me. Safe people who could put together the cash, but that much money takes time. Also, we must keep people from talking in Bogotá, especially about Ponce, and especially with the bribes to buy information from housekeepers, drivers, delivery guys. A lot of moving parts."

"Let's sell to a foreign dealer or collector. The farther away the better." An idea came to her. "Would you like to flip them quickly? I might have a buyer, not perfect but he does deals like this."

"You could do it yourself? Why do you need me?"

"Ponces are not my thing. A buyer will trust you about their authenticity. And for obvious reasons, my name can't be associated with the sale."

Enrique nodded with a face that showed more gravitas. But he didn't know this deal could stop more weapons, more killing in his country.

She continued. "If collectors think I am paying the bills by flipping high-end works, they'll stop believing in my young artists. Collectors are quirky. It's all a head game."

"True, never about the talent, no objectivity about quality. It's smoke and mirrors, who's hot and who's not. Look at Barbara Gomez. Will she ever make it?"

Barbara made stunning, hazy constructions of high heels, lipsticks, and other cosmetics hidden deep inside shoebox-shaped frames, mounted flush with the wall and covered with parchment paper. She would have bought them all for her gallery, for herself, if she had money. The best job in art is collector, but those dreams were gone with Nick's death.

"Do you want to hear my idea for a buyer?"

He nodded. "You've got my ear, *guapa*."

"Jake Klingman."

"Ugh. God no." Enrique turned away, revulsed. "Hate that guy. He's a *cabrón*."

Whoa. Restrained, elegant Enrique had a boiling point.

"I agree. Klingman is sleazy. But he's got these wealthy buyers."

"Not trustworthy. Not at all."

"Focus on how this might transform our businesses, our lives, and the artists we represent."

"Or get us killed. Not worth it."

"Speaking of prices. The two paintings—about 60"x 48"—what do you think they're worth?"

"Each? $20 million, maybe more."

These numbers shocked her. She hadn't kept up with the prices, only knew what Santi had told her. "Give him a great deal. If the two paintings are worth $40 million, tell Klingman you need $30 million net for the two. The owner probably will take $15 million, and you and I split the remaining $15 million with $7.5 million each."

Lying to Enrique about who was getting the owner's share wasn't right, but neither was getting him killed.

Enrique shook his head and placed his hand on his forehead. "Provenance? Where are they coming from? Violent people are involved here."

"Another reason to sell to Klingman. He won't ask, he won't care. He just wants money, whatever the consequences." That was not kind. No matter how reprehensible Jake was, he was not a gangster. At least, she didn't think he was. "You've seen more Ponces than anyone, except Ponce. Jake will trust you. He can't know I'm in the chain. Maybe I can steer him to you though."

"What about keeping quiet? Klingman will brag all around the fair."

"Tell him that he's playing in the big league with dangerous people involved. If he wants more top works, he must zip it." She pulled her fingers across her lips in the universal symbol to shut up. "Klingman's a lot of things, but he's not stupid."

Enrique shook his head. "I don't feel good about this."

Klingman was standing in the corridor, skulking, trying to overhear their conversation. She nodded with her head toward Klingman to alert Enrique and raised her voice to be sure both men heard her next remark.

"Mateo's work has a great future. You're smart to get in now. I'll see that Mateo's paintings are delivered today after we get the confirmation of the wire transfer to our account." She put her hand out for a confused Enrique to shake it. He played along, kissing her hand.

"Pleasure to do business with the best-looking dealer here." She stepped back.

Klingman hovered closer now, joining in. "You mean the only female dealer here!"

They pretended to be amused by Jake's remark. Yeah, the only female dumb enough and so desperate for sales that she'd come to Bogotá. She left Enrique's booth.

"Al-lay-son. Al-lay-son." Jake ran behind her. Predictability in opponents, loved ones, and everyone in between made life easier to navigate.

"Did you sell the Mateo Lugano paintings? To Enrique?"

"I guess I can tell you since it's a done deal. I set up an exhibition for Mateo with Enrique." She'd done so much lying in the last few days, it had become her new normal.

"But, but you . . . I told you I loved them."

He'd taken no interest in Mateo's work for the last three days they'd been booth neighbors. "I would not write an invoice just because you admired them. Enrique commissioned two paintings for a client, and he took an interest in Mateo."

"Can I have the Mateo works hanging in your booth? I have buyers and the funds all set up."

"How is that possible? You don't even know the prices." She shook her head but was secretly pleased with this new opportunity. "Mateo's prices are moving fast. I probably need to hang on to those works, not sure I can get more."

If she sold the paintings at a higher price, it wouldn't matter how Klingman played with the numbers, what discounts he'd give. Mateo's collectors would be thrilled at the price increases, and higher prices created buzz in the market and new buyers. And he'd have money to live, to buy food to survive.

Klingman's face turned red, and his tone shifted to dark. "Look, babe. I need to deliver to my clients."

She paused for a minute to show her displeasure. "If I let you in on these prices, you can't claim you represent him, exhibit his work, or play with the prices. Just place the works quietly into your clients' collections. Can you commit to that?"

He answered, "Of course." Too quickly. He had no intention of complying.

She needed to finish and get out of the country. "Are you able to keep something else quiet? Not talk with anyone? If I could trust you, I could share something I heard, just a rumor, you understand."

He nodded like a sycophant, and she cringed understanding that she could not trust he would keep a Ponce deal quiet.

She'd mastered the technique of insults with a smile. "Stop nodding like a dog waiting for a treat and prove you can be trusted." She took his arm, guided him out of the aisle and the traffic to a side exit door where she stopped.

"What, what?" Jake ignored her *honest* words and went with the drama of the secret conversation.

"Would you please go get me some coffee—*por favor.* Let me finish the deal with Mateo and Enrique. We'll talk about both getting you some work and that other . . . thing."

He scampered off.

She took a moment to write down the deal on the Ponces and the Mateos in cryptic calculations without words, before she forgot the numbers. All those zeroes. Then she looked around and pulled all of Mateo's paintings out of the back room. She placed them under the ones hanging in the front of the booth and picked up a clipboard with an invoice and pretended to be calculating.

Jake returned faster then she expected. "I brought you two coffees—one black and one with sugar, milk. Didn't know which you wanted."

"*Gracias.*" The ink-colored coffee scared her. "I'll take the one with milk and sugar. It'll sweeten me up for the deal." She winked, disgusted with herself and her manipulation of him but justifying both with notions of a greater good, again. She was becoming the sleazy art dealer she deplored. Keeping her ethics in the face of extortion, violence, and situations that might destroy her, slipped down her priority list.

Jake pulled up a chair and sipped the other coffee while he glanced over at his empty booth.

She reached for the clipboard and completed the invoice while she stirred her coffee. "Which Mateo paintings do you want?" She pointed to the display.

Without turning his head, he said, "I'll take them all."

"You can't have them all. We want a broader market, not just your Guatemalan collectors."

"I have them all sold to my loyal collectors, all over the world."

She shook her head and gave him that look, the one she saved for Nick or the kids when they exaggerated. "How? I just brought them out."

"I have people, clients who buy what I find for them." Paintings were just commodities to him. Mateo's career mattered to her, and she did not want Jake to have a big role. Then she knew what to do, for herself and for the artist.

"You'll have to pay a premium if you want to take say . . . six of the eight."

"Don't change the deal, *guapa*."

Aggressive, no more flirting. Okay, game on.

"Then no deal. I'll sell them myself once the word is out about Enrique handling Mateo in Bogotá." Stone-faced, her heart beat faster as she waited.

A standoff silence hung in the air. He broke first. "What do you need?"

They went back and forth.

A big guy with a crew cut paced the aisle around the around the booth. They, whoever they were, had arrived to follow her again.

She returned to Jake. "A 50 percent premium."

"Can't do it, my clients trust me to negotiate a fair price."

She tossed the clipboard back onto the desk and stood. Klingman followed her to the storeroom of the booth.

"I told you I had a special deal I was offered. I've tapped my people out, so I had to pass. You might have clients though."

"What? What? Tell me."

"You're wasting time. I'm not telling you anything until you agree to Mateo's price and transfer the money. If I hear anything about you trying to represent Mateo or steal him from my gallery, hell will rain down on you, Jake Klingman. I only work with people I can trust. Don't misrepresent your role. Agreed?"

"Yes, yes."

She could have asked him to run naked through the fair and the answer would've been the same.

She shrugged and said nothing. Scribbling out an invoice for six Mateo paintings at $15,000 U.S. each and pausing to do the math, then considered $50,000 each was easier to calculate, but too greedy, maybe $25,000 dealer cost. Putting prices on art was funny money; she knew, and so did most collectors, that the market drove the value.

She had trouble holding the pen and suppressing her joy — for Mateo, for Enrique, and for herself.

She put the invoice in front of him without saying the amount, as was the practice of a well-mannered dealer. "How will you pay?" She said it with aplomb, although she wanted to do a few flamenco twirls and shout, 'Olé!'

"I need your bank routing number in the U.S. Quick. We can transfer funds before the bank closes international transfers."

He looked at his watch and started to take the paintings.

"Stop. Not until the funds transfer is confirmed."

Klingman scribbled his name on the invoice. "Okay, *mujer*, what is this deal you promised to let me in on?"

She wrote down the wire instructions for him. "Move the money now, before the bank closes, and then I'll point you in the right direction."

Klingman went to call his banker on the landline phone installed in his booth, a luxury she could not afford, along with the private fax machine the fair installed for Jake.

He returned with a paper that had the bank numbers showing he'd wired the money to her account.

She went to the desk and picked up Enrique's card, wrote her name on the back and handed it to Jake, who nodded. Nothing more was needed. When Jake showed up, Enrique would offer him the Ponce paintings.

Dealing in this kind of money, well beyond her experience or what she'd imagined, happened in art all the time. Well maybe not *all* the time, but more frequently than one might think. But not to her, until now. She had deals where big money came into her bank and big money went back out leaving a small commission in the account. When the total sale increased, so did the commissions. She made a note to talk with her banker when she returned to explain how her business had changed and avoid any kind of bank holds, investigations or worse, an IRS audit.

Jake's chatty persona would work to Mateo's advantage as Jake would broadcast the deal to the entire fair within the hour. She grabbed an adhesive sheet of red dots and began to put them on Mateo's paintings.

Maybe Enrique was right about him; he couldn't be trusted to flip the Ponce paintings. He would do those things she forbade him to do, but with Mateo's paintings Jake's indiscretion would help her artist's career, his prices, and his bank account.

The Ponces were different. The consequences of Jake talking could be lethal.

"Quite a sale. Congratulations."

She jumped, dropping the adhesive sheet of red dots as she turned around to the person behind the voice that made her cringe.

Frankie stood two feet away beaming.

Ally folded her hands between her arms to keep them from shaking.

Frankie had overheard her talking to Jake. Relief swept over Ally that she'd not uttered the name Ponce to Jake, that there was no way Frankie could know about Enrique, about the location of the originals Frankie's people had dumped in her crate, and she would never know about the copies Mateo had made.

The U.S. operatives had to believe their plan to earn dark money from the auction sale of the Ponce works was in place. Ally had that part handled; the plan for the copies to be shipped off and disappear was well underway.

"Red dots, lots of sales of . . ." Frankie adjusted her purple reading glasses to focus on the label. "Ah, Mister Lugano, Mateo Lugano."

Ally said nothing, not wanting to open the door for chatty Frankie.

Frankie continued anyway. "You look tense. Is everything all right?"

"No, Frankie, not all right." She whispered her anger. "I tried calling the number on the card you gave me without reaching anyone. Where's David?"

"What card, dear?"

"Don't be coy. Where's David?"

"He should be here somewhere, at the fair." She scanned the aisles, pretending to look for him.

What a ridiculous act. Hopeless waste of time. Frankie was a pro and would focus on her job to get the original Ponces to auction and have the proceeds sent to the untraceable bank account to use for whatever covert purpose the conspirators needed.

The big man still lingered on the outside walls of the booth near where Klingman dialed madly on his phone, looking for money for the Ponce deal with Enrique. She assumed it had happened. She'd have to live with it. One slip up by Jake and the whole deal would crumble.

She left Frankie, hoping she'd leave.

The big man who lingered near the entrance of the booth studied a painting. She approached him and said, "I'm here alone and don't want to ignore you." She studied him trying to determine who he was. "Can I answer any questions about these paintings?"

"I can wait."

"I have time to help." She almost begged him to engage in a dialogue, a conversation he didn't want to have. He thanked her with a 'maybe later' and drifted down the aisle.

She turned back toward her booth, disappointed to see Frankie still there, now comfortably positioned in the chair at the desk, looking a little like a badly dressed collector.

"Frankie, are you resting your feet?"

"We have a deal to talk about." Frankie leaned toward her, as close as her large chest, spilling onto the artist catalogues on the desk, would allow. "The auction deal?" Frankie raised her eyebrows.

"All set. I was going to tell David at breakfast, but he didn't show."

Frankie continued. "The chief is worried the paintings might have gone missing."

Oh God no. Did these people know about her deal with Enrique?

Enrique would not have betrayed her. She trusted him, and it was not in his interest to lose out on the sale of the artworks. Jake hadn't known about them until minutes ago and could not have blabbed around the fair. Did someone overhear her and Enrique? Oh geez, please don't let this fall apart.

"It's Colombia, Frankie. Rumors. You said yourself— booth to booth. Art fair gossip."

Frankie shook her head. "It would be bad, a dangerous thing, Allison, if those paintings didn't end up at auction where they need to be sold."

A silent stand-off rose between them.

Ally leaned over. "The Ponces are in that storeroom." She pointed to the closet. "Would you like to see them?" She mopped the sweat with a tissue praying for a negative response. Please say no, say no. Ally couldn't show her the copies, copies that smelled like fresh paint and were twenty percent smaller.

"Why yes, I'd like to see them."

Damn. "Ah they're half packed but I guess I . . ." She stood up, took a couple of breaths, straightened her spine, and motioned for Frankie to follow her to the storage closet where the crate was.

Frankie poked her head in the door while Ally removed the top of the crate to reveal two large paintings wrapped in brown paper.

"Is that paint I smell?

Ally stumbled to respond. "I . . . I complained to fair management, didn't want to breathe the fumes. But they said when they paint the walls of these little closets the odor stays trapped in the small space. So annoying."

"Can you unwrap the works?"

"Oh, it's hard to get more packing materials, I'd hate to have to find more to rewrap them."

"No need. Could you pull the tape off the paper? I need to report back all is in order."

Ally's hand trembled as she picked at the edge to lift the Scotch tape off the paper.

Frankie waited without any show of impatience.

The tape came off and the end of wrapping paper opened to reveal a section of the painting.

Ally waited in silence, depending on Frankie's ignorance about art, and her inability to compare measurements of these works against the originals.

Frankie said nothing. She leaned the paintings away from the wall and looked at the backs, pulling the paper lower. Frankie had done her homework, earning a new and worrisome respect.

Ally's heart pounded.

Finally, Frankie spoke. "The colors, so vibrant. Just takes your breath away."

True, both about the colors and taking her breath away.

Frankie whispered. "I read your record from Santiago. Like David said, you're a team player, Allende, and all that. Despite our set back, you'll do what we need you to do. Isn't that so, dear?" Frankie winked.

A wink really? She stared at Frankie. A team player or tool? In this dirty world there was no difference.

The Ponces had passed Frankie's muster, but Ally had almost missed her remark. "Set back? What set back?"

Frankie moved her awkward body, squeezed past her out of the little storeroom. "More galleries, booths to visit. Have you seen that Picasso?"

Ally asked again, "Is David the set back?"

Frankie turned around. "I'll return tomorrow and review the auction paperwork. I'll bring the bank numbers for Ellsworth to forward the proceeds of the sale."

Ally needed to find David.

Frankie had to believe, and Ally had to make her believe, everything was being done to sell the paintings to get them their dirty money. But Ally knew no bank account numbers would be needed.

She'd been so worked up over getting the art moved around she'd not thought about how many people were aware of her involvement. More than David and Frankie. Mark. The station chief and maybe the ambassador.

The maze grew more complex—and more urgent. Government bureaucracy—right hand and left hand don't recognize they're part of the same body. Missions conflicted with each other, the alphabet agencies, CIA, DEA, State worked against each other with no one in control. This was the worst scenario for her.

Didn't matter what the conflicts were, even if she could get to the truth. She had to move the paintings as Frankie and the others had asked, or let them believe she had, and if possible, use the contradictions and infighting to her advantage.

Klingman smiled and blew kisses across the aisle, looking very pleased with himself. He must have sold something. She hoped Enrique had not done the Ponce deal with him. Not yet.

She returned a weak nod and left, strolling toward the cafeteria to keep him from coming to talk to her.

She needed a salad, empanada, something to keep her strength up and to look normal to those watching her.

Enrique waved from his booth. He was with clients, and she couldn't tell him to kill the deal with Klingman. She motioned with her finger for him to meet her in the cafeteria when his clients left.

A long line of people waited to buy food and provided a calm moment to assess options. If Frankie's people knew copies were being sent to the auction house, they would know she'd scammed them on the real ones. Once, art crates had arrived in a jumble to her gallery from abroad through customs. They had that yellow inspection tape crudely rewrapping everything and a note stating the inspection date with a scribbled signature. Maybe the gallery's history of shipping and passing random inspections would get the crate through without them opening it. She couldn't let that happen. The DEA needed to seize the crate and impound it forever.

Sitting solo at a small table with her back to the art fair traffic, she picked at the empanada and sipped a soda. Someone squeezed her shoulders from behind.

"Party tonight!" Santi startled her out of her thoughts.

She kissed and hugged him like the old friend he was. "I've missed you." She hugged him again. "Where've you been?"

"Out late with my tribe." Santi cleared his throat and didn't elaborate. But she was certain he wasn't referring to art people. If he wanted her to know, he'd tell her.

"You're the queen. Garcia Márquez hanging out in your booth, Gabo, your new best friend. So jealous, Mami."

"He'd love you too." His gushing emotions, so out there, drew her like a bee to a flower.

"We're friends, serious friends. Gabo comes by the gallery whenever he's in New York, and we go out with the literati." He continued. "Sold him a Warhol and an Ana Mercedes Hoyos he'd admired. Ana is friends with Gabo too. But you, *chica,* you're the star."

"Call me next time you're planning to get together. Maybe I'll fly to New York." The words were hollow. That was her old life, the one that included Nick. As dear a friend as Santi was, she couldn't share the mess she was in. As intuitive as he was, he appeared to know nothing about what was happening under the surface.

"So how are sales for you? Is the fair good?"

"Okay, we'll survive. But you, word is out about Mateo. Wow. Terrific for you and for him. He's destined for the big time."

Didn't even take an hour for Jake Klingman to boast and circulate the exaggeration.

She was glad of the praise for Mateo from someone like Santi whose opinion mattered, counted in New York art circles. Regardless of the manipulative way she'd achieved it, Mateo deserved the recognition and the success. "Want something to eat?"

"I'll pass. Haven't been feeling great. Would Mateo consider a New York show with my gallery?"

"Are you kidding?" She grinned at him and chuckled to herself.

Santi continued with the updates he'd gathered while circulating the fair. "The Japanese gallery didn't sell the Picasso, a painting on paper, not a canvas. Around $30 million."

"Yikes, that's the price for a work on paper? Is it a good work?"

"Small. A gouache. The signature looks good, and that's all that's needed for that price."

Hard to wrap your head around how the scribbled pencil marks of a signature could change the value by millions.

"Too bad they didn't sell it." She rotated her head around the open area of the convention center. Where was Enrique?

"The Japanese understand the long game. They hold onto things in secure vaults until the right moment. A different way of running an art gallery."

"Must be nice to have the cash to pay the bills while you wait."

"Are you celebrating with everyone tonight, our last night?"

"Another party! Can't. I'm exhausted."

Santi's face fell in disappointment.

She squeezed his hand. "Exhausted in a good kind of way—phenomenal sales. Thank you for convincing me to come." She couldn't crush him with the truth of how Bogotá had landed her in the most dangerous situation of her life. All she cared about was getting out of here to protect Claire and Mikey. But now, she needed to tell Enrique that he couldn't do the Klingman deal. She never should have suggested it.

"Life's too much fun. So many cute guys and so little time. Quittin' time at the fair, *mija*. Only artists and students left."

She studied his face and hesitated before she decided to ask him. "I need a favor."

Seeing her perplexed look, he rotated his hand urging her to speak.

"Could I stay with you tonight? Share your room, the couch or something."

"Didn't expect that." He took a deep breath. "You wouldn't like my hotel. A lot of crazy things happen in this type of hotel. A guy place if you get my meaning. The suite is beautiful—top of the world—jacuzzi tub, baby, but the rest of the hotel, well . . ." Santi had a sparkle in his eye, the energy was returning to the Santi she loved.

She didn't want to share much. "I can't go back to the Tequendama. Someone . . . don't ask. I need somewhere to stay, a place they can't find me."

"What—who's bothering you chica?" He paused for a long moment and then added, "I'll figure something out." He reached for her hand and kissed it.

She tossed the napkin onto the table.

He took her elbow and walked out of the café down the aisle.

Another one of those guys with the earpiece and the out-of-place suit stood by the cafeteria exit. "I, ah, I . . . a guy is chasing me." True but not exactly.

"Guys are chasing you?" He laughed. "*Guapa, intelligente,* and gracious. Now, single. Go for it."

"No, you don't understand. He follows me everywhere. So creepy. I'm exhausted trying to ditch him. He'll be looking for me at Tequendama."

"What about the Casa Hotel?"

"No. Too touristy, predictable that an American would go there, and they'd look for me there. Your hotel sounds perfect." She needed him to stop suggesting other places and just agree to let her hide at the Morada.

"Wait. You said 'they.' Who's they?" He elevated his tone to the alarm level. "Don't answer. Let's get your stuff."

Enrique had not come to the cafeteria, and she still needed to talk with him. She gathered her purse and duffle from the closet. She locked the door and switched off the art lights.

Santi steered her double time toward the exit. She loved him for not requiring more details.

Enrique headed toward her. "Hola, Santi. A private word with Ally, please?" Enrique pulled her toward his unlit booth.

Santi gave her a raised eyebrow look with an unspoken question: is this the guy chasing you?

She shook her head and stepped with Enrique to the back of his booth.

Enrique spoke fast. "Don't be upset. Can't sell Ponces to Klingman. Just can't."

She embraced him. "I'm so relieved." She hugged him again. "You were right about him. He can't be trusted. But he was so happy, I worried you'd done the deal."

"I told him you had admired Barbara Gomez's works and might handle her in the U.S."

"Hurry, tell me quick. Santi and I need to get out of here."

"Jake bought all of Barbara's works. Tried to cut you out."

"No worries. I'll get the next series she creates." Her smile evaporated as the Ponce tsunami returned. "What the hell are we going to do with the Ponces? Can we do a cash deal with someone outside the art sphere?"

He shook his head. "Maybe. We'll think of something."

"I'm leaving tomorrow, early as possible. Meet me here, first thing." She gave him a quick kiss.

She and Santi exited the main entrance where Santi lifted his arm to signal a white limo. Brutus, the driver, recognized Santi and provided him with an over-the-top welcome.

"White. So, so Vegas, Santi."

Santi sang, wagging his head. "Goin' to the chapel, gonna' get married."

She joined him, in tempo, the urgency and anxiety blew off with the breeze into the Bogotá night and with Jake Klingman out of the Ponce deal.

Santi leaned over. "Who are you running from?"

She shook her head. "Can't tell you." She studied all the dark corners of the entrance of the convention center as the limo pulled out. The entrance was empty, there was no one. Maybe Frankie had called off the thugs once she saw the paintings, or Mark had convinced them he had the mission in hand. She hoped so.

Santi switched on a speaker and spoke to the driver. "Brutus, take us for a drive around the city." He kissed her hand. "Drive by the best new hotels."

Santi put his arm around her shoulder. She was glad the limo would drive around a bit. When she was sure they hadn't been followed, they could go to the Morada.

"I just want a clean place to sleep. Be left alone. Is there space, a couch, a chair?"

He paused and looked at the roof of the car, out the window, and then took her hand in his. "There's room for you, my lady. Santi protects Maiden Allison." He kissed her forehead. "Belieeeeve me—no guy will bother you at this hotel. But promise me you won't go to the bar in the basement. That could scare you worse than the guy following you. If you stay in the room until morning, the hotel will be empty by then."

"I promise. Thank you, Santi." He was taking a risk not related to his wild behavior and getting found out. She had her secret too and they were both twirling, together.

"Do you want to swing by your hotel to get your suitcase?"

She'd left her suitcase in the booth's closet. "I have what I need in this duffle. Do you have a t-shirt I can sleep in?"

"*Por favor!* You theeenk Santi even owns a t-shirt? Nothing without cufflinks, Mami. Buy anything you need in the hotel shop. They plan for impromptu guests."

"Don't you own a *Gay and Proud* shirt, maybe in Spanish?"

He chuckled at the idea. "Not in Bogotá, too risky to be out." His face turned serious. "Brutus, take us to the Morada."

After a few more blocks, the white limo pulled in behind another white limo at a hotel she'd never been to or even heard of. A doorman, in a purple uniform with a feather plumed cap, opened her door.

"You'll feel like a stranger here."

She already knew that and was glad for it. "I want to be invisible."

The lobby exhibited an array of hip, well-designed features she rarely saw in South American hotels. Still the place was dowdy inside, just in a different way. The dozen or so people in the lobby stared at her. Other women were around, mostly waitresses at the bar. She surveyed the rest of the lobby and lowered her shoulders down from near her ears. The thugs pursuing her, whoever they were, would never look here.

Before he left for the night, Santi changed into an outrageous paisley blazer with an ascot around his neck. He sauntered into his world, king of that universe, unafraid of the perils lurking in the darkness.

She wanted to protect Santi, keep him safe, but withheld her motherly advice. He provided his wisdom, knowledge of the art scene and New York savvy. And yet she held back, not wanting to judge. In a way she envied his freedom, a freedom she once had but now could barely remember. Nothing in her repertoire helped her understand that he would risk life itself for moments of pleasure. He chose to ignore the experts and the critics, those adjudicators with flawed judgments of him and his friends that time would surely eclipse into a verdict of acceptance.

Mateo and Santi balanced their world of worries with laughter and pleasure. She wanted to feel loved, yes, an evening of feeling loved could be magic. Now more than ever, she missed and needed a partner she could trust. Maybe that would never happen again, but the love of her two babies would be enough, more than she needed. The worry for them left no space for her own needs.

DAY 5

CHAPTER 24

BEFORE SHE'D LEFT HOME, ALLY HAD put a red circle on the kitchen calendar around Sunday, the fifth day of this trip, the day she would return. Claire and Mikey were meant to cross off the days to count down until their mom would be hugging them again. Day five had arrived, but the kids wouldn't have crossed off the days.

They couldn't. They weren't eating cereal from their turtle-shaped bowls at the child-sized table in the kitchen. Instead, the kids were in hiding, bundled off to the cabin. Her heart broke thinking the calendar, meant to connect them, sat untouched.

Today she'd leave this place, end the hellish schemes surrounding her, finish this nightmare. She'd return to those little ones, fill their cereal bowls, and join their laughter as they welcomed a new day.

She sank down into the bath water filled with lavender scented salt and buried herself in bubbles from which she could emerge restored. Restored to what? It had taken years to push Santiago from her memories, but scars remained. Bogotá had terrorized her beyond Santiago and might never be purged.

The elephant that remained was to finish the sale of the Ponces, and time was running out. She couldn't leave Bogotá with those paintings not safely in a distant collection, hidden somewhere. If Enrique had sold to someone that couldn't be trusted, someone like Klingman who would reveal their secret, it would be a disaster. If embassy operatives discovered that she'd tricked them, there would be payback. Placing the Ponce paintings was priority number one, the last puzzle piece to solve before she could leave.

Her strategy had remained as fragile as the bubble froth surrounding her, a plan that would disappear with a whisp of a breath or explode when touched.

She sipped hot coffee from a porcelain cup, left in the suite by a discrete butler, and returned the cup to the saucer balanced on the marble rim around the bath. She closed her eyes and inhaled the calming lavender scent. In this world of competing and confused forces, each believed they could dominate the other and, in the end, everyone would lose. Except her. She could not end up the loser.

The phone in this hotel room would be safe to use. But the other end was not safe. Gossip in the Baldy Café could hit a new crescendo if a call came in from Colombia. She was so close now, almost home, no reason to take a risk.

The sun rose over the mountains surrounding Bogotá and spread its warmth through the window into the bathroom. A thick towel absorbed the water droplets from the bruised skin on her wrists and upper arms. Flashes of the shack where she'd slept two nights ago returned like a PTSD episode. The thugs were operating on their own plan, or their non-plan, and they wouldn't bother to kidnap her this time. They'd kill her.

She'd heard that Escobar's men feared extradition to U.S. prisons more than they wanted whatever they thought she had. Sketchy people like Horny and his boss didn't want paintings sold at an auction like Frankie did; they just wanted the money. They wanted those paintings for themselves as a source of cash to continue their fight or maybe enrich themselves.

Whoever still pursued her, maybe it was the Cali cartel people with whom the U.S., Mark, and others shared a common goal to kill Escobar. But a lousy twenty million dollars, when rumors said the cartels burned cash to stay warm, wouldn't seem worth their trouble. Perhaps the people who hated Escobar waited and watched all night, or FARC rebels who wanted that cash for their political objectives. She considered departing from the Morada Hotel to the airport now that she had her passport and credit cards, take a flight to anywhere outside Colombia. But dismissed the idea, circling back to the logic she'd repeated more than once and returning to the same place: The only permanent exit door was through the plan, not by abandoning it.

The towel had loose hairs all over it. Her hair. Stress. The face in the mirror, not even hers. But alive. She brushed her hair and tied it up like a warrior ready for battle. She needed to find Enrique and secure a buyer for the original Ponces. Time had run out.

The same black dress came off the hanger, looking less wrinkled. She left the purple t-shirt she'd had sent up from the hotel shop, a shirt with the English words *Meet Me at the Morada*. One large 'M' captured all three words with the result being 'eet e at the orada." Funny. She placed a note next to the shirt addressed to Santi, thanking him, with the comment that she knew t-shirts weren't his style, but this one was a classic worth keeping.

The business center was listed in the hotel phone directory. They were there on Sunday, and she went downstairs to give them four envelopes, each containing the same documents to be sent by Federal Express with overnight service. The clerk asked for her passport number.

She searched her purse.

Oh God. Her passport was missing. She unloaded every-thing on the counter, frantic to find the one thing she had to have. It wasn't anywhere. "Sorry. I must have left it in the room. I know the number, is that enough?"

The clerk was reluctant but took the number and entered it on the form.

She retrieved everything from Santi's room and wouldn't have lost the passport in the limo. Her room at the Tequendama was the only possibility. Ugh. She had to return there to get it.

The doorman insisted that she take the Morada's white limo to the Tequendama.

Brutus wasn't driving this time. If anyone followed her or waited at the hotel, the driver might protect her from someone waiting, someone to come find her if she didn't return to the limo. Maybe the driver had a pistol like the one Santi told her Brutus had in his belt.

The passport had to be in the room. At the hotel, she'd run to the room, find the passport, return to the limo, get to the booth, find Enrique to finish the Ponce deal, and rush to the airport for the 7 p.m. flight.

The limo pulled into the Tequendama entrance, and she exited before the driver came to a complete stop.

"Check-out time has passed." The slimy clerk corrected his rudeness with a tardy 'Good morning.' She took the key and said nothing, but added a quickness to her step, in case he was the snitch who summoned those looking for her.

She put the key into the lock, opened the door slowly. Her clothes were in the same disorder, nothing out of its random place, scattered as though she'd never returned. She searched the desk and the floor. The safe was empty when she left, but she reopened it anyway. Her passport sat at the back, the same color as the interior of the little safe. Geez. Moving fast was essential, but making mistakes like this could cost her.

The photo of the kids was still on the bedside table, she picked it up and kissed it. She reached for the phone, wishing she could call them. Instead, she dialed the front desk to make sure both her bill and Mateo's had been charged to the card and check-out was complete. She did not want to linger in the lobby.

A large hand grabbed hers and slammed the receiver down.

She dropped the photo and released the phone.

"Keep quiet. I'll let you go." That voice. Mark Bingham. She trembled, nodding to signify she'd cooperate. He removed his hand from her mouth, pushing her onto the bed, and blocking her from reaching for the phone.

"You ran. Made big problems for me. I've been trying to talk to you alone."

She couldn't breathe. "I've been working at the fair. You saw me, and your guy did too."

"What guy? I work alone."

"Well, there's spooks watching me every minute."

"Did you tell someone about the paintings?"

Mateo and Enrique knew, but neither of them would be so stupid. "Embassy people know about them."

Mark pulled back. "Where were you last night? I thought someone grabbed you."

"With a friend."

"I don't give a shit about your sex life. You know this mission splintered. Guys are not cooperating, out of control."

"No surprise." She stood up and had to ask. "Where's David? What happened to David?"

"Dead. Didn't you see the papers?"

Dead. Oh God.

Not a surprise, but she'd hoped that it wouldn't be true. David did not deserve to die, even if his idea of serving his country was wrong-headed.

Rage bubbled up and overflowed. She dropped the photo of the kids and slapped him. She beat on his chest. "You're a killer. No matter what you believe, you are killers."

"I didn't kill David . . . didn't kill anyone." Mark stopped, unable to defend or clarify what happened to David. He sat next to her on the bed, mumbling, and then reached to the floor to pick up the photo of her kids. He stared at it.

Her talent as a salesperson was reading faces. In a voice as calm as she could make it, she brought him up to speed. "I've arranged what you wanted. The paintings are shipping out this morning to Miami. All the paperwork is complete." She paused, taking a breath. "You'll get your money."

His eyes darted back and forth between her face and the door and then he handed her the kids' photo. "Thought I understood this mission. I don't know anymore." He shook his head in despair. "We could all be dead."

"David deserved—we deserve to live. Just like the little boy in that photo. What's worth dying for in Colombia? No reason for you to be working here. Bright young person like you, a family that wants you home. Safe."

Some nerve in him reacted. He stood up and touched his finger to her lips to keep her from saying more. He lifted the bottom of the telephone and removed something. Turning to the ceiling light, he raised his arm but couldn't reach. Finally, he removed a tiny device and took it to the bathroom.

This was her chance to run for the limo, then the airport. She had her passport, but she hesitated when she heard him throw the device into the toilet. He flushed the toilet several times. She waited.

He returned to sit next to her on the bed and spoke in a low whisper. "Mission's unraveled. The people, U.S. people, who hired me lost control. A partnership with Colombian criminals was a bad idea to start with." He shook his head.

Taking a page from David, she turned the television on to high volume. She whispered near his ear.

"We can get the hell out. Run."

"Marines don't run."

She touched his arm. "What's this fight about? It won't stop American kids from taking drugs. The opposite will happen. Our government is subsidizing the drug business, using dirty money. They are exhorting us to get that money from the sale of the paintings. Yes, us."

He sighed and nodded, confirming what she'd guessed. Misery overtook him.

"There's only one you, your mother's son, a brother, your girl's guy."

His voice cracked. "I've got a son."

That she didn't know. "A son? A little boy who needs you, to teach him baseball, take him fishing, put your arms around and read him stories. You threatened . . . I hope not you, but those other guys threatened my kids' lives and my life. David's dead because he wouldn't use my kids to terrorize me. We mean nothing to them, nothing to their government or to our own government. You'll die, rot in this foreign place. No medals. No honors. Nothing for your son to remember. Collateral damage to them, but we're everything to those we love."

He mumbled under his breath, slipping back into that mode she knew too well. "In too deep. No way out."

She shook her head. As an extra precaution, she took the pad by the desk and wrote, "I have a plan. But I need you."

He shook his head and whispered. "Only way out is to get them their money. That chick at the embassy needs weapons, weapons not on Congress' radar."

"Frankie?" She swung her legs off the bed preparing to stand. She turned the paper over and wrote, "Listen to my idea."

He wrote a question mark on the pad.

She scribbled, "Frankie'll believe she's getting what she wants. But she won't get it."

With a perplexed face, he studied the words on the notepad.

She poured water into two glasses and offered him one.

He chugged the water, breathing heavy. She tried to remain calm.

He nodded and pointed to the door.

She turned toward the desk where her purse was and took the kids' photo. Mark held the door open, and together they walked to the elevator.

She called the elevator and when the empty carriage arrived, she hit the hold button to give them time to talk without being overheard.

"What's your plan?"

"I need you to go to Miami and stop the crate with the paintings. It'll have drugs in it. Make sure they seize it."

"Shouldn't be a problem. But why?"

"Those paintings can't make it to auction." She pulled ten one-hundred-dollar bills, her emergency stash, from the compact in her purse and gave them to him. "Is this enough to get you to Miami? To get you out of Colombia?"

He counted the bills and nodded.

"Alert the DEA that a shipment with drugs is on its way. They need to seize it." She handed him the tracking numbers. "And impound the crate." She pointed to Frankie's return address on the forms. "Keep eyes on the crate, no bribing nonsense, no one can sell the paintings inside if it's part of a drug seizure. Correct?"

"You'll need to have real contraband, real drugs inside or this plan will backfire."

"I can get some zip lock bags of marijuana. I'll have artists find it for me."

He smirked. "Those Miami guys don't bother with a few zips. Too much paperwork. Colombian cocaine. That's their objective."

"Don't the dogs sniff out marijuana?"

"Not what those dogs are trained to find."

She shook her head at her own stupidity. The elevator pinged open and fortunately, no one got on. "Okay then. Can you get cocaine?"

"Are you kidding? Every ounce of powder I have access to is measured, accounted for, and locked up. The guys get drug-tested constantly. Keeps U.S. agents honest."

She only needed a few ounces, not truckloads. A country full of cocaine, and she couldn't get her hands on enough for a dog's nose. "I'll figure it out. Somehow." An art fair, all that partying, drugs were somewhere. Her head ran through a mental Rolodex of contacts, searching for likely sources. Only six hours until she had to be at the airport.

Mark pushed another button on the elevator to delay their arrival to the lobby.

She added, "Keep that crate in DEA seized property lock-up in Miami. Can you do that?"

"Got it. Next assignment?"

"Might be the toughest of all. But the most important."

His face reflected a concern.

She continued. "Go home to Ohio." She smiled. "Have nothing to do with these people—no matter what they offer you. Get a job, a real job, sell copy machines, lease farm equipment, anything. Away from these deadly, little boy games."

The elevator door opened into the lobby. "Mark Bingham, or whatever your name is, go be safe with your son."

Mark nodded in a way that seemed he believed it was possible.

She too had to believe and convince herself she could exit this corrupt world. For now, she'd needed to behave like them, without becoming them.

Almost everything was in place, finally. Now all she needed was some cocaine and a buyer for the Ponces.

CHAPTER 25

ART FAIR ENERGY HAD MOVED TO the wrap-up drill. The center was crazy busy, with people bustling in the aisles, but the space was eerily quiet. Mateo sat in the booth flipping through an avant-garde magazine, probably given to him by the Wilson curator. He set the publication down with a smug face. "The paintings are dry, packed in the crate, and ready to screw on the top and ship, Comandante." He saluted.

She had no comeback for his sarcasm. "Thank you."

"How much?" Mateo rubbed his thumb on the tips of his fingers in the international symbol for money.

She'd share more with him, including his record prices as soon as she pinned Enrique down. He wasn't in his booth and time was up. Until he got here, she'd work on the second priority: buy cocaine.

Mateo had been talking, and she hadn't listened to a word. He continued, "Got to pay Lobo for the paints and return his key. He's not here at the fair."

She handed Mateo some cash. "You still have the key? Are you returning it to his studio?"

He nodded. "I guess so, since Lobo's not here."

A long shot idea developed, but if it worked, a big problem would be solved. "I'm going with you. I promised Lobo I'd see his paintings. He was generous, sharing his studio with us."

Lobo was clueless about what Mateo had painted. A puzzle might be pieced into an artful whole with this new alliance between the three of them.

Klingman walked up, buzzing, flashing something in front of her. "Did you hear about your friend?"

She took the tabloid from his hands. She gasped.

Mark had said 'dead,' but she did not expect this gore. A photo of a bloody mess, a face with one eye missing. The shirt and pants were David's.

David. A spread of four views of the same scene covered the front page. A 100-point headline screamed *Diplomático Asesinado*. DIPLOMAT ASSASSINATED.

Dizzy, she reached for a chair and sat down holding her head. "Water, could I please have water?"

Jake scampered away in search of water, mumbling something about not wanting to upset her.

She forced herself to breathe and concentrated on translating the article. Short on facts, there was no 'when' and no 'where.' The 'why' was understood, except he was an American. An American government employee. Killing an American would involve a U.S. investigation, and the feared extradition to the U.S. if a suspect was identified. Killing a foreign official was beyond an ordinary American, off-limits for most terrorists. It was odd that the article did not have a comment from the embassy.

David Martinez, political attaché from the United States Embassy, was found murdered in the parking structure of the Tequendama Hotel, shot in an apparent robbery of his watch and money. A hotel security guard found the body. No suspects have been identified. Anyone with information, please contact the local police.

David's life gone, snuffed out in a dingy Bogotá garage. The thugs or agents, she couldn't be sure, had murdered him. She hadn't believed Mark, but the news story made it real. A tragedy would be covered up as another casualty of a crime-ridden country, but people in Washington, maybe Congress, would ask questions. And they would expect answers beyond excuses like Colombian crime.

But it was weird that it happened two days ago, and the news story came out today.

At least, she had clarity. The people Mark declared out of control would kill her to get what they wanted. She'd planted protection, permanent, foolproof protection that would keep embassy people away from her. She didn't understand what motivated David's killers or who was their leader. There was no plan to escape them, except get back to the U.S. where they did not want to be caught.

"Your water." Jake held out a paper cup and stared at her.

She'd been burned and now could trust no one, including Jake who waited expectantly for some gossip about her reaction.

She mumbled thanks.

Jake shifted his weight from one foot to another, said he was sorry and thankfully, finally returned to his booth without the newspaper.

Mateo stood in the background, having withdrawn his tall frame to the back of the booth, peeling labels off the walls. The two of them needed to talk.

He came near her chair to throw the unneeded labels into the trash and looked at the newspaper. "David Martinez! What are you—what are *we* involved in?" He fumed. "Don't fucking say I can't know."

His anger was justified. Murderers kidnapped her, hunted her, nearly shot her. He didn't even know that. "I am so sorry; it's complicated and dangerous. I wanted to protect you."

He backed off when he saw tears in her eyes and handed her a tissue. He bent over and placed his arm on her shoulder.

"Sorry, Roba. Too many close people dying . . . I want to help, to protect you, protect both of us." He stumbled on his words, unable to say more.

The comment was meant to comfort her, instead drew her into the losses over the last year, the struggle for survival. To right the family ship, to make a new life, had been challenge enough, even before threats from the narco-spooks, and the not-so-clever U.S. operatives. Her legs shook, and she teetered on emotional and physical collapse.

She took a napkin from the wine tray on the desk, wiped her eyes. The news of David's death would spread throughout the fair, and everyone would turn their attention to her when she most needed to be invisible.

She whispered to Mateo, "Let's get out of here." She picked up her purse and walked toward the exit.

He trailed behind until she turned and walked back toward Jake's booth.

"Jake, a favor, watch the booth?"

He nodded and seemed wounded by her request.

She added a limited explanation to ease her guilt. "Mateo and I need to be gone for a couple of hours."

"Can I talk with my new artist? Before we all leave Colombia?" Jake leaned his head toward Mateo who waited closer to the exit.

She pulled Jake aside. "I sold you some paintings. We did not, I repeat, did not, agree that you will represent Mateo over any territory." She lowered her voice, thinking she'd been too harsh. "Are we clear?"

"Fine, fine. Go do your errand. I'll cover your booth."

Jake was . . . well she didn't have the word for him. She rushed toward the exit with Mateo, hoping her hunch about Lobo was correct.

Mateo slowed her down. "Where are we going?"

"Lobo's studio. In a taxi. You can return his key." Screw the embassy's safety myth that hotel drivers were better than a random taxi.

He shrugged and hailed a cab with a meter and opened the door for her.

She looked around to see if someone was following them. She had to be sure. At the old marketplace, she told the driver to stop. They got out of the taxi, walked across the market to the taxi stand near where the funky bus had dropped her. They got in line and took the first available, heading in the opposite direction.

Mateo got in behind her. "What's up?"

She didn't answer and told the driver to take them to Lobo's address in Candelaria. The driver continued down the main street driving between cars, moving fast as she'd requested.

She held back the good news from Mateo. It was exactly what he dreamed about. "First, would you like to know you're the talk of the fair? You were off painting and missed that Klingman bought and paid for a selection of your paintings. Because Enrique bought some also, I was able to push your prices up. Higher prices might get you a show in New York. I'm talking with Santi about it."

He was stunned, covered his mouth with his hand in disbelief, and then laughed a hearty roar. "What are the prices? A show with Enrique and in New York? Incredible."

"No, all credible, the truth. You've broken through. I was always convinced you would. I've been working hard, got your back. When we return, I'll send you the details, but you'll have plenty of money."

She'd asked a lot of him and was glad she had something for him in return. But she needed his help for a couple more hours. If he'd realized he was rich, he might jump out of the taxi and run all the way to Montevideo to tell Christina.

From the outside, the yellow taxi looked like a random taxi anywhere. Inside, little flags hung from the mirror and sun visors, promoting a soccer team and honoring saints, or was it the other way around? The violent culture affected their beloved fútbol, too. Miss a penalty shot, get death threats, or worse, be killed. She had one chance, one final score she had to make.

The taxi waited in the traffic and faceless people paraded to get to their jobs. They plodded ahead, like figures in a painting by Antonio Sequí, trodding toward their daily grind. She and Mateo shared that, those money worries that made them envy a predictable life of a 9-to-5 job, a paycheck, and stability.

She ran her hands through her hair, could sense a victory was near, but the game wasn't over. Intense pressure to get to Enrique, to finish the job before the clock expired. "Can we go on a street without so many stoplights? Go faster?"

The driver peered at her in his rearview mirror.

"You ok, señora? Are you having an emergency?"

His tone was kind, and she believed he wanted to be helpful. Humanity existed, even where life was short and cheap. Scratch the surface and find compassion and understanding.

She uttered one word. "Bogotá." She shuddered, unable to speak without breaking down.

She took several breaths, settled the rising panic, telling herself she wouldn't cry until it was over, until she was up in the air on the plane home.

The driver spoke up. "We are good people. We laugh and cry. Love our children, kiss our wives. Work hard, sing, dance, want the same things you do—to be left alone to live our lives."

Simple wisdom. The three of them shared these goals, beyond which everything else was secondary. Without a quality crust, the pizza toppings meant nothing.

Mateo, the cynic, rolled his eyes and said nothing, but squeezed her hand, his face glowing. His look was something that she'd never seen before, a recognition, a vision of a life he dared not imagine.

The driver pulled up to the studio on the narrow street in front of the colonial house. She paid him twice the fare they owed and asked him to wait.

Mateo rang the bell, but no one answered. He used Lobo's key to open the lock box and retrieve the large key to the antique door. They wandered through the dark foyer to the studio.

A heavy odor of acrylic, paint thinner, three-hundred years of tobacco, and whatever else lingered in the studio, created a pungent soup that convinced her what she was looking for had to be here.

Lobo's work, the paintings she'd not yet seen, lined the walls. Serious works, not representations of quotidian objects or landscapes, but original expressions from his imagination. They were complex abstractions about surface and texture that she'd be pleased to show in her gallery.

She studied Lobo's paintings making notes of the titles written on the backs of the canvases as she rotated her head, looking for what she really wanted. Minutes she couldn't afford to lose, ticked by.

Mateo stood in front of her, waiting. "I'm not moving until you tell me why you're here. It's not to look at paintings."

"Okay. Okay. So not for me, but we need . . . for complicated reasons . . ." She lowered her head, drew in a breath to find words. She raised her head to meet his eyes. "Do you think Lobo has cocaine somewhere?"

She expected him to object, strongly. But that reaction didn't erupt.

"Of course, there's cocaine. These crazy artists." He chuckled and, in an instant, his face turned sour. "Wait. You're not thinking . . . no, come on! Taking it back? Through U.S. Customs?"

"No. Not exactly."

"There's not a middle ground, either you are, or you aren't." He shouted.

"I'm putting the drugs in the crate with the copies to make sure DEA seizes them." There it was, out into the world. "The cocaine will make certain they seize the shipment."

"What the hell?" Mateo's eyes grew large. "The DEA will seize my copies? And you'd promote the corrupt economy of this place. We're all going to jail."

"No. No one will know about our connection." She struggled to explain. "Your copies will never hit the market, never be seen again."

He reacted like a lightbulb went off. "Ah ha, the originals. You can sell them elsewhere, but to who? What about the owner?"

"Do you really want to know? This is why I kept you away from danger."

"Yeah." He paused. "But now I deserve to know."

"The originals, the ones that appeared in our booth, were seized by the government in a raid on Escobar's place."

"Holy shit. Those paintings belonged to Escobar!"

Hearing him say it out loud made her tremble. "What we are doing is going to trap some awful criminals, who want to sell them and use the money for weapons, but—" She tried to convince him and herself.

"Stop." He held up his hand. "No more. I don't want to know."

Better not to know, especially because there was nothing to know. She did not have a buyer for the Ponces. Yet.

He looked at her. "Let's end this. Get out of here, out of Colombia."

He continued shaking his head as he went to a shelf where jars held different types of powdered compounds for preparations, glues and paints. He pulled a jar labeled gesso, which appeared to be the classic form, a glue from animal hides and white pigment.

"I saw this when I was looking for a base for the canvas. It's not gesso powder." He unscrewed the jar and tasted a bit on his little finger. He winced. "Ugh cocaine, more bitter than mate."

Mateo never drank the bitter tea Uruguayans sip all day long.

She hated mate and there was no point to taste it. "Can you be sure?"

"Don't ask." He smirked, mimicking her.

She knew, just knew Lobo had more going than art and artifacts, with strange people surrounding him, bringing him things in dark night. The money he needed for his lifestyle could not have come from art sales. "Put the jar in here." She opened an empty shopping bag that someone had left on the desk. "Can you do something else?"

He sighed, like he was annoyed, but his trembling hands showed her something else. "You have some nerve, Roba, to ask for more."

She winked. "I'll tell you in the taxi."

He slipped the jar of 'not gesso' into the shopping bag, avoiding getting dust on their clothes. Before they left, he washed his hands in the sink with artist's turpentine.

Three of the clay whistles from Lobo's artifact collection sat on a shelf above a jar holding used paint brushes. She added two of the clay figures with hollow centers to the shopping bag, left a note thanking Lobo—their unsuspecting host—for the use of the studio, and added two one-hundred-dollar bills, double the amount she'd paid the other night. She wrote, "For the supplies and the whistles."

She stopped, and then took out her pen again to add, "Let's talk soon about your paintings."

When he missed the jar, Lobo wouldn't ask about the cocaine, maybe think Mateo had taken it. Lobo didn't seem like a coke user, maybe he supplied other artists, but lately, her judgment about people sucked.

"I'm hungry. Coffee and cigarettes make a lousy diet."
Mateo likely had no money left from what she'd given him.

"We have no time now. Eat at the airport." She pulled
an old chocolate bar from her purse, an emergency stash for
hungry kids.

Mateo handed her back half of the chocolate bar. Her own
grumbling stomach brought memories of the shack, the kidnappers, David's killers. David dead, she couldn't believe it
was true, those gruesome photos. She wanted to crawl into a
soft bed, cover her head, and never leave.

But she could not. Not yet.

Keep going. Keep friggin' going. Finish strong.

The taxi driver rolled down the windows, letting in not
fresh air but thick pollution from cars and buses. He wove
through the streets of the Old Town into the modern city and
the uncertainties that waited at the fair.

CHAPTER 26

THE LOADING DOCK ENTRANCE OF THE convention center buzzed with trolleys, forklifts, and trucks heading for places across town and across the globe. She asked the taxi driver to take them to the rear of the center, to avoid anyone still looking for her. She flashed her Exhibitor's badge at the guard, but Mateo had left his credentials in the booth. The guard accepted the five-dollar bill she handed him and waved Mateo through. Her principles had evaporated with the urgency to leave Colombia. Despite its rich culture and lovely people, this country could corrupt anyone.

They reached the booth and there was Jake holding court, as though he owned her gallery. He was surrounded by a few collectors talking about Mateo's paintings, explaining this was a new artist he'd be representing in Guatemala and around the world.

She shook her head. A clear attempt to steal clients, using her brand. Damn him. Everything she'd asked him not to do.

She did not want to confront him in front of collectors or undo what was a huge sale for Mateo. Instead of throwing a fit, she honored her promise to meet together with Mateo so he could hear the news from Jake. Beyond generous, she thought, given what she'd just caught Jake doing.

The collectors dispersed, and she pulled Jake next to Mateo. "Jake has placed six of your paintings with his collectors, and you'll be impressed with the new prices."

Jake interrupted her. "Biggest increase in prices I've seen in a young artist, six digits each. You'll need a good accountant to manage the funds from me and continue our representation." He held out his hand to Mateo on the vague deal he was offering, stealing her artist right in front of her.

Mateo stood numb, confused by these stratospheric, *desorbitado* numbers, and mumbled something about life changing. He took Jake's hand and shook it, but then recovered to clarify what the deal was. "Thanks Jake. Allison represents me, you can get work from her. Pay me through her so she gets her ten percent."

Mateo knew the drill and understood she did not work with artists who failed that loyalty test. If they went behind her back, used her as a steppingstone, she dropped them, or they were de facto dropping her. It happened.

She paused just long enough to pretend to be worried. Compared to the other opponents she faced, Jake frightened her at the level of an annoying gnat, a bug taking up her time.

She needed to finish the crates and find Enrique. "We must pack up to leave. We can talk more later."

Jake left and returned to his booth.

Mateo said, "Roba, all the details now, please. Did I hear him right? My paintings for over $100K?"

She pulled out Klingman's invoice and set it in front of him on the desk. Mateo lifted his arm and placed his palms on his temples and started to laugh. He turned himself around once and then again and slid into a chair to keep from falling. "Really serious money."

She nodded.

"A car. An apartment. I can marry Christina." He choked up with the words describing a life that only yesterday had been out of reach.

"Wow I had no idea you two were so serious." She glowed. This is why she did what she did, helping artists create their work and build a life. In a normal world, it would have been the pinnacle.

"I love you, Ally Blake." He picked her up and twirled her around.

A high note, an interlude, but not yet the end. This financial roller coaster plunged to the lows of nefarious extortion, negotiating for their lives, to the highs on the fringes of economic liberation. They teetered on the precipice.

He nodded, unclear whether in agreement or shock. He paused. "Christina is pregnant."

She hugged him at the happy news. During the whole fair, she had not even taken the time to find out about his world. "Congratulations, Papa. Why didn't you tell me?"

"Didn't want to burden you with my challenges, make you worry about me along with whatever is going down."

She wanted to tell him to leave, immediately to go home, get out of here. She struggled to ask more about that curator, and how his family was, but with only a few hours left, she had to get the job done. She couldn't handle the cocaine shopping bag and finish the deal with Enrique to sell the Ponce originals.

She pulled Mateo to the back of the booth. "Can you fill the whistles with the powder and place them in the shopping bag? Before you leave for the airport?"

He swallowed and nodded.

She hugged him and said, "I appreciate you and all your help."

"Are you sure you don't need me to stay?" He withdrew the question. "Ok, I know, I know, don't ask. Truthfully, I can't wait to be out of here." Mateo took the contraband and headed toward the men's room, a place he could flush the residue down the toilets.

She looked up to see a buff man with a shaved head. His back was to her as he examined the artworks.

If Frankie had put the word out that the Ponce paintings were on their way to auction, all these types should back off, go away.

Unless she didn't know them. They'd entered a perilous phase, with random operatives answering to many *jefes* or maybe there was no boss at all.

Ally excused herself and hurried to Enrique's booth. No Enrique, no one to ask. No time to waste waiting, she had to find him.

She returned to the booth and noticed Morini's works. They had to be removed from the stretchers and rolled in a tube to be picked up by Galván's driver. She took the Morinis off the wall.

Mateo returned after a few minutes with the shopping bag.

She grabbed Mateo's arm before he said anything and led him to the crate in the closet to keep the buff guy from noticing them.

Mateo set the shopping bag on the storeroom floor. "I emptied Lobo's jar into the figures, put tape on the bottoms, flushed the extra down the toilet, and tossed the jar in the bathroom trash."

"Don't speak too loudly. That guy. Did you see him yesterday?"

"Don't think so." He caught her nervousness, and his words were strained.

"I need you to do something else."

"Ahhh. See? You do need me." His modus operandi to lighten her mood failed, and he switched and saluted again.

"Pack up the Ponces in the crate. Put the shopping bag back in there with them."

"The other thing you need?"

"Go to the hotel, shower off all the powder. I already paid your bill. Leave for the airport."

He started to protest, his ticket was for later in the day, and he had more time.

"Don't wait. Get the first plane out of Bogotá. To any airport that has flights onward to Montevideo." If the renegades Mark feared were wanting to hurt her and her children, or anyone else she cared about, she needed to protect Mateo and get him out of Colombia.

"When you get home, open a bank account in your name. Fax the wire transfer instructions to the gallery. I'll send the amounts to the accountant, and she can transfer the money into your new account." She wanted it done urgently, in case . . . just in case she . . . if something happened, she wanted him to have his money. She pushed the thought from her head, thinking the bad karma would lead to something worse happening.

He held his forehead. "Hope I can remember all that."

She grabbed a card out of the packet with Frankie's embassy address, pulled the business card for Lisa from Ellsworth Auctions, and taped them to the outside of the crate. "Write these addresses with felt marker on the outside of the crate. Leave the lid loose without the screws tightened."

Without comment or reaction, he copied the address on the crate and adjusted the lid without screwing it shut.

She avoided stepping on flakes of white powder on the floor, walked around his six-foot frame to hang his jacket on him, and finished by placing his messenger bag on his shoulder. "Thank you for everything. You're a great friend." She gulped in the sadness, wondering if she'd see him again. "One more task, the most important one."

He rolled his eyes. "Ok sure, what?"

"Tell Christina I send hugs for her and the little one."

She walked with him past Enrique's booth toward the exit.

He kissed her and gave her a quick hug. She watched him leave toward the taxis and whispered a wish, a silent prayer, for his safe return. Then said the same prayer for herself and her little ones.

From a distance, she could see Enrique was not yet in his booth. He'd agreed to meet her early, and she began to have memories of David not showing for breakfast. The young, maybe not out of high school, gallery sitter didn't know when he'd return. That was not like him. She wanted to ask if the paintings were still in the storeroom closet but decided to say nothing to this inexperienced stranger.

She rushed back to her own booth. The guy outside her booth, the one with the crewcut had disappeared. Frankie stood in his place.

No longer playing the game, she yanked Frankie's polyester clad arm and steered her to a chair, directing her to sit.

Ally took the chair across from her and wanted some answers. "David is dead, murdered. What do you know about that?"

Frankie cleared her throat. "Very little. We're devastated, of course, to lose one of our own. The violence and crime here, it's terrible. He got caught in a crossfire between some thieves."

Ally shook her head. A lie, right out of the Agency playbook. She needed the truth, but also wanted to test Frankie. If Frankie suspected that Ally had witnessed David's murder, Frankie would not have lied.

"Didn't you get that packet from us at your hotel check-in? There'll be an investigation—high profile. Gaviria has a lot to answer for. The ambassador is meeting with the head of the National Police. Everything will be done to find the killers." Frankie paused and feigned an effort to suspend her emotions. "We need to talk about other things. About the deal."

Frankie wasn't going to tell her anything.

"The deal is done, paintings are in the crate, ready to be picked up, on their way to Miami and the auctions."

"Good. Very wise of you. Here's the info."

Frankie slipped her a piece of paper with the contact information of a customs broker in Miami.

She took the paper, even though she wouldn't need it. "This is the end. Leave me and my family alone. I don't want to hear from you again."

"It's not up to me."

"I expected you'd say that. Some invisible, never to be revealed chief makes these decisions. You could be more original, Frankie." She tossed the paper with the broker's name onto the desk. "Tell the puppet master to command his thugs to back down, tell him that dossiers have been sent to attorneys on three continents. If anything happens to me or my children, the truth about this mission, the U.S. in partnership with the Cali cartel to kill Escobar, will be released to the press." She paused and then added, "With all your names."

Frankie flashed an angry look.

Ally paused to breathe. "Congress, the Colombian government, the cartels, everyone will know about the dirty money used to buy illegal arms. To fund people who kill American kids with their drugs."

Silence. The power of silence.

Frankie stiffened, smiled a frozen smile, and walked out of the booth toward the exit.

Ally would have wished her dead, but she needed her to carry the message, to spread it around, let it drift down to official and not official players, to the lowest echelon, to stop pursuing her or there would be consequences. She hoped to hell that Frankie would carry the message that the U.S. had to control the thugs chasing her, or their scheme would be exposed.

CHAPTER 27

A DARK-HAIRED BOY AROUND EIGHTEEN stood in front of her with a vase containing a couple dozen red roses. "Miss, for you. Sign here."

Flowers? On the last day of the fair, who would do that? Maybe it was an explosive. The boy struggled to put the vase down on the small desk.

Seeing her confusion, the boy pointed to a plastic stick with a small envelope.

She nodded. The flowers had to be something else.

From a few steps away, still not trusting the suspicious gift, she noticed the name written on the envelope: *Linda flor.*

Stunned, she couldn't believe it.

She grabbed the card and placed it in her pocket. She headed toward the restroom, one foot in front of the other, smiling, trying to appear normal and not break out running.

Inside the cold tile refuge with the flickering fluorescents, she entered a stall and locked the metal latch.

David was alive!

The words proved it. *Linda flor.* Only two people knew García Márquez had written those exact words. Mateo was gone and would not have sent flowers.

David. David was alive! He was alive.

She'd seen the photo, photos of a violently mangled body. A body with an unrecognizable face. His clothes, his shirt, convinced her it was him. But the photo had been a fake.

Shaking her head, she concluded if she believed he was dead, so did everyone else. That's what he had wanted, a smart way out. Maybe the Agency had helped it happen.

Faking her own death wouldn't work for her. She and the kids would be hiding forever. She could not do that to them, but who knew what she'd do if she had to.

Inside the empty restroom, she tore open the gift card envelope. She focused her eyes on the message.

Don't trust Enrique. Bracing herself, she read the card again.

Enrique had been her stalwart in Bogotá, the only confidant she had; he knew more than anyone. But what did she know about him, really? Today he'd disappeared when he'd committed to meeting her first thing.

She ripped David's card to pieces, threw them in the toilet, flushed, and watched them circle down into the sewers of Bogotá.

Enrique, not a friend, not trustworthy. Her world, the one where she trusted one person, shook like an earthquake collapsing the ground underneath her.

Those Ponce paintings could never be seen in public. If they were out there, there would always be a risk the copies would be found out. The card might be a ruse, or maybe something else, someone who wanted to spoil her deal with Enrique.

But where was he?

The route from the restroom to her booth went by Enrique's booth. She wanted him to be there, look into his eyes, probe for lies.

But he wasn't. Enrique's absence, the words on the florist card, it was all starting to develop a narrative that meant she had to alter the plan.

The gallery assistant, the same girl that had been there earlier, sat at the desk, only this time she was busy. Busy adding a coat of polish to her nails. "Enrique's not here," she said without looking up.

"Tell Enrique the McGraw paintings he's taking to his gallery are in my booth waiting to be picked up."

The girl blew on her nails to speed the drying and looked up for the first time.

"Could you cover the booth while I take a break?"

Ally almost said no. She changed her mind and answered the gallery assistant. "Be quick please." Quick was not going to happen, not with this gal.

She needed to verify Enrique hadn't taken the Ponce originals and sold them for his own purpose.

Once the teen disappeared, Ally tried the handle on the flimsy door. It was unlocked. Not a shock, given the ineptitude of Enrique's staff.

The wrapped Ponce canvases were there. What a relief to see them leaned against the back wall. She undid the paper to verify she had the right paintings, and without pausing, she stacked the two works fronts facing each other and lifted them. The bundle was awkward, but it wasn't the first time she'd done this. With her foot, she closed the door to Enrique's storeroom and took off for her booth.

Once there, she placed the canvases in the back of her storeroom, behind the crate, and locked the door before Klingman's or anyone else's prying eyes discovered the duplicate paintings. She slid a chair in front of the door. Anyone trying to enter the storeroom would need to move it, and she would know.

Enrique had some scam going if she believed the note. If he'd abandoned their project or maybe something worse, he would have returned the paintings. Or maybe not. Maybe Enrique was in trouble, too.

David had disappeared, and yet somehow, he'd known about her project with Enrique. If David knew, others associated with this hideous mission did too. No more waiting for a partner who was either compromised, not trustworthy, or both.

She left her booth and walked the back aisles of the fair in a circuitous route toward the Japanese dealer's booth. She waited just inside until a few visitors departed and had cleared the space in front of the Picasso. She didn't know the Japanese gallerist who greeted her graciously, with a deep bow.

She reciprocated, with a bow lower than his as she'd been taught and asked him to tell her about the Picasso. The dealer shared details, including the provenance of the little gouache. It had come from a friend of Picasso's family in Málaga, Spain. The water-based pigments created a soft portrait, maybe the subject was Picasso's partner Francoise Gilot or their daughter Paloma. The documentation listed the title as *Portrait of a Girl*. The girl looked like an older Claire might look. The little painting captured her heart, and she wanted it for many reasons.

"There's a lot of interest. However, we must pack this painting to return to Japan as the fair is ending."

"So, it's not sold. I might have a collector."

"We will be honored to discuss with you, Mrs. Blake." He bowed, again, and subtly handed her a plain white card on which he had written the number $30 million.

They chatted another five minutes about details, about flexibility, and the dealer wrote some numbers on a paper but never said them out loud. She studied the numbers and nodded.

This time the dealer bowed and shook her hand. "*Arigato*." He smiled.

She thanked him too and left. Men moving crates created an obstacle course for her to return to her booth.

A man with his back to her waited in the booth. He turned. Enrique!

He gave her another one-kiss Colombian greeting and added a hug. She sensed a coldness, a distance, but maybe it was her. Then she looked into his eyes. He turned aside and stared at the artworks remaining on the walls.

"Where have you been?" She took his arm and walked him back by the storeroom but didn't enter it. "I came to your booth twice. What are we doing with the Ponces? Banks are closed on Sunday. Can we do a cash sale?" She tested him.

"Not possible. Do you know how much $20 million is?"

"Yes, at least what it could buy, in art." She waited to see where he was going with this.

"No, not the purchasing power, but the *volume* of all that cash. Picture a large pallet with fifty boxes holding cases of water, larger than you are tall. You can't receive cash like that, can't hide it, or move it without the quantity screaming crime."

She wasn't surprised but in fact had not considered the logistics.

"It doesn't matter." He was silent for a moment. "We have a worse problem, a real big one."

How could things be worse? With the clock ticking, she could only shake her head.

After a deep breath, he spoke with a lot of discomfort. "Escobar's men found out I have his paintings." His face was ashen, grim, eyes averted. "They want them back."

Why didn't he tell her immediately about Escobar's men instead of the nonsense about piles of cash? He was lying, keeping the money from the sale for himself. What a slime.

She invented a surprised look. His acting wasn't as good as hers. "But how? How could they know?"

"Doesn't matter. They know."

"You said they had rooms full of cash, that they wouldn't care about $20 million."

He nodded. "Escobar wants to get his family out of Colombia. He can send the paintings, like clean money, with his wife and kids. The paintings are insurance in case the government freezes their other accounts."

Interesting. His story sounded plausible. After all, she was trying to do the same thing, except for the part about frozen bank accounts. She mulled over this new scenario and felt oddly connected to a drug lord, protecting his family with valuable artwork. God, she'd lost it, thinking her family was like Escobar's.

One thing was clear, Enrique hadn't discovered the paintings were missing from his storeroom.

He folded his arms and unfolded them, in a nervous tick. "I must be quick. Shouldn't be seen talking to you. Too risky for you." Enrique started to walk away.

That was odd, he'd not worried about that before. She went after him. "Wait a second."

Enrique's shirt collar was open, his tie undone. This different Enrique did not morph from reliable Enrique. He'd played her since the beginning. Or maybe there was something else. Laura Ellsworth demanding a Ponce from him for her auction. Maybe Enrique had thought to use these paintings to protect his artists' works Laura had threaten to pull.

Ally had to test him. "We've run out of time. What now?"

Desperate looks between them, combined with acting on both their parts, contributed to anxious words and fuzzy thinking.

"No choice. I must return the paintings to Escobar's guys."

She nodded but wanted to tell this traitor that he should be afraid of the many people who wanted money from those paintings. "Will you handle the return to them?"

Enrique nodded like he would need to abandon the plan to sell the paintings with her and was being forced to hand them over to Escobar's people. Regardless of what he was up to, he was going to cut her out of the deal.

Enrique started to leave.

She put on her sober face. "Wait. I need you to move these McGraws to your booth. Remember the show you are doing for him? We can save the shipping if you take them." She removed one from the wall and handed it to him. "I can't leave the booth. You'll need to come back for the rest."

Enrique was minutes away from discovering he no longer had the Ponce paintings in his storeroom.

CHAPTER 28

SHE NEEDED TO MOVE THE PONCES before Enrique finished
transferring the McGraws. She didn't dare take the paintings
out of the storeroom while Enrique went back and forth.

She cleared up papers from her desk. The fair's public
relations people had put a newspaper with the photo of García
Márquez holding the McGraw painting on her desk. She
folded the newspaper and placed it in her duffle bag to give
to McGraw. The artist would be pleased and happy to have a
show in Bogotá at Enrique's gallery.

The prospect of working with his gallery didn't give her
the joy she might have once felt to land such an exhibition
for her artist. She was never good at faking relationships. She
smirked at this lie, a lie to herself. Every relationship at this
fair had been an act, if not a complete falsehood. Except Mateo
and Santi and maybe even David.

Well, she didn't tell them the truth either, but for different
reasons. She wanted to protect those she trusted. Values she'd
taught her children had been abandoned to survive. This wasn't
who she was. This confused persona she'd become made her
question whether it was reversible if she managed to survive.

The buff guy appeared near the booth again. She no longer
cared about the man's identity or his motives for hanging

around. She just needed to get the Morinis packed and picked up. He stopped and studied their labels.

"These works are sold. We're waiting for the collector to retrieve them."

He removed his cowboy hat and bowed to air kiss her fingers. "Señora Blake, I represent los Señores Galván. Paco, the Galváns driver, at your service."

Stunned to learn he was just a driver, she smiled. "I'm pleased and relieved to see you. Are you picking up these works?"

He unfurled the receipt she'd given Galván and handed her a copy of the bank transfer showing the balance had been wired.

She hadn't verified that the funds arrived in her account, a significant oversight on her part. The canvases hadn't been removed from their stretchers to transport. All those little staples—it would take some time and there was none.

"I've been so busy, they're not ready. How are you traveling?"

"I'm driving. In the Galván's Explorer with some other purchases. All the way back to Panama."

Oh, good. No need to un-stretch them. "We need to wrap them. Do you mind helping me? It'll go quicker."

"Of course. Do you have wrapping paper in there?" Paco headed toward the storage closet.

"Ah. No, no." She grabbed Paco's arm to stop him from entering the storeroom. "We have our special ways of protecting the paintings for travel. I'll get some bubble wrap and come back."

She returned with supplies from a shipper in the next booth, who was kind enough to give them to her. Paco returned his cowboy hat to his head and picked up the plastic bubble wrap and began to work. Together they were holding, wrapping, taping, and stacking, like they'd done this dance before.

"You're good at this. Do you want a job in the gallery?" She felt lighter, could manage a chuckle. No need to make things worse with a stranger whose boss had become a big client.

"Would you like a ride to the airport? I can drive you on my way out of town. Taxis and even limos aren't safe in Bogotá."

"I'd appreciate it." She could leave as soon as she finished one last thing.

She rotated her head to survey what was left of the fair and who was watching. Exhibitors rushed around, either closing deals, delivering art, or breaking down their art installations. Others were in deep conversations with each other, trying to organize exhibitions or dealer sales for low discounts to reduce shipping costs on the return. There was an urgency, a stampede to an ending that could not be stopped.

She stood on the edge and had to jump across a chasm to make it to the other side of her plan.

The last of the Galván purchase had been wrapped. "Anything else?" Paco asked.

Now or never. "Could you help me with an errand?"

She opened the storage room. Against the wall were the two Ponce paintings she'd stolen—ah, she'd *recovered* from Enrique's booth. Hell, she didn't know who owned these paintings. The only clear fact was these paintings were like radioactive material, needed to be buried until their half-life expired and they could no longer hurt anyone.

She took the canvases out of the closet. "Could you take these two works to this dealer?" She gave Paco a paper with the name of dealer, the gallery name and booth number. "Give him this envelope, and he'll give you a package."

Paco took the note, folded it into his shirt pocket, and lifted the two paintings.

She smiled and thanked him. "I'll finish here and when you return with the package, we'll leave for the airport."

Paco, cowboy hat on his head, disappeared in the chaos of booths being disassembled.

CHAPTER 29

ALLY KEPT HER SUITCASE UNDER THE desk, away from the cocaine in the closet. She'd go to the restroom to exchange her clothes and shoes for something cocaine-free from the suitcase. Bogotá customs didn't check for cocaine either coming or going; if they did, it would be the joke of the century. But the big problem was U.S. customs and their dogs. She could not get tripped up entering the States.

On the way back from the restroom, she visited Santi's booth. He wore sunglasses and did not look well.

When she asked, he confirmed her impression with a scowl. "Not doing so good."

He was hurting. Physically sick. In a tight black turtleneck, he looked thinner than she'd ever seen him.

She put her mother's hand on his cheek and forehead to see if he had a fever.

He squeezed her hand, took it away and kissed it. "I'll be okay, Mami. Going to NYC tonight. My love, Tom is waiting for me."

Santi's sad face added another worry to her list. This serious, sober Santi was a stranger. He managed a weak turn of his mouth for a smile, and with a lot of effort offered a generous compliment. "You sold so much. I'm glad for you."

"It's been terrific, and I'm happy, yes." The hypocrisy of her own words amazed her. She couldn't wait to leave. "I loved meeting so many new contacts at the parties."

"Great partying, and partying never disappoints. Living life well has its own payoff." He laughed without the usual energy. "Let's do a Mateo show in New York. That would be a party. Life is short, *mi amor*."

"Mateo would love that. I'll call you from California." She gave him another hug, a single *abrazo* could not be gratitude enough for how he'd turned her finances around with all the sales, not including the Ponces.

No more fairs for her. Once she held her kids in her arms, she was not leaving them again.

She returned to the booth, gathered her belongings for the flight home, and waited for Paco to return from the delivery.

The shipping broker arrived. With forms in hand, he paced in the booth waiting for her to fill out the one for the crate. The man offered to send for the forklift to remove the crate in the closet.

"Only one crate? When you came, you had two."

She studied his face, hidden under a baseball cap. Maybe the guy from the customs station downstairs? She couldn't remember what he looked like from only four days ago, a face so repugnant to her then. He was probably just a worker, a Colombian earning a few bucks at this job.

She moved papers around the desk tossing out old invitations, publicity flyers, and useless paper. Put some cards she wanted to keep in her wallet. García Márquez's card fell out and again she tucked it into her wallet where she wouldn't lose it. They'd meet again, maybe in New York instead of Bogotá. She made a note to ask Santi to invite him.

"Who gets the invoice for the shipping and insurance?"

The shipper's question interrupted her reverie of the few good memories that had transpired during the fair.

She was certain now the guy was not the creepy one she'd met in the garage. He stood, pen aloft over a clipboard, ready to write. Each person who circled inside her orbit got the twice over, no one was exempt. She couldn't shake suspicions and maybe never would.

"On the form. That address at the top." She pointed to Frankie's embassy address. Ally needed to take care her own name, her address, her fingerprints would appear nowhere on this shipment.

"Is it ready now?"

"Go get your forklift, and I'll close up the crate before you return."

She put on her cotton gallery gloves, lifted the lid, used the hammer to lift the shopping bag, without touching it, closer to the center of the crate. The cocaine filled figures needed to be covered like someone cared that they survived intact. She did care about them but had a different priority. If these figures were authentic antiquities, they deserved a respectful resting place. It was wrong to rob graves, but being buried in the impound storage might make a better resting place than being traded on the black market.

A wad of bills popped out when she pushed the figures toward the center of the crate.

Yikes. Galván's deposit. She'd lost track of this sale and the money, which was not like her. She flipped the bills, still in a little plastic bag, out of the crate. She pulled the money out, hoping there was no cocaine on the bills, and placed the cash in her pocket. Thousands of dollars, enough for a house payment, was a nice bit of cash to ease her trip home.

Forklift guy returned with the customs broker, and the latter reviewed the forms.

"What's the value?"

A loaded question that had her calculating the strange contents, although original art was duty-free coming into the U.S. Fake paintings were still original art, probably, she guessed. Was the coke worth more than the fake paintings or maybe the clay figures would be the most valuable objects she was shipping? Funny word 'value.'

"Insure it for $25K. How much are the fees?"

The broker said nothing, not believing the value she'd assigned. She studied his clipboard and pointed to a number, $2700 U.S. for shipping and insurance.

She asked, "Will you take cash?" The dance of the non-bribe bribe began with a simple question.

She turned her back to avoid showing him how much cash was in her pocket and turned back again to hand him $3000. He marked the invoice paid. Didn't even offer the $300 change for the ridiculous processing charge.

She no longer cared. Moving this art to Miami, avoiding the paper trail to her, and finally executing the plan, brought her closer to ending this ordeal.

He walked away toward the underground storage locker, the place where this nightmare had begun.

Where was Paco? She had trusted him too quickly. But with everyone gone, she had no one to lean on and no options. Treating the errand, the exchange she sent him to make like it was routine could work and was her best play at this point.

"All packed up, Allison?"

Enrique.

He stood behind her and asked the question a little too loud. He looked forlorn or angry, she wasn't sure. She shuddered and scanned the aisle for Paco, wondering if Enrique had discovered the Ponces missing from his booth.

"Glad you came back, Enrique." She handed him the consignment form with the McGraws listed and asked him to sign it.

He wrote his name and took a copy. She reached to hug him good-bye, but he lingered, raising her suspicions about why he'd come to her booth. She needed to know. "Did you give the Ponces to Escobar's people?"

He wrinkled his forehead, hesitated. "The cartel people took them. When I was out of the booth."

She sucked in a long breath. "Wow, I guess that's that." She considered saying more, expressing regret that reflected the magnitude of losing this sale, but decided against it.

Enrique didn't seem surprised at her lack of distress. He didn't seem disappointed that he'd gotten nothing for the paintings. If he'd made up the whole Escobar thing, who did Enrique think really took the paintings? The best outcome for her would be that he'd just give up.

Paco walked into the booth, returning from the delivery. A look darted between the two of them as he handed her a parcel about twelve by eighteen inches wrapped in brown paper and tied with string. The swap had happened.

Enrique watched the two of them, while she tried to hide her nervousness. He could not know about this.

"Thanks, Paco." She took the package with aplomb and tossed it in her duffle like it was an unimportant catalogue.

Paco looked Enrique up and down. "Ready to go? It's four o'clock. We've got to leave. I'll carry Galván's paintings. You take the luggage." Paco reached under the desk for the suitcase and grabbed the duffle from her hand and placed it on top of the rolling suitcase.

Enrique asked, "Do you need a hand?"

"No thanks." She brushed him off with one kiss and moved away so he wouldn't feel her racing heart.

Enrique said good-bye and returned to his booth, walking faster than normal.

Workmen finished disassembling the booth next door and marched into her booth. Without saying anything, they began to take down the walls and remove the empty storage closet. One guy stared at her, and she stared back.

No. She recognized him.

The guy from the shack in the mountains, the one who could have shot Horny, wearing an art fair employee's uniform, stood in front of her. Was he working for the anti-Escobar people to get the paintings?

Without a word, the man pushed Paco out of the way. The guy moved toward her, took hold of her arm, and started to drag her toward the parking garage exit.

Paco, bigger and stronger, stood in his way and removed the guy's hand from her arm. He parted his jacket to display a pistol in his belt to kidnapper guy, who took a step backward.

Paco shouted, "Leaving. Now."

He picked up her things from the desk, pushed her blazer and her purse into her hands. Like a small child leaving for school, she stumbled, balancing her bags. The thug stayed behind, steaming, wondering what had hit him. She turned to catch a glimpse of him as he dashed toward the front entrance.

CHAPTER 30

EXHIBITORS, WORKERS, AND EQUIPMENT crowded the loading dock. The guards inspected the paperwork and then released Galván's paintings. Paco hurried to load them in his Explorer. She presented her suitcase and duffle, and the guards passed them out onto the loading area. As she expected, they never opened the small package in her duffle bag.

She craned her neck to look behind her. The thugs who tried to grab her were nowhere.

Paco held open the Ford Explorer door in the VIP section next to the dock, and she climbed in. He dashed to the other side of the car to climb into the driver's seat. "Don't know what that was all about, but you've got some dangerous friends." He pulled his gun out from his waistband and put it on the console.

Paco was no ordinary driver, taking her on no ordinary trip to the airport. He peeled out of the loading dock parking. Without looking, he crossed three lanes of traffic, cut down a side street, and headed for the Old City.

"The Old City? Is this the way to the airport?" She asked as the gun slid from side to side on the console with each sharp turn. Accepting a ride from a stranger, an armed stranger, broke all the rules, rules now in such shambles she no longer remembered them.

"We have an errand. For the Galváns."

"Right. Do you think we can make it to the airport . . . on time?"

He wove in and out of traffic. "I'm a good driver, used to compete on the track. We'll make it or die trying." He chuckled at something not funny, like his regular routine included outrunning thugs.

She pointed to the gun on the console. "Why do you carry a gun?"

"I take care of Galván and his interests."

"What interests?"

"We don't ask that question."

Those interests could mean life or death. If she'd learned anything on this trip, the players and their alliances drove the story. "Who was that guy in the convention center?"

"You tell me, *guapa*. He's after you, not me."

She gulped to swallow the story she could not tell. "I'm not sure, but I'd like to get to my plane. Do you have to stop?"

"The boss needs me to do a quick pick up—a package. Then straight to the airport."

Her only option was to stick with Paco. The detour to Candelaria might throw off the guys chasing them, maybe it could work.

She checked in the side mirror. Wrong again. A beat-up Range Rover, the same car from the shack where they'd held her hostage was behind them. These guys pursued their own agenda, without direction from Frankie or the U.S. government agencies. The U.S. never learned deals with the devil have consequences.

"Relax. I got this." Paco studied the rear-view mirror. "*Sí*, that car, something with the Americans. This'll be fun." He laughed, sped up, and continued to whip around corners.

She grabbed the hand strap to steady her torso and keep her head from bouncing against the window. Paco drove the

Explorer into Candelaria's twisted streets, shifted around sharp corners, and reversed directions, backtracking to lose the Range Rover.

The gun slid to the floor on a wild turn. Paco grabbed for it to secure it in the little depression between the seats, and then straightened his cowboy hat, a weird concern in this moment. When the Range Rover missed them after they'd pulled into an alley, Paco backed out and sped in the opposite direction.

Paco, now breathing hard himself, ranted. "Tough guys, sick enemies, between the cartels and the U.S. Americans need to get out of this business, stop doing business with bad guys, and get out of Colombia."

Yes. Out of Colombia was *all* this American wanted.

Paco braked, jerked them both, throwing her head forward. He parked the Explorer on the sidewalk, so close to the stucco wall of the old house she could not open the door. Paco hustled out of the car and rushed to a familiar antique door ten feet away.

That door—Lobo's house. The antique door creaked open. She watched in the rearview mirror.

Paco stood at the door talking, then took a package from someone hidden in the entrance. She didn't see Lobo and didn't want too.

A lullaby she'd sang the kids stuck in her head, and she sang it over and over while one knee shook. She counted down the seconds of the eternity of Paco chatting, yes chatting, with the person at the door.

Oh no. The beat-up Range Rover pulled in behind them.

She locked the doors, slid to the floor to hide. She grabbed the gun Paco had left between the seats and hid it underneath her blazer, with her finger ready on the unfamiliar trigger.

She covered her head with her blazer, hand still on the trigger, hoping to be invisible.

A thug approached the door, tried the handle, and then pounded on the tinted window. He shook the door, and she put her head under the dashboard to make herself small, but ready to shoot, if she had to.

Paco came running. "Fuck off!" Paco pushed the guy off the window.

More obscenities. She couldn't look.

The two men fell to the ground in a scuffle. She could hear them, but not see them. She raised her head and stretched her torso to see through the edge of the window. They'd rolled onto the sidewalk toward the stucco wall.

Paco beat on the guy's head. Seemed to be winning.

The door was locked, and Paco wouldn't be able to jump back in. What to do? Unlock the door? Stay put? She could not move.

A second guy, the driver, got out of the Range Rover.

No way Paco could handle two of them.

She unlocked the car door, barely squeezed between the car and the wall, and held the gun in her trembling hand.

She pulled the trigger.

Nothing happened. The safety was on. She fumbled to turn it off and aimed the pistol at the guy coming toward them. Closed her eyes.

She heard the shot. It hit the wall.

Both men stopped, looked toward her.

Paco, only four feet away, reached out his hand. She tossed him the gun, crawled back toward the door, slipped into the shotgun seat, and locked the door.

Paco took the gun and squeezed back through the narrow opening between the wall and car door.

Whoosh, whoosh, shots flew by her head. Both missed.

God, *please.* Fine time to learn to pray. Whatever force governed the universe needed to intervene, now, yes now.

More shots.

Paco. Paco.

She scrambled, reached to hit the button to unlock the door.

In one motion, Paco jumped behind the wheel and threw the package on her lap. He shifted the Explorer into drive and peeled out.

She stared at the package, amazed he still had it. Within a second, they were down the block, around the corner, onto a highway.

She gasped for air, panting, her chest pounding.

"*Jode.*" Paco expelled the obscenity. Then turned toward her with a smile broad enough to show a gold molar. He exhaled and said, "That was fun."

She mumbled like a deranged person. What was that? The horror of what had just gone down hanging over her, consuming her. Killing people over some damn paintings?

"Sorry about the swear words." Still smiling, he added, "Guess that wasn't the ride you expected."

Ah yeah, not the ride she expected. His jovial attitude shocked her. Apologizing for swearing vs. killing two people. Not her planet.

"You missed the shot."

"Are they dead?" She had to know.

"Maybe." He looked at her and changed his answer. "Nah. Not dead. Those *cabrones* will be back up in two minutes, a lot smarter though." Paco hooted a big laugh this time. He pulled a cigarette pack out of his pocket and put one unlit between his lips. "Can happen any minute, anywhere. A war. Everyone, a soldier. Even you. Ha, ha." At a stoplight, he lit the cigarette and then rubbed his head. "Lost my hat! Shit."

Geez, his hat? Shoot somebody, leave them for dead in the street, and what matters is a hat. A cowboy without a hat, in a lawless country. Business as usual, life goes on.

She could take no more. "Get me out of here. Airport *rápido*. Tell Mr. Galván . . . well, ah." Hard to say she was grateful. The box wrapped in white paper stared up from her lap. The package was so familiar she didn't need to ask what was in it.

Galván a drug king? With that elegant, sweet wife. Impossible.

Paco continued. "Galván knows the score. It's why he hired me. He'll be glad to hear I got some target practice." He chuckled, showing the gold tooth again. The Mr. Toad's Wild Ride between cars, up the shoulder, around any traffic continued even though no one followed them. "Having you here in the shoot-out, nah, he wouldn't like that. Maybe we don't tell him that part."

In the dying daylight, the silhouette of the Bogotá skyline appeared majestic against the dark blue mountain. Beauty and tranquility fell onto the city at twilight, a peaceful illusion that obscured the harsh reality that she was still being hunted. No plan could engineer an escape from the complex tangle of competing evil forces, but she had to try.

Paco dusted the sleeve of his shirt. She leaned over to help brush the dust off his shoulder.

"You're not so bad, señora, for an American. Need target practice though." He turned his head. "Gotta lot to learn about surviving here."

Skills she hoped she'd never need, never hold a gun again. But she needed to know what to expect next. "Will they hunt me down in the U.S.? Ever leave me alone?"

"Depends on why they want you."

Quiet tears rolled down her cheeks. Paco handed her a tissue from the center console.

"Nah, don't think so." He seemed unsure and then added, "They wouldn't take the chance of getting locked up in a real prison."

"What if it's not Escobar?"

He took a big drag from the cigarette and released a plume of smoke. "Same answer."

Freeway signs signaled the next right for Aeropuerto El Dorado. Before the Spanish came, El Dorado was the golden place. Artisans made gold treasures like those little bells, not for profit but for art and ritual. Beautiful cultures were lost when Spaniards slaughtered natives and melted down objects for the treasuries of Seville, Toledo, and Madrid. The legacy of Spanish greed morphed into today's power-hungry criminals, who fed the world's insatiable demand for coke.

Paco shifted in his seat and turned his head toward her. "All Americans are not bad. Neither are all Colombians or Panamanians. Best thing that ever happened to Panama, you guys took the canal away from Colombia." He reached for another cigarette. "Hundreds of years of history. What do you think García Márquez wrote about?"

She rolled down the window to let the cigarette smoke escape. "He autographed my book." A random remark, that created imaginary distance from the mess she was in. She put one hand on the duffle bag under her feet that held the book, the two remaining gold bells, her children's photo, and the flat package.

"Are you driving to Panama?" She looked at the package he'd risked so much to pick up from Lobo's house. How was he planning to get the parcel across the border?

"After I drop you at the airport I will head north." He puffed on the new cigarette.

Traffic slowed at the highway exit. Their Explorer approached the airport entrance. Cars backed up in traffic. Two armed soldiers stopped and checked each car. Paco waited, inching forward.

Looks darted between them, she panicked, he relaxed. "It's routine. Everyone's checked."

Paco's package, the drugs still on her lap. "What about this?"

He howled with his peculiar laughter. "Doubt art supplies will bother these guys." He continued chuckling between cigarette puffs.

Her cheeks flushed red and hot. "Art supplies? We almost died to pick up art supplies?"

"Señora is learning to paint. Lobo teaches her. Lobo told Galván you're a trusted dealer, one of the best for Latin American art, and Señor Galván thought maybe you'd look at photos of señora's paintings."

Freaky. After what had happened, she could not pivot to the ordinary. Represent Señora Galván's paintings? No wonder la señora was shy at the Art Fair.

She shook her head and attempted to be cavalier like him. "Lobo would be a good teacher."

Paco pulled the Explorer up to the guard. The guard motioned with his automatic weapon for Paco to get out of the car.

Paco stood spread eagle, hands on the car for a pat down. A second guard poked his head in the window.

"*La pistola?*" The gun. He looked at her, pointed at the console.

Her heart beat faster. She shrugged like a native, 'doesn't everyone have a gun in their car?'

Ignoring her, the guard picked up the pistol.

The guards discussed the gun with each other. Then they talked with Paco. In the side mirror, she saw a car cutting around the others in line.

The Range Rover! One guy was in the passenger seat. Someone else, maybe the third guy who stayed in the car for the shoot-out, was driving.

She gripped the door handle, frozen.

Paco stuck his head in the driver's door, rummaged around the console looking for his wallet, his permit to carry the gun and some kind of badge he had.

She motioned her head toward the road and whispered, "Look behind us."

Paco looked back, then with his eyebrows raised, he looked at her. He returned to the guards and within a few seconds, got back into the car, threw the gun on the console. "Ha, ha. No worries."

"Your badge got you through?"

"My badge kept 'em talkin. My wallet got us through."

"What about the guys behind us?"

The Range Rover had exited the checkpoint and closed in on them. Both cars pulled up to the curb by the entrance to her gate.

She shook her head. "No, not here. I can't get out here."

Paco returned a hardened look as he surveyed the situation.

She grabbed his arm and pleaded, "Could I ride with you to Panama?"

CHAPTER 31

PACO WENT PAST THE ENTRANCE TO American Airlines, swerved through traffic, found the highway headed north, and then immediately exited on an unmarked off ramp. He drove down a dirt road behind the cargo warehouse of the airport, not far from where she'd tried to claim the crates.

The Range Rover had disappeared.

Paco parked and turned off the engine. "Driving to Panama is not easy, there's no highway to cross from Northern Colombia into Panama. The jungle owns that piece. Caravans of poor migrants carry drugs, mules on their way to the U.S. border. I use a ferry for that section."

She looked behind, back toward the airport to check again that no one had followed them.

"Another option—over there," he pointed to a landing strip with private planes.

"Does Galván own a plane?"

"No, but you have a friend who has friends with friends."

He couldn't mean Ponce; she hadn't even met him. She waited for Paco to clarify with details. Before he said more, it occurred to her, "García Márquez?"

He nodded.

How could she ask him? But stuck in Colombia, the Range Rover, Escobar, Frankie, Enrique, one or all of them would catch up to her. Desperation eclipses social etiquette. She pulled the card with the assistant's direct number from her wallet.

From under his seat, Paco took out a contraption with a strap and a battery pack, a satellite phone he said, something he no doubt needed to cross Panama's jungle roads.

She called out the numbers from the card. He dialed and then handed her the receiver.

"Hi, Ally Blake. From the art fair?"

"Of course. Mr. Márquez loves the painting you gave him, hung it in his office. He is not here. Can I help you with something?"

"Ahh, a problem with my flight home . . . I really need to get to California, back to my children. I apologize for imposing, but is there any chance you know of someone or maybe even Mr. Márquez, who has a plane, or a friend with a plane, flying to the U.S.?"

"Oh, too bad you didn't call yesterday. He flew in a friend's plane to Mexico. Mr. Márquez is at his home there."

Paco whispered, "Ask if any other plane is available?"

She scrunched up her mouth and gave him the angry eye and then asked, "Maybe if you hear of anything . . . " She managed the words. "Thank you for taking my call. Give my regards to," she hesitated, "Gabriel."

"Is there a number I can call you? I could reach out to some friends or if I hear of someone traveling."

"I am calling from . . ." She looked around. "The airport. Could I call you back?"

"Yes, I'll work on it." The assistant hung up.

"What now?"

Paco thought for a moment and started driving. "We have to go back, but there's a door for VIPs to get to their gates. I don't think those guys will find you."

She gulped.

"Once inside, you'll have to go through security, and once you're through passport check, those guys won't be able to touch you. I need to leave now, or I'll miss the ferry that takes me around the jungle." He paused. "Once inside, stay alert."

Great. She nodded. Nodded and hoped luck was on her side.

Paco drove to the VIP door, a plain grey door at the far end of a parking garage, and slipped some bills to the guard. Would it be that easy for the Range Rover guys to get in or maybe they'd just shoot the guard? She had to make a run for it.

Paco opened the car door and handed the duffle and the suitcase to her. "Go up the stairs and through the glass doors into the main airport. Got your ticket, right?"

She didn't stop to check anything.

"Straight to passport control. After that, security. Head to the first-class lounge."

She shook her head and was too paralyzed to talk.

"Okay, if you're not first class, just hand them a $100."

She had the cash from the Galván deposit in her purse. Then, as an afterthought she gave him a hug, this driver, body-guard, gunslinger, partner in crime, with whom she shared a terrifying experience.

Her weary body struggled to lift the duffle bag and the rolling suitcase up the stairs to the next level. With a big exhale, adrenaline pumped her upward, and she added a mantra of 'go-go-go.' The passport control sign hung from the ceiling at least fifty yards down the long airport corridor. Adrenaline propelled her forward, double time toward the beginning of the twisted line.

There should be no line for VIPs, and she looked around to see if she was in the wrong place. The faces up and down the line appeared to be ordinary travelers, not the people she feared. The many couples in the line reminded her of her place in the world. No Nick, no Mateo, no David, no ally to reach out to for help. No one would miss her if she vanished. At least she'd told her sister she'd gone to Colombia, and Dawn could send searchers for her if she never returned.

Finally, she stepped forward, passport at the ready to hand to the agent.

A young Colombian asked, "Purpose of your visit?"

Her answer, the truth matched everyone else who traveled to Colombia in this dangerous time: to get money, money to survive. Her household bills impressed her now as a shallow mission, such a small thing to have taken the huge risk of coming here.

"Art fair. The Bogotá Art Fair."

"What do you do in California?" He studied her face as though he expected she might reveal an insecurity or a lie. That look alone produced the nervous tick in her eye.

"Own an art gallery." Please hurry. Please.

He flipped through the passport pages to study where she'd been, stopping on a page with Argentine stamps and another with Uruguayan stamps and one trip to Paris, the last vacation she'd had with Nick. He lifted his arm with the stamp that would mark her exit from this country and brought it down with a thud.

With the first step of the gauntlet finished, she hustled past the sign to the VIP lounge, pretending not to be searching for it. Then she turned around to check who was behind her. No one had followed her. She ducked into the hallway to the door marked with the logos of airlines the lounge served.

Before she reached the door, two uniformed customs guards overtook her and stopped her.

"Señora Blake? Come with us."

No! She sputtered, then relented. So close to escaping. So close.

To protest or struggle would have been futile. She no longer had energy to be terrified, mostly she was resigned now with no fight left.

The guards walked, one on each side of her, steered her down several long hallways and a short corridor with fluorescent tubes flashing, reminding her of her walk to Substation 1109, her baptism into this Bogotá disaster.

The guards opened a non-descript office with a key. It held a desk and three chairs like those rooms where police interview suspects. They locked the door and disappeared.

She expected that Horny's killer or another thug would appear and drag her out, once again extorting her for money from the damn Ponce sale.

She waited, an hour or more, too spent to feel anything. Thirsty she stood, paced the small room.

Finally, the door opened. She squeezed her eyes shut in anticipation of being gagged or tied up again.

"Dreamin' darlin? Helloooooo?"

That voice. Unmistakable. She opened her eyes and smiled with joy.

Santi!

He squeezed her hand and tears that had been quashed for days could wait no longer.

Tears flowed all over her, the seat, him, his jacket.

"Look at you, Mami. Niagara Falls." He put his arm around her, gave her a strong hug, she felt his bony torso through his winter coat.

"You, I mean . . . how did you know, why are you . . . ?"

"Later, Mami. Your flight, your plane awaits." He pulled out the handle of her rolling suitcase and handed her the duffle bag and her purse. "Let's go. Now."

Santi tottered a bit, still weak from his illness, and led her to a parking garage. A security guard waited in a golf cart used to monitor the parking structure. The guard sped away and parked in front of a different grey door. He used a key to open the door and left.

Santi nudged her through the door and down a hallway until they arrived in a small waiting lounge next to a staircase. They went directly downstairs, double time, and exited onto the tarmac, next to a Gulfstream.

"Your carriage, Highness."

"How did you. . . ?"

"Pilot needs to leave, now. Wheels up, chica."

She took a seat, buckled in. The plane backed onto the runway, and Santi sat across the tiny aisle from her. She reached to squeeze his arm with the desperate affection of someone who had been trapped in a shaft and finally, emerged into light and air.

He puckered his lips, blowing two air kisses her way.

The pilot asked them to remain seated because of expected turbulence. Turbulence, ha. She'd survived the mother of all turbulence. A bouncing plane was nothing.

She smiled at Santi. "How are we together in this plane?"

Moving his arms in classic Santi style, he overdramatized even that which could not be exaggerated. "I'm an art dealer, a schlepper. Got to get to Los Angeles. Whatever the collectors want—clean their house, dust their frames, polish the Plexi, rearrange furniture, choose their clothes, style their hair. Or favors, even for my friend Gabo." He sighed an extended breath with a smile. "Is LAX okay for you?"

She nodded and leaned her head toward him. "You're not going to explain, are you?"

"All questions don't have answers. Some are better without answers." He winked and squeezed her shoulder. He continued, "I can tell you things happened that we didn't expect, but we've had your back all the way like those guys shadowing your booth."

She laughed out loud. "Why didn't you tell me you'd organized my bodyguards?"

"Right? A flaming gay guy." He laughed and then coughed. He put his finger to her lips. "Shh. No more worries for you." Santi reached in his coat pocket, drew his hand out to squeeze her hand, and dropped something into it.

She opened her hand to see her Cartier watch. Stunned, without words, she didn't ask how, because the answer would be the same.

CHAPTER 32

STEAM ROSE FROM HER COFFEE CUP, drifted into the air, and disappeared above the desk. Through the gallery window, beyond the jacaranda trees, she saw the San Diego city bus driver stop and get out to light a cigarette. He waved at her as he paced up and down the street, puffing until the precise departure time. The passengers he waited for never appeared in a city too in love with its cars. Joe, she never knew his last name, once visited the gallery on his break for a two-minute exhibition tour. She loved his energy and how he pointed out the gallery to his riders, nudging them to go see the art.

Lethargy had sunk into her days, a welcome tedium. Work piled up, art to unpack, inventory waiting, but she did get the payroll out and notify artists of the good news about their sales. She greeted clients and talked about exhibitions. The fair, even without the big Ponce money, had been the success she'd needed for her family.

Claire and Mikey enjoyed their time at the cabin, unaware of why their aunt had taken them there. They played the old Candyland board game with Dawn and Margarita and never asked why. Like most children their age, they lived in the moment and found joy in small things, something she'd be always grateful for.

Dawn never asked questions and made up a story that their mom had arranged a special adventure in the mountains.

Ally had arrived in a rental car straight from the LA airport just as the sun came over the hill. They drove from the cabin directly to Dawn's sailboat in the Oceanside harbor. The next few days were idyllic, cruising up the coast and then across to Catalina Island. Whales and dolphins, not creepy guys, followed them. The kids searched for urchins in tide pools, and everyone slept in peace, rocking on the boat where no goons would know to look for them.

She'd imagined the details of what had happened. The scene in Miami must have been something with dogs sniffing through the large shipments including art crates. An agent with a dog on a leash making a pass through recently arrived shipments from Colombia, commanded the customs officers. "Open it."

A guy with an electric screwdriver went to work. Pieces of little clay whistles and white powder spilled onto the concrete when the lid came off. The agent returned the contents to the crate, put crime tape across the inside, screwed the lid back on, and wrapped the entire thing with special tape marking it as seized goods.

When the DEA inquired, Ellsworth and State would move quickly to disavow the crate. Government infighting, never a good day. This impounded art would die a dusty death in an evidence room as the government ran around to cover its ass, transferring people like Frankie Brown. The copies of paintings that would eventually be destroyed by the DEA had served their purpose.

She finished her coffee and didn't need a second cup. The energy from one dose of caffeine eased her into her routine, the tranquility of the ordinary.

She picked up an exhibition invitation from her desk and dialed New York.

"Santi, how are you feeling? What do the doctors say?"

"Some experimental drug, AZT, has side effects, but I have more energy. Mami, did you get the invite to our exhibition? Are you coming?"

"Not this time. You'll have a huge success."

He lifted his voice and his spirits. "Let's go to Uruguay, see Mateo, and organize the show. Yes, please say yes."

She paused for a minute, remembering her commitment to take Mikey and Claire out of school more often. Uruguay, it's beaches and rolling hills; Brazil with Iguassu Falls, butterflies, the Rio Plata; Spanish lessons, geography without a map. "We'll see. Maybe."

"Mateo is opening an artists' co-op, a center to help other artists in Uruguay."

"He told me. Has a baby coming, too. He's becoming boring."

"Did he tell you he has hired a director for the center? A fellow you went to school with at Stanford. I think he said you dated him."

She laughed. "Are you sure? That would make me so happy to know they're working together." She checked the watch Santi had returned to her.

"Got to pick the kids up from school. I'll call you next week. Let me know if you need anything, anything at all, Santi."

He sent mushy sounding kisses over the phone. Lots of them.

The big transaction, the plan she'd engineered, re-engineered at the last minute when Enrique betrayed her waited in the safe under the stairs. Nick had bought the safe to protect important papers, but now it held the most valuable piece of paper she'd ever owned. Smaller than a pallet of cash, more valuable than the useless life insurance policy, the deed to the house, or the retirement plan, the unassuming little portrait protected between conservation-quality board stood by until the day she needed it. The name Picasso, scribbled in the lower right-hand corner, was an ally she could depend on forever.

Time was a friend in these matters. For now, she would do nothing.

AUTHOR NOTES

IN 1991, I FLEW FROM SAN DIEGO to Bogotá to exhibit at the first ever Feria Internacional de Arte. Our art crate had arrived but could not be found. Fernando López Lage, a terrific artist, agreed to help me at the Fair and had brought art works from Uruguay on the plane with him. Eventually, the crate was delivered with the contents intact.

That experience became the spark of an idea for *Five Days in Bogotá*. Many scenes came from experiences on that trip, including meeting Colombian President Gaviria. Gabriel García Márquez did autograph a rare copy of *One Hundred Years of Solitude* I had brought with me. I consider that edition — which I had purchased in Madrid around its original publication date — to be a prized possession in my library.

The works of some artists named in the story, like DeLoss McGraw who creates works inspired by literature, are available in a variety of galleries and museums for art lovers to enjoy. Other artists, like Bernardo and Morini, are imagined by me and, like the remainder of the book, do not reflect my personal experience or anyone I knew or have met. I want to give a nod to so many who work diligently and ethically in the art world to be the links between the creators of art and the public. This hard work, often done without financial reward, is sustained by the passion these professionals feel for the work they do.

When I returned to San Diego after a successful art fair, I pondered how cavalier I'd been to go to Bogotá, one of the most dangerous cities in the world. The experience led me to begin in-depth research about the political dynamics between the US and Colombia and our mutual goal to control the drug trade and the mountains of money that benefited criminals. The dynamics of the various agencies and organizations in the story are informed by this extensive research and interviews with former State Department and DEA personnel who lived or worked in Colombia, or were familiar with it, in the early 1990s.

I wanted this book to showcase the beauty of Colombia and its people. Pre-Colombian history, including the little bells and clay whistles from that era, fascinates me. The food, the music, and the many talented visual artists make it easy to love this country and its capital city. I hope readers will be inspired to travel there and explore this gorgeous place. I've been back numerous times and would love to return. Perhaps we can meet up for a strong Colombian coffee or a drink of aguardiente.

ACKNOWLEDGMENTS

A BOOK PROJECT REPRESENTS A LONG journey filled with doubts, reversals, and revisions. The challenges can be overcome and drudgery can be transformed into publication joy with the support of friends, writers, mentors, and family. They become like the people handing out water bottles during a marathon, cheering you on to make it to the finish line. The book launch finish line offers the opportunity to recognize those who ran the race with me and made all the difference.

Readers spearhead the top of my gratitude list for this second novel. As a debut novelist, I had no readers and waited anxiously to learn what they thought of *Attribution*. Generous comments about *Attribution* from readers who wrote that they "could not put the book down" and those who even lost sleep to finish reading it helped propel the book for other readers to discover in book clubs, at book events and signings, and through postings online. This generous feedback gave me the courage, and it does take courage, to complete another novel. *Five Days in Bogotá* is for all of you who read, wrote reviews, and asked for another book. Thank you.

My writer community has expanded beyond the resolute group that nurtured each other over several decades. The

Asilomar Writers group and the De Luz Writers group inspired me with their steadfast commitment to the writers' life. The San Diego writers group, including Carl Vonderau, Suzanne Delzio, Eleanor Bluestein, Peggy Lang, Louise Julig, Barbara Brown, and Karen Johnson, read many chapters and offered insights to improve the book.

Stanford Novel Writing Cohort friends—especially Karen O'Connell, John Maly, James Burnham, Maryam Soltani, Michele Morris—and members of the faculty, including Angela Pneuman, Caroline Leavitt, Malena Watrous, Joshua Mohr, and Stacey Swann, have generously supported my efforts. I appreciate the help of Richard Russo and Ron Currie Jr., who provided commentary about this book. These wonderful writers made the book better. Its shortcomings are mine alone.

This writer community has grown to include the wonderful writers I have met through the publishing and book marketing process, especially Lyn Liao Butler, Gina Sorell, Leslie Johansen Nack, Suzanne Parry, Jodi Wright, Anastasia Zadeik, Suzanne Moyers, Lindsey Salatka, Margaret Rodenberg, Barbara Conrey, Rebecca D'Harlingue, Jesse Leon, Adam Sikes, and Mark Pryor.

Friends new and old have congregated around this writing journey. Success Team members came together to support the first book as beta readers, book club members, with photos from around the world, and the word-of-mouth network that helps readers to discover books. I reconnected with Madrid classmates Paul Chitlik, Linda Tarpley Hales, Cynthia Dusel-Bacon, John Powk, and Kendall Mau, and reminisced about those extraordinary years. Neighbors, college roommates, and volunteer friends from various good causes and service clubs, including Rotary and Junior League, all stepped up to spread the word about *Attribution* and have invited me to tell them about *Five Days in Bogotá*. The above-and-beyond award belongs to many, but special appreciation goes to Susan

McClellan, Patty Gravette, Beth Rowley, Iraina Hofsteede, Kim Swecker, Barbara Enberg, Marcia Littler, Pam Palisoul, and Vickie Mogilner.

The publishing team at She Writes Press—Brooke Warner, Lauren Wise, Tabitha Lahr, and more—produced a beautiful book and provided advice at every step. Ann-Marie Nieves has been a delight as a publicist with her good humor and positive outlook. Caroline Gilman has worked diligently, and has been a dependable partner in the never-ending work on our platforms.

My protagonist, Ally Blake, believes family is everything, and I agree. Siblings and their partners Karen Anderson, Rob and Colleen Moore, Jim Anderson and Lois Fisher, nieces Meredith Anderson and Catherine Moore organized book clubs, showed up at bookstore events with friends, and supported me and these books in so many ways.

Over the last few years the Moore family has become a publishing enterprise, using their talents to help their mom when she needed it, which was often. The tech, marketing, social media, legal, editing, and accounting talents of the incredible Craig Moore, Gina Moore, Adrienne Wetmore, and the extraordinary Terry Moore gave these books the heft they needed to succeed. You all mean the world to me.

ABOUT THE AUTHOR

LINDA MOORE is an author, traveler, and recovering gallery owner. Her gallery featured contemporary artists from Latin American, Spain, and the United States and she has exhibited at numerous art fairs, including in Bogotá, Buenos Aires, Chicago, and Madrid. *Attribution*, her debut novel won the National Indie Excellence Award for Literary Fiction, Independent Publisher Book Awards Gold Medal, Eric Hoffer Award winner among other distinctions. She has published award-winning exhibition catalogs and her writing has appeared in art journals and anthologies. She resides with her book-collecting husband in San Diego and spends time in sublime isolation in Kauai.

Author photo © Daren Scott

SELECTED TITLES FROM
SHE WRITES PRESS

She Writes Press is an independent publishing
company founded to serve women writers everywhere.
Visit us at www.shewritespress.com.

Attribution by Linda Moore. $17.95, 978-1-64742-253-0. In this fast-paced novel full of imaginative art world revelations, betrayals, and twists, an art historian desperate to succeed leaves her troubled parents to study in New York, where she struggles to impress her misogynist advisor—until she discovers a Baroque masterpiece and flees with it to Spain.

Beautiful Garbage by Jill DiDonato. $16.95, 978-1-938314-01-8. Talented but troubled young artist Jodi Plum leaves suburbia for the excitement of the city—and is soon swept up in the sexual politics and downtown art scene of 1980s New York.

Beautiful Illusion by Christie Nelson. $16.95, 978-1-63152-334-2. When brash and beautiful American newspaper reporter Lily Nordby falls into a forbidden love affair with Tokido Okamura, a sophisticated Japanese diplomat whom she suspects is a spy, at the Golden Gate International Exposition, a brilliant Mayan art scholar, Woodrow Packard, tries to save her.

Peregrine Island by Diane B. Saxton. $16.95, 978-1-63152-151-5. The Peregrine family's lives are turned upside-down one summer when so-called "art experts" appear on the doorstep of their Connecticut island home to appraise a favorite heirloom painting—and incriminating papers are discovered behind the painting in question.

Estelle by Linda Stewart Henley. $16.95, 978-1-63152-791-3. From 1872 to '73, renowned artist Edgar Degas called New Orleans home. Here, the narratives of two women—Estelle, his Creole cousin and sister-in-law, and Anne Gautier, who in 1970 finds a journal written by a relative who knew Degas—intersect . . . and a painting Degas made of Estelle spells trouble.

Waterbury Winter by Linda Stewart Henley. $16.95, 978-1-64742-341-4. Barnaby Brown, a wannabe artist, has had enough of freezing winters, debts, a dead-end job, and his lonely life with his parrot in Waterbury, Connecticut. He promises himself he will start anew—move to California and find inspiration to paint—but he has more than a few obstacles to overcome first, including debts and a drinking habit.